The Last Bride

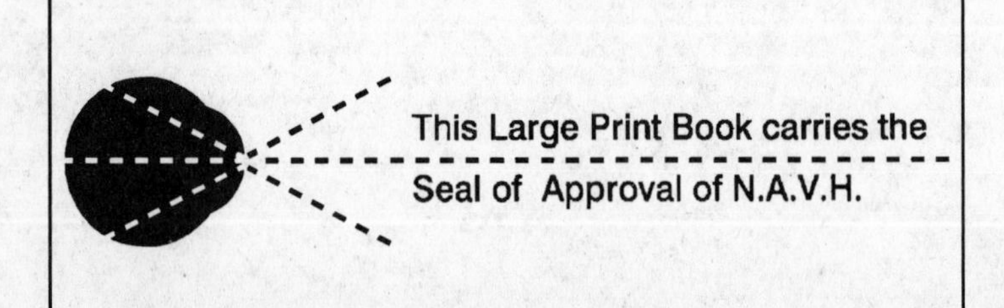
This Large Print Book carries the
Seal of Approval of N.A.V.H.

THE LAST BRIDE

BEVERLY LEWIS

THORNDIKE PRESS
A part of Gale, Cengage Learning

GALE
CENGAGE Learning

Farmington Hills, Mich • San Francisco • New York • Waterville, Maine
Meriden, Conn • Mason, Ohio • Chicago

Home to Hickory Hollow Series #5.
Scripture quotations are from the King James Version of the Bible.
Thorndike Press, a part of Gale, Cengage Learning.

Thorndike Press® Large Print Christian Fiction
The text of this Large Print edition is unabridged.
Other aspects of the book may vary from the original edition.
Set in 16 pt. Plantin.

LIBRARY OF CONGRESS CATALOGING-IN-PUBLICATION DATA

Lewis, Beverly, 1949-
The last bride / by Beverly Lewis. -- Large print edition.
pages ; cm. -- (Home to Hickory Hollow series ; #5) (Thorndike Press large print Christian fiction)
ISBN 978-1-4104-6470-5 (hardcover) -- ISBN 1-4104-6470-9 (hardcover)
1. Amish--Fiction. 2. Large type books. 3. Lancaster County (Pa.)--Fiction. I. Title.
PS3562.E9383L37 2014b
813'.54--dc23 2014004113

Published in 2014 by arrangement with Bethany House Publishing, a division of Baker Publishing Group

Printed in the United States of America
1 2 3 4 5 6 7 18 17 16 15 14

To Debra,
delightful friend
and former marketing manager.
New blessings ahead!

Prologue

I did everything right. *Everything.*

I faithfully attended baptismal classes and listened carefully to Preacher Yoder's instruction last summer. I bowed my knee to God this past Sunday morning and received holy baptism at the Hickory Hollow church. Then and there, I vowed to follow the rules of the *Ordnung* all the days of my life.

All of that, and yet I suddenly found myself in this terrible pickle and hurrying to meet up with Marcus King tonight . . . with such *miseraawel* news. I recalled my father's response to discovering my long-standing courtship with Marcus. *"He just ain't the man for ya!"* he'd said decisively, his expression ever so stern. *"You need to trust me on this, Tessie Ann."*

My bare feet fairly flew across *Dat*'s grazing land, since I didn't dare be seen, 'specially this late on a weeknight. It would reflect poorly on my honorable beau. Even so, I knew from his letter he was impatient to see me, to tell *me* something, too — unwilling to wait till the weekend, like most Amish courting couples.

Oh, such urgency. What was on *his* mind?

In the midst of my sadness, I couldn't help noticing the orange-red harvest moon, its delicate light a balm for my troubled soul. *Dearest Marcus, if I didn't love you so, this wouldn't be so awful hard!*

Determined, I ran silently, darting in and out of the birch grove at the far end of the meadow, where I sometimes went to pray. Yet never a prayer like this one: *Lord God in heaven, are You there? Do You see my breaking heart?*

When I arrived at the spot just off the road, near the one-room schoolhouse, Marcus opened his strong arms and I ran straight into them. He held me near, then lifted me into his courting carriage, getting me settled beneath his lap robe. His long blond bangs ruffled beneath his straw hat as he darted around to the driver's side and leaped into the seat. "Tessie Ann, wait'll ya hear what I have to tell ya."

"Jah?"

"I've found us a place to live once we're married — gonna sign the lease this coming

Monday."

I sighed. He sounded so pleased; I couldn't bear to put a damper on his plans.

"And . . . I've had lots more hours workin' in the vineyard out yonder, so I'll have plenty to support a bride." He smiled wistfully. "Won't be long now till wedding season, love."

I held my breath. He sounded so confident, and before I could say more, Marcus clicked his tongue to signal Prince, his beautiful black road horse, to move forward. That quick, Marcus slipped his arm around me, drawing me closer. "I've been prayin' about this step for us, and with late November little more than two months away, I have plenty to do to get ready."

I listened, heart pounding in my ears.

"I want to make a nice home for ya, Tessie. Can't be too careful 'bout such important things, ya know."

I couldn't have agreed more. But now was the time to open my mouth. "*Ach,* but we can't wed, Marcus."

"Wha-at?" His handsome face was marred by a sudden frown.

"I guess I should say, *I* can't."

Stricken, he looked at me, straight through to my soul. "What're ya sayin', honey? I thought —"

"I *do* want to marry you." I bowed my head. "Ain't that."

There was a dreadful pause, awkward and long, like he somehow guessed at my father's harsh words before I could even speak them. Dat disapproved of Marcus for me. Not only him, but *Mamma* did, too. And none of it made a whit of sense, since I'd never known my parents to hold a grudge or show narrow-mindedness toward anyone. Why they didn't welcome my hopes for Marcus was beyond me.

"My father forbids us to wed," I said, my throat tight and hoarse.

When Marcus spoke at last, it was so soft I wasn't sure I'd heard him right. "Your father's still got his heart set on another fella for ya, is it?"

Honestly, I didn't care one bit for my father's choice. Unlike my sister Mandy, I was determined to make my own decision about a husband.

"I really hope you're not sayin' we can't make up our own minds, with God's help."

"I'm just tellin' you my parents are sorely against it, even though I've prayed up a storm."

He pondered that for a time. Then, "Maybe I should go an' speak directly to your father."

"Won't help none, believe me."

He slowed the horse. "We know this is the right thing for us. After all, we've looked ahead to this day for nigh unto three years."

"Jah, 'tis." My heart sank, hearing the twinge of pain in his voice, a pain that matched my own. Ach, how I'd pleaded with God to let us marry!

"I'll win your father over in due time." He paused, his right hand gripping the reins. "But I don't think we need to wait to wed."

"I don't understand."

He drew in a slow breath. "We'll elope if need be."

"Run away?"

Marcus nodded firmly. "The only way I can see. That way, your father will have no other choice but to accept our marriage."

The only way. His words slammed into my heart. I yearned to be united with Marcus as his bride, and I'd been taught not to squabble with the men in my life. Even so, wouldn't I feel cheated out of a wonderful-*gut* Amish wedding — a *real* one?

Tears sprang to my eyes. Oh, I loved him so . . . but to give up saying our sacred vows before almighty God and the People?

"You know you mean everything to me, Tessie Ann Miller. Don't ya?" Marcus's blue eyes played havoc with my emotions. "We can't let anything stop us."

We'd waited such a long time, or so it seemed. We'd first fallen for each other at sixteen, at the start of our *Rumschpringe* — the running-around years in Hickory Hollow. And we were both church members, too, baptized in anticipation of our wedding day.

"Next week we could get our marriage license at the Chester County courthouse. That way we'll keep it secret, since it won't appear in the Lancaster paper, ya know."

"But we ought to honor my parents, ain't so? According to Scripture."

His eyes probed mine, searching . . . his gaze caressing me. "Sweetheart, the Good Lord put us together. I believe that. We're the ones makin' our way in life now, don't ya see?"

I breathed in a mere half breath. It was all I could manage. "Are ya mighty sure 'tis the right thing, love? Under *Gott*?"

He pulled me even closer to him there in the open buggy. My face pressed hard against his shirt, and while we hadn't let ourselves share a kiss just yet, it took all my determination not to let him. *"Wouldn't ever wanna spoil things,"* Marcus often said, so I turned my head, denying our affection till it was safe. And right.

"Marcus," I whispered, ever so torn. Such a thorny spot to be in, but we were in it together, and somehow that made it more bearable.

"I think I should at least try to get your father's blessing." Marcus flashed his winning smile. "I'll go tomorrow morning."

I bobbed my head, but my toes curled inside my shoes. Truth was, Dat would never change his mind — I knew him. And come morning, Marcus would regrettably experience the selfsame sorrow I carried now. Still, he could try. I surely wouldn't stop him.

In the end it all boiled down to my decision, and that alone. Would I respect my father's unwavering will or yield to my beau's steadfast love?

Chapter 1

Tessie Miller would be the first to admit that living at home these days was not nearly as much fun as it used to be. Not since her older sisters — Miriam, Molly, Marta, and Mandy — all married and started families of their own. Their staunch and opinionated father, Ammon Miller, often commented that the evenings had grown quieter and more manageable with the nest nearly empty. All the furtive whispering had nearly vanished, as well as Tessie's sisters' hushed urgings to follow in their matrimonial footsteps right quick, *"before all the best fellas get hitched!"*

Her father, on the other hand, wasn't too talkative on the subject of Tessie's marriage, even though for the longest time he'd had his eye on the Smuckers' only son, just down Hickory Lane. As a serious church member and an assistant chief for a volunteer fire department, Levi possessed every desirable attribute, and his family was highly regarded in the Lancaster County Plain community.

Presently, Tessie sighed as she scattered feed for the chickens Saturday morning, startling when two of the more feisty ones — Obadiah and Strawberry — flew up too close to her head. She'd insisted on naming them, though her father disapproved of assigning names to animals that were destined for the dinner table. Three other rambunctious chickens began pecking at one another, vying for the desired feed. But Tessie's mind was scarcely on the chickens. Truth be told, Tessie knew she'd break her mother's heart if she eloped with Marcus or any man. Even so, she let her beau's words filter through her mind. While she was willing to embrace his thinking, she wished they could wait to earn her father's favor.

She finished feeding the chickens and went to the barn to check on water for a handful of goats. Tessie still terribly missed the farm where she'd grown up, just two farms away. Oh, the beloved tall, redbrick farmhouse where she and her sisters had learned to follow God's commandments while cooking and helping their mother to clean, sew, and make all kinds of jam. They'd learned to recite the Lord's Prayer in German on the sweeping back porch after eating homemade ice cream on sultry summer evenings. And how could she ever forget the wonderful old two-story barn where leisurely Sunday afternoons were spent swinging on the long rope in the haymow?

But all of that had changed when her sister Mandy married Sylvan Yoder, who promptly took over Dat's steer-raising business. The newlyweds had moved into the coveted old house, kept pristine and in the family for four generations.

Oddly enough, Dat had not waited for Tessie to marry — saving the farm for the youngest son or son-in-law was more typical of Amish families. Why Dat had overlooked her, Tessie still did not know. She had her assumptions, though, and one was that Mandy had been greatly rewarded for yielding to Dat's wishes, marrying the man he'd practically handpicked for her. *"Sylvan's like a real son,"* Mamma qualified once when Tessie timidly inquired as they snapped sugar peas. Tessie had tried not to feel slighted that her father had pushed ahead and not waited till *her* future husband had the opportunity to accept or reject such a wonderful-good offer. But it miffed her more than she cared to admit.

Wiping her hands on her black apron, Tessie made her way back outside to the picturesque potting shed not far from the one and only *Dawdi Haus,* where her widowed grandfather lived. The little shed needed a bit of redding up before the cold weather snuck up on them here before long. As she often did, she glanced wistfully across the expansive back lawn near the well pump to survey the house's southern elevation, where verdant vines still scaled the wall. It was much smaller, this house they'd lived in for two years. And merely a house, in her humble opinion. A home was the treasured place where you made family memories retained for always.

The former family home had many more charms. One in particular was the large oak tree that shaded the back porch, with its immense low branches strong enough for a person to climb up to perch and ponder there, something Tessie had been known to do more frequently than Mamma thought necessary.

The trees here weren't nearly as ancient, nor as sturdy, so Tessie occasionally snuck over to Sylvan and Mandy's to sit in her favorite tree. Well, *theirs.*

She looked now at the pebbled walkway near the potting shed that led over to the woodshed and Mamma's tiered flower gardens, actually kept up by Tessie more than Mamma this past summer. The same path meandered back out to the small horse stable, where they sheltered two chestnut-colored driving horses, Agnes and Bonnie. More like beloved pets, the mares were gentle in spirit and nimble as the wind. Tessie was tempted, at times, to take Agnes out riding, but she couldn't abide her father's certain rebuke, so she avoided riding bareback altogether.

When she'd finished sweeping out the potting shed, Tessie ran back to the house, up the back steps, and through the small mud room just inside the large porch. Dat preferred to wash up there before entering Mamma's tidy kitchen, with its black-and-white squares of linoleum. They'd left the floor as is after moving in, since Dat was a frugal man and redoing the flooring made no sense.

Other aspects of the kitchen looked more modern — the off-white appliances, all gas powered, though one wouldn't know it by their outward appearance. And there was an exceptionally sturdy built-in bookcase on the far wall, near the foot of the table. Mamma had filled it with her large collection of Grace Livingston Hill and Janette

Oke books. Mamma had never been warned against reading fiction, and she'd placed the books up front and center. Of course Dat had no idea they were made-up stories, and Mamma, wise as she was, hadn't clarified that one way or the other.

I guess what Dat doesn't know won't hurt Mamma, thought Tessie as she hurried to the large basin to wash her hands.

"Would ya run this over to Dawdi Dave's for me?" Her mother held a casserole dish, her light brown hair bun mussed a little.

"Sure, I'll do it now, Mamma." Carefully, Tessie took the hot dish in its quilted carrier. " 'Tis always a *gut* excuse to go over there an' visit, jah?"

"And your Dawdi will be happy to see ya, dear."

"I love makin' him smile," Tessie said.

"He misses *Mammi* Rosanna something awful." Mamma stood there in the doorway to the kitchen, wiping her brow with the back of her hand.

Tessie nodded. "They were so in love."

Tears sprang to her mother's eyes, and she brushed them away. Mammi's death had come so suddenly three months ago. "Thank almighty God for the blessed hope of seein' our loved ones again one sweet day."

Tessie agreed and headed outside and

around the stone walkway to the cozy little Dawdi Haus attached to her parents' larger home.

"*Kumme* on in," her grandfather called inside the house. "Door's open."

Tessie smiled; of course it was. They never locked their doors. "*Wie bischt,* Dawdi?"

"*Besser,* seein' ya here." He raked his callused hand through his graying hair, emphasizing the cowlick on the right side. "Where's your perty Mamma today?" He looked around, his gaze settling on the casserole dish in Tessie's hands. "Ain't she with ya?"

"She sent me over with this."

"Well, ain't that nice." He muttered something she couldn't hear, then smacked his lips. "*Gut* thing, too, 'cause the last batch is nearly all."

He continued talking while Tessie placed the hot dish on the back burner, then turned the gas to simmer. "It'll be ready whenever you're hungry, Dawdi."

"*Denki* so much." He sighed loudly, his lower lip trembling. "Sure do enjoy your mother's cookin'. Awful hard round here sometimes."

Tessie felt sorry for the dear man. "I miss Mammi Rosanna, too," she whispered.

"Sometimes I feel like I'm lookin' for my

right arm — callin' to her in the next room 'fore I realize again she's not there."

"Can hardly imagine it," she said, going over and sitting near him in a chair next to his rocker.

"Nothin' but Gott's mercy and love lasts forever."

She nodded.

"Say now, best be talking 'bout other things, jah?" he suggested. "Saw your beau, that tall fella, Marcus King, wander out to the barn not but a few minutes ago." There was a glint of mischief in his gray eyes. "Made me wonder what's on his mind."

Tessie remained silent.

Dawdi drew in a long, deep breath. "Ya know, your father's downright opposed —"

"Ach, Dawdi, if ya don't mind, I'd really rather not discuss it. All right?"

He frowned. "So you must know something."

Despite the sudden stir of emotions inside, she willed herself to be still.

"Not to step on any toes, Tessie Ann, but there's more to your father's resistance than you might know. Much more. And that's all I best be sayin'." By his words and his stern look, she knew enough to believe him.

Why hasn't my father told me?

■ ■ ■ ■

It was on the way back to the house that Tessie saw Marcus marching down the driveway toward Hickory Lane, shaking his head. He'd obviously just talked with her father, exactly as planned. When Marcus was determined to do something, he went right ahead and did it.

Remembering her grandfather's remarks, she scurried around the side of the house, where dazzling golden mums still flourished in the ground and the stately purple martin birdhouse stood high at attention. "Marcus," she called softly. "Marcus!"

She didn't dare arouse anyone else's notice. She made herself wait till she was nearly on his heels, running as hard as she could barefoot, before she called louder. "Marcus . . . did ya talk to Dat?"

He slowed, letting her catch up. "You were right. He's already made up his mind and won't say why." Marcus folded his arms, eyes serious. "If he weren't your *Daed,* I might have the nerve to say he's unreasonable."

"Puh!" She said it louder than necessary.

He reached for her hand and raised it to his lips, his eyes searching hers. "Have you thought any more 'bout what we talked about?"

"Eloping?"

He nodded solemnly, as if he were as hesitant to do so as she was — a church member in good standing, after all.

"Shouldn't we pray 'bout it?" Her chin quivered.

"I've been talkin' to the Good Lord a-plenty about our marriage. Wouldn't be *schmaert* not to."

She stepped closer, intent on his strikingly handsome face. She stood on tiptoes and brushed her lips against his clean-shaven cheek. "Aw . . . Marcus, don't be glum 'bout my father. You mustn't be."

"Ain't easy walking this fence 'tween pleasing a difficult man and doing what you believe is God's will." He removed his straw hat and pushed his hand back through his hair, from his thick bangs clear to his sun-tanned neck. He stared at the road for a moment, silent.

"I wish Dat were on our side." Tessie struggled with a lump in her throat. "Truth be told, my father is stubborn. He did this with my sister Mandy, too, for no *gut* reason, and now he wants to do the same with me."

It occurred to her just then that her beau's

part-time work in a nearby vineyard might pose a problem to her parents. Could that be? But many Amish church districts made their own wine for communion services. It wasn't as though Marcus was the occasional moonshiner who kept his brew secret until found out and reprimanded.

"Come here to me, Tessie Ann." He pulled her into his arms and held her in a fierce embrace.

She felt the pounding of his heart against her face. "Marcus, I . . ." She stopped right there, unable to say it. He must decide first what to do for their love and speak it into the air. She honestly could not make such an important decision for them.

Then, just as quickly, he released her, put on his straw hat, and gave a glance toward her father's house. Tugging on his black suspenders till they snapped, Marcus stood straighter just then. And without a word, he leaned down and cupped her face in his hands, kissing her lips softly. Then again, ever so tenderly. "I'm goin' to marry ya, Tessie . . . you just wait and see."

Her heart nearly stopped at the kiss. Oh, such joy! *Dearest Marcus . . .*

"Let's talk again tomorrow," he added. "Meet me behind the house I'm goin' to rent — in faith that we'll move in sooner rather than later."

"You'll sign the lease, then?" She was surprised but very pleased.

"Sure, I'll move in an' get things set up for us right quick." He paused. "You'll join me there, once your father sees the light." With that, he turned to head up the road.

Tessie watched him go, the fingers of her right hand resting lightly on her lips.

In the near distance, she heard her father calling. She cringed, but his call was meant for Mamma. And Tessie was ever so relieved he hadn't seen her rush out here after Marcus — or witnessed their first kiss!

CHAPTER 2

Mandy Yoder was hanging out a small last-minute washing when she noticed Marcus King swiftly making his way up Hickory Lane. By his determined stride, she assumed he was angry. Then, lo and behold, her youngest sister, Tessie Ann, suddenly appeared, her apron flying as she ran, calling after him.

Goodness, thought Mandy, a wooden clothespin stuck firmly between her lips. She paused and studied the couple from her somewhat hilly spot not far from the spread of land that presently belonged to her father. Truth be told, she wished her parents hadn't moved in so close to her and Sylvan, considering how she sometimes felt about Dat's insistence on her marrying a man of *his* choosing. It was downright uncomfortable. And she and Sylvan had her parents over for supper more often than she preferred to, really. It was Sylvan who was enamored with the idea of bonding the two generations.

Sighing, she shook out her husband's sopping wet shirt before pinning it securely to the long clothesline that stretched between the large house and the horse stable. She ought to be more grateful, Mandy knew, and it wasn't that she disliked having her family so near. The struggles, the memories were still fresh at times. So many things had transpired to bring her to this point — married to Sylvan Yoder two years this November.

Certainly her husband was a kind enough man, and Mandy was trying to make the best of things. She glanced back at the road, hoping she was inconspicuous as she watched Tessie touch her fair-haired beau's hand, smiling up at him. Their kiss stirred up past recollections, and Mandy remembered too well the endearing look on another young man's face. How he'd commented so often on her *"perty flaxen hair."* She shook her head, brushing away the memory.

"Be ever so happy, Tessie," she whispered wistfully. "When ya find your heart mate, never let him go. . . ."

But she must not let herself fall into the trap of remembering, mustn't think back to her whirlwind courtship with Norman Byler, cut short by her father's harsh decree.

Just last week, Norm's older sister Hallie had received word from her long-lost brother and came rushing over to tell Mandy while Sylvan was gone to the barn. *"Norm might be comin' for a visit sometime this fall,"* Hallie told her, eyes bright with the unexpected news.

"For how long?" Mandy had asked. It had been three years since Norm left with a dozen other young men for Nappanee, Indiana, the lot of them quietly traded for the same number of Nappanee fellows. All for the purpose of strengthening the gene pool in both locations. Sadly, four more children had succumbed to fatal genetic diseases in the Hickory Hollow area in just this past year.

Hallie's brown eyes had penetrated Mandy's as she said she didn't know how long Norman would stick around. After all, he hadn't been home but once since he'd left, and his family surely missed him. And Hallie hadn't stayed even long enough to sit down and have some sweet bread and coffee. Mandy had wondered at her visit; Norm's whereabouts really didn't matter to Mandy. Not anymore.

Whatever their problems — especially

their beginnings — she and Sylvan were married now, and Mandy's loyalty was reserved solely for her husband. "Till the Lord separates us at death," she reaffirmed as she admired the neat lineup of washing fluttering in the clean autumn breeze. She carried the empty wicker basket to the house and set it down in the outer room, where Sylvan's work boots and their other shoes were placed neatly in cubbies he'd built along one long wall. The minute Mandy stepped into the kitchen, she flung wide the windows there and in the front room. Every single one.

"Honestly, have ya ever heard of a father forbidding his daughter to marry?" Marcus tried very hard not to raise his voice. He'd gone walking after his encounter with Tessie, out there in broad daylight, and somehow or other he'd ended up near the Wise Woman's place. Going to see Ella Mae Zook was something he'd never thought of doing in his nineteen years, counselor though she was to many in the neighborhood. Still, he'd spotted her out tending to her orange and gold mums, lean as kindling. When the elderly woman waved him over, inviting him to sit with her for a moment on the porch, Marcus found himself following his feet.

"Well, now, maybe you could fill in some of the cracks for me." Her gentle voice was just what he needed. He'd already mentioned his disappointment with his sweetheart-girl's father, trying to be vague and discreet — till he'd let the name Ammon Miller slip.

"I believe I've told you all I know," he said, which was the truth. You couldn't lie to a woman like Ella Mae — anyone knew that. "Her father's put his foot down, and that's that."

"Without an explanation?"

"*Kenner* — none."

"I see." She slowed her rocking some. "Must be a bit unnerving."

"Not even Tessie knows what's up."

Ella Mae jerked her little white head around to face him. "Say, now, wouldn't have anything to do with her bein' his last daughter, would it?"

"Well, you'd think he'd want to make sure she gets hitched up. Ain't?"

"Might be he's overly protective 'cause she's the youngest, though."

He could see that. *Just maybe.*

"I 'spect you've talked this over with the Good Lord."

"Wouldn't think of movin' forward otherwise."

"Sounds like you've decided *something,* then."

Marcus gave a nod, but he wouldn't reveal what.

Rolling her eyes, Ella Mae waved her delicate hands in front of her. "Far be it from me to probe." She laughed softly, and he did, too.

To his surprise, Marcus realized he wasn't nearly as wound up as before, sitting there in the morning sunshine and talking right slow with the hollow's well-liked sage. Small but mighty. A woman who very well could have been his own great-*Grandmammi,* if she weren't already related in some other distant manner. After all, weren't they all closely connected in Hickory Hollow? By faith and by blood.

"I 'spect I could use any *Gscheidheit* ya might have for me."

"Wisdom, you say? Well, now, if I walked in your shoes, I'd prob'ly let patience 'have her perfect work.' "

"So you think I should back away from what I believe is right?"

"Didn't say that." She gave a faint smile. "But it'd be a mighty sensible thing to have your in-laws-to-be on your side if the time comes, ain't so?"

He wasn't sure that would happen very soon; Ammon Miller's piercing look was still too fresh in his recollection.

"At least think 'bout not rushing ahead with something that can't be undone," Ella Mae suggested.

"I've pondered this so hard, it feels like boulders pinning me to the bed at night. I *want* to marry this girl," he insisted.

"And nothin' will stop ya?" Ella Mae frowned. "Not even the lack of her father's blessing?"

"I *love* her," Marcus declared. "No one else will do: I want Tessie Ann Miller for my bride."

"No need shedding a tear," Mamma said as Tessie sat across from her at the kitchen table, mending a pair of Dat's work trousers. "Ain't like there aren't plenty of single young men your age just waitin' to get to know a nice girl like you . . . including several fellows from Indiana."

The traded men, Tessie thought with annoyance.

"And don't forget 'bout Levi Smucker," Mamma added. "Your father thinks a lot of *him.*"

Tessie struggled to conceal her disgust at

her father's meddling suggestions. He'd already spoiled Mandy's life. *I won't let him ruin mine, too.*

Her mother peered over her glasses, big blue eyes accentuated by the recent new prescription. "You all right?"

Tessie wanted so much to say what she was thinking and get it over with: *"You don't understand, Mamma. How could you suggest such a thing?"* Instead she merely said, "I 'spect so," then pressed her lips together real hard and tried her best to make small, tidy stitches.

"*Gut,* then." Mamma nodded as if satisfied. "Heard tell your cousin Emmalyn Lapp and her Mamma are hosting a hen party next Wednesday . . . makin' big batches of cookie dough and tending to a few other chores, ya know."

Tessie loved this particular first cousin and wouldn't think of missing out on spending time with opinionated but sweet Emmalyn — more like a sister than any of Tessie's other girl cousins. Nearly seventy, and counting.

Might be one of the last times I'll go anywhere single. She surprised herself at the thought — had her heart already agreed to elope with Marcus? His eager kisses signaled his unwavering commitment, and she was willing to follow his lead. *Anywhere at all.*

Chapter 3

For an instant, Mandy was befuddled as to what she saw out on the road Monday morning. She'd taken two circle letters to the mailbox and had just pushed the flag up when she heard someone humming. When she turned to look, she waved at Tessie, who was wearing her pretty plum-colored dress and matching apron as she came this way.

"Hullo, *Schweschder*!" Mandy smiled, still more curious as she noticed her sister's for-*gut* shoes. "Where ya headed this fine sunny day?"

"Just up a ways."

"I see that." She waited a moment for Tessie to say more. When it seemed that she would not, Mandy added, "Well, have yourself a right nice time, wherever it is you're dashing off to."

"All right, then." Tessie gave her a half-hearted wave.

"Say, are ya plannin' to go to Cousin

Emmalyn's party this week?" Mandy called after her, hoping for a chance to delay her.

"Not sure." Tessie kept going, her head down now as she pressed onward this lovely fall morning, which served up all the wonderful scents of harvesttime.

Well, don't that beat all? Mandy had never known Tessie to be so standoffish, even though they hadn't been close since her marriage to Sylvan. Mandy sighed — she had a peculiar feeling that something wasn't altogether right between them. She headed back to the house to check on the three Dutch apple pies cooling on the counter. One pie for Sylvan, for their noontime dessert, and one to take over to *Mamm* for supper tonight. Her mother would see to it that Dawdi Dave got a nice big slice. The remaining pie was for dear Ella Mae, who'd helped Mandy through several trying seasons.

Mandy made a mental note to go to the cold cellar and bring up a jar of chow chow, one of Sylvan's favorites. Meanwhile, she wandered out to the front porch and planted herself in one of the two chairs, relishing the wondrous aroma wafting through the screen door. It was still warm enough to sit outside without a shawl or jacket, unseasonably mild for late September. It was the ideal spot to just catch her breath and wait for the mail to arrive. She wasn't really expecting anything, but it was always fun to receive another circle letter, especially those from upstate New York and Marion, Kentucky, where a number of her married second cousins were living, having one baby after another. *Like my own sisters are . . .*

As of yet, Mandy hadn't conceived a baby, and her anxiety increased monthly. She wondered if Mamm didn't think something was the matter.

I'd hate to disappoint Sylvan, she thought, knowing he wanted a whole houseful of children, especially boys. In fact, Mandy had overheard him talking to her father soon after their wedding about all the sons he wanted. Recalling that, she realized just how often her husband and her father sat and chewed the fat together, far more frequently than Sylvan seemed to talk with her. Even now, there were unresolved things between them — the way their marriage had come about, for one. And they never talked about their infertility, either, though Mandy sometimes saw the hope in Sylvan's eyes when she cradled a little nephew or niece in her arms.

Leaning back on the porch chair, Mandy yawned and wished she hadn't stayed up so late reading last night. Dat had always said there was more time for prayer and early devotions if you went to bed on time. But with most of her morning chores finished, she knew she could doze off for a few minutes.

She closed her eyes and dreamed of holding her own first baby, soft and tiny. Until that moment, she hadn't realized the intensity of her maternal yearnings. But now, in the solitude of this haze, the baby's sweet little face drew her deep into the dream.

She awoke with a gasp. "Oh, dear Lord, may Thy will be done in this," she prayed, the longing growing stronger as she thought of her older sisters' dear children.

Mandy was dismayed by her empty nest. *It's probably my fault. . . .*

Quickly, she rose and stumbled toward the front steps, then made her way around the north side of the house, where she noticed the bare places on the old rose arbor, the last roses of summer all gone.

How much longer must I wait, Lord?

At the sound of children, she turned to stare up the road. Here came the cutest little boy pulling a wagon with two smaller children, a girl and a boy, tucked inside. Straining into the morning light, she shielded her eyes and saw that it was Hallie's three youngest. Goodness' sake, if the blond boy pulling the wagon and walking confidently in his little black suspenders and blue button-down shirt wasn't nearly a miniature of his uncle Norman.

She waved at them, and the older lad towing the wagon turned into the driveway. "Hullo there," she called, delighted by the company. "*Wie geht's,* young Perry?"

"Mamm said we could come over and visit for a while," Perry replied with a slight lisp. The boy looked down at his younger brother and sister. "Gracie and Abe like to ride in the wagon."

"Well, yous are just in time," Mandy said, thinking of the tasty pies. They might have to cool a bit more, but she could offer the children some with ice cream, if Hallie wouldn't mind them eating between meals. "Hungry for a snack, just maybe?"

At the mention of food, Gracie and Abe scrambled out of the wagon, and all of them filed up the front porch steps and into the house. Perry sniffed as he followed the tempting aroma.

Truth be told, their being here was a treat. Sure, there were plenty of opportunities for visits with Mandy's nieces and nephews, but the days could be terribly lonely with Sylvan out managing the steers.

She got the children seated at the table, then went to check to see just how hot the pies were. "Do ya like apple pie?" she asked as she poured them each some milk.

At their unison "jah," she explained that they'd have to wait a little while, till the pies were cooler.

"Put one in the fridge, maybe," young Perry suggested. His blue eyes sparkled as he tugged on his thin suspenders. "Might hurry it up, ya know."

Mandy laughed right out loud. "Why, of course it will." And she did just that.

Marcus waited till that evening to write in his black ledger-like journal, a habit he'd indulged in since beginning to court, even though none of the men in his family or circle of friends did so — unless one counted his father's running account of the weather, feed prices, and suchlike.

Monday, September 23

Went to Chester County with Tessie Miller to apply for our marriage license. Now comes the three-day waiting period . . . though I'm uncertain yet if we'll marry at the end of this week or wait till after the Lord's Day. Tessie wants me to choose the actual date. May the time pass quickly!

My bride-to-be is the prettiest and kindest young woman in Hickory Hollow, and even though her father is against our marrying, I feel honored that Tessie will soon become my wife. I'm mighty sure it won't take long for Ammon to see that we belong together — once he knows. Meanwhile, we'll wait to declare our marriage till the time is right. Tessie will stay put, living with her family, and I'll move into the rental house and get things set up for her to join me. I'll have to disconnect the electric right quick. Wouldn't want Bishop John upset at me for anything such as that, not when he'll eventually hear that I ran off to marry Tessie in the English world.

One thing's certain: There's far less planning and expense involved, which makes me wonder why more young couples aren't tempted to do this. Of course, I daresay most don't have to put up with such resistance from a future father-in-law! And what Amish couple wouldn't prefer an Amish wedding?

God sees my heart . . . and Tessie's,

too. Things will be just fine, given a few more weeks.

Chapter 4

The next morning, Tessie kept busy pressing the hand-washed *Kapps* — hers and Mamma's. While she ironed, she considered yesterday's trip to West Chester and relived her feelings as she'd walked into the courthouse, feelings of excitement and also trepidation. There was no question that she and Marcus were pushing the boundaries of the Hickory Hollow church, being there in the first place.

After the noon meal, she helped clean, skin, and cut up a whole chicken for supper. Tessie did not make eye contact with Mamma, because one cautious look from her and Mamma might suspect something. She was known to read Tessie like the books lining the kitchen shelves. And up until she'd started seeing Marcus King seriously, she and her mother had been very close.

Tessie thought fondly of her overflowing hope chest, wishing she might use the many homemade items right away to set up housekeeping with Marcus. Even so, patience was a true virtue. *"Good things come to those who wait,"* the Wise Woman was known to say. Tessie must wait for Marcus to say just when, and try to keep an agreeable attitude, too. *Sometimes the hardest part of all.*

Mamma finally broke the stillness later that day, after supper. "You're quieter than usual, dear."

"Maybe so." Tessie kept her eyes on her devotional book as she sat in the front room. They were waiting for her father to return from visiting Dawdi Dave, where he'd gone to share a slice of Mandy's gift of apple pie. The tranquil, reverent hour for family Bible reading and evening prayers was upon them, yet Tessie's thoughts were a whirl. She felt both nervous and giddy about her and Marcus's plans — the most peculiar combination of emotions she'd ever experienced.

"Cat's got your tongue?" Mamma said, tilting her head and eyeing her further. "What's a-matter?"

"Nothin's wrong, Mamma."

"Ach, you can't fool me."

"I'm fine, really." She made the mistake of glancing up and seeing Mamma's deep azure eyes still studying her from across the room.

"Goodness, Tessie girl, you look awful pale. Are you sure you're not ill?"

"I feel all right," she said, thinking the more her mother kept at it, the more likely she *would* feel sick. She changed the subject. "I wonder if Mandy's busy tonight."

"Well, you can go on over and see, I 'spect. Unless you're more interested in the old oak tree out back." Here, Mamma smiled.

Tessie decided it might be a good idea to visit Mandy after silent prayers. But what if *she* started asking questions, too? After all, Mandy had seen her dashing up the road yesterday to meet Marcus. No, the more Tessie considered it, the more she knew that a visit to Mandy was not at all prudent.

Oh, if only she could talk to Marcus, even for a brief time. That would help calm her some. She felt so guilty. Would Mamma discover she'd disregarded their wishes? Her mother had a way of fishing things out of her.

My joy might be fleeting, she realized as she heard the back door creak open and Dat shuffle onto the porch.

The following day, Mandy enjoyed the

familiar prattle of dozens of first cousins, all women between courting and middle age. She searched her aunt's kitchen and adjoining rooms for Tessie, hoping to sit with her. Mandy had brought along a generous supply of ham-and-cheese sandwiches to share at the noon meal, carrying in a food hamper from her carriage just as others had.

"Ach, there you are!" she said, touching Tessie's elbow.

Her sister turned and smiled. "Hullo, Mandy."

"I see you made it. 'Tis *gut.*"

Tessie nodded, but her smile was less than convincing. "I decided to come at the last minute."

"Well, glad ya did."

Tessie was tight-lipped today, and her eyes scanned the room, which made Mandy wonder what was wrong. Was Tessie nervous about seeing someone, maybe? For her friendly, well-loved sister, this was so out of character. What had happened to the carefree, self-assured Tessie Ann?

Together, they returned to the kitchen, where the large table was already filled with cousins. Seeing that, the two of them went to sit at a big folding table set up at the far end.

"It's like we've been shunned," Mandy

whispered, smiling.

"Sister, for goodness' sake!" Tessie rebuked her.

More cousins were already upstairs sweeping and washing floors, and some were outside beating throw rugs. Still other young women sat at tables in the front room, working on various mending projects and jabbering in *Deitsch.* It was going to be a wonderful-good frolic, to be sure.

Mandy and Tessie sat alone for only a few minutes at their separate table before two more cousins came in the back door. "We're eager to get our hands into some dough," Emmalyn's older sister Faye said happily as she and her sister Becky sat down with Mandy and Tessie. These married cousins lived on the far east side of Hickory Hollow, and it was good to see them, since it wasn't often Mandy got over to either of their homes. Becky, especially, had a talk on, telling about her four little ones, including a set of twins. Faye, too, seemed to want to share about her babies and even hinted that she hoped she was expecting yet again.

Tessie glanced at Mandy, her expression turning sympathetic, and Mandy appreciated that, guessing her sister understood what she must be feeling. Yet Mandy wished they might have had time alone before these chatty cousins arrived, because Tessie was definitely not herself. Mandy had never seen her so *verleedich* — downhearted.

Tessie wished she'd stayed home from yesterday's hen party even as she retrieved the letter that arrived in the mail the following day. She'd felt as if everyone could guess she was up to something — Mandy in particular had seemed concerned.

She sighed and opened the letter. Marcus had written to say he was moving into the rental house that very afternoon, once he returned from helping fill silo for Paul Hostetler up the road. Marcus evidently had received some nice wood furnishings donated by relatives. *Most of my family suspects I'm getting hitched later this fall, but I haven't confirmed that, not even with Daed.*

What matters most now is that you'll meet me tomorrow morning near Maryanna Esh's grove of trees. If you're still in agreement, I've got a van driver lined up for us.

Since there was so little time, Tessie would have to write back and slip the letter into his mailbox yet today. Busy as he was during daylight hours and after — and now with setting up the house, too — there was just no telling how to track him down. "I need to give Marcus my answer," she whispered, holding the letter against her heart.

As soon as possible!

Marcus opened the pages of his journal later that night. He felt an urgency to document their elopement since he and Tessie were missing out, not having a typical Amish church wedding. Keeping such an account would in no way help that, but it might be something to show their children someday.

Thursday, September 26

My last day as a single man. I found a letter from Tessie Ann tucked into the mailbox on my front porch. Her words were exciting, just knowing she truly wants to become my bride tomorrow. She has always had an encouraging way about her, and I'm grateful. Some men's wives are just the opposite.

I am considering when we'll manage our first night together, since tomorrow is Friday. We cannot afford to have Ammon wondering why Tessie's out late on a weeknight. If only we could have gone to the courthouse on a Saturday!

At least everything else is set in place. I have cash to pay the judge and I've told my boss I'll be off work tomorrow. I've also made reservations at the Kling House Restaurant, where I've requested a table near the wood-burning fireplace — more private there, I think. We'll have us a wonderful-*gut* meal to start our happy life.

One thing is up in the air: two required witnesses. There is no one from Hickory Hollow I want to entrust with our secret. I'm looking to God for this necessary detail.

Tessie waited till after dusk, then hurried up the road to her childhood home, needing some alone time in her favorite old tree. The gas lamp burned gaily in Mandy's roomy kitchen as Tessie ran past the east side of the house, glad for the solitude. Going to the splendid gnarled oak, she deftly climbed to the familiar branch.

So many happy times here as a girl.

Once she was settled, she tucked her long dress and apron tightly between her knees and leaned on the strong limb, feeling the lingering warmth from the sun-drenched afternoon. Tessie recalled how terribly skinny she'd been, no matter how much she ate, back when she'd first managed to clamber up this high. Even all those years ago, Mamma had called her a dreamer of many dreams. *"Ach, so many,"* Mamma sometimes would add with a shake of her head.

"She could have said I was an odd duck," Tessie whispered aloud.

From her lovely spot, she could see the fair moon rising in the distance, just above the Wise Woman's little house. "Denki, Gott, for this special haven," she whispered into the twilight, wondering what Marcus would think if he could see her this minute.

She prayed more fervently in her perch, asking the heavenly Father to permit things to go smoothly tomorrow. It troubled her that Dat had mentioned Levi Smucker again just today, but if he was holding out hope for a match between them, it was a poor excuse for him to reject Marcus, she thought with a grimace. Just look at how her father had finagled things with Mandy, getting the upper hand in her marriage! But Mandy wore a mostly cheerful face, and she rarely talked about what was basically an arranged marriage. *Unheard of around here,* thought Tessie.

Yawning, she stared at a glimmer of lights coming from a buggy as it made its way down Hickory Lane, the sound of the horse's hooves muted in the growing darkness. Over yonder, at Bishop John Beiler's farm, she saw what looked to be a large flashlight bobbing along — the bishop must be out checking his barn animals once more before heading inside for the night.

She imagined the lights of Bird-in-Hand farther to the west in the distance. And Tessie realized this was the last time she would sit up here praying and thinking her private thoughts as a single woman.

"Some things happen exactly once," she murmured, thinking of the moment she'd first noticed her beau's contagious smile. It had been on his eighth birthday, as he received a pony from his grandparents. The sight was something akin to spotting your first-ever sunrise or the joyous, breathtaking birth of a brand-new calf.

Or . . . uniting in marriage with your one and only love.

Chapter 5

Tessie awakened the next morning to the soft, lamenting sound of mourning doves . . . and prickles of anticipation. She flung off her quilt and flew out of bed, heading downstairs to wash and dress.

Swiftly, she returned to her room, where she pushed the only chair over near the window and looked out at the nicely landscaped flower beds she and Mamma had created together when Dat purchased this new place. So many satisfying hours spent with her mother, talking about what to plant and where.

Sighing, she turned to the Psalms in the Good Book. *Cause me to hear thy lovingkindness in the morning; for in thee do I trust: cause me to know the way wherein I should walk; for I lift up my soul unto thee.*

As she read, she kept her ear tuned for sounds of life in the kitchen below. Her fondest thoughts were of dear Marcus, and she prayed for a blessing on this, their rather strange wedding day. With all of her heart, Tessie hoped this was God's will for her.

For us, she thought.

When it was time, she made her way down the long staircase to help her mother make oatmeal and sausage patties for breakfast. She mentioned the mourning doves, and Mamma said she, too, had noticed quite a few flitting about the trees down near the road, singing their haunting song.

Later, Tessie dusted the entire upstairs, paying special attention to the many windowsills and making note that the windows all needed cleaning soon, inside and out.

By that time, Mamma had taken their fastest road horse and family carriage to run errands, which was a godsend, since Tessie wanted to bathe and put on her best blue dress and matching apron before leaving to meet Marcus. She wouldn't wear her white for-*gut* apron, though, not wanting to call too much attention to the nicer clothes. *Ach, I'm breaking with Amish tradition in every way possible.* She didn't recall Marcus saying anything about dressing up for the day, although typically he dressed better when going to town, just as all the men did — Tessie's father included.

Oh, Dat. She struggled with apprehension.

I hope you can forgive what I'm about to do. . . .

She made her way down their long paved lane to the main road and glanced at the sign her father had constructed the day they'd moved in. Mandy's husband, Sylvan, had helped dig a post hole to secure the pole at the end of their driveway, and Dat had painted the words *Ammon's Way* in perfect black lettering, large and bold enough to see for quite a distance.

Ammon's way, she thought. "In every way," she whispered, conscious yet again that she was defying her parents' wishes.

Turning onto the wider road, Tessie walked toward Marcus's house and purposely pushed away such thoughts. She lifted her gaze to the remarkably clear blue of the sky and saw not a puff of a cloud anywhere.

Perhaps it's an answer to my first prayer today, she mused.

She spotted a buggy coming toward her and soon recognized round-faced Rhoda Kurtz and her friendly neighbor Rebecca Lapp, both women waving and smiling. "Isn't that one of your best dresses?" Rebecca asked when the carriage drew near. "It's too late for market, so you must be goin' visiting, ain't?"

Tessie dipped her head and raised her hand to wave, not commenting.

"Have a pleasant day," Rebecca called behind her as the buggy continued on.

Not far behind Rebecca and Rhoda was another buggy. Tessie was surprised to see Levi Smucker with his towheaded twin nephews — little Jake and Joey — perched on Levi's knees. The horse began to slow to a trot, then halted. "*Guder Mariye,* Tessie Ann." Levi grinned, his light brown hair blowing in the breeze, a straw hat on the front seat beside him. "Ain't the Lord's Day, is it?" he teased.

She couldn't help but laugh, though she hoped he wouldn't ask more questions.

By now the two boys with him were waving and grinning, as well. And young Joey pushed his little hand into his pants pocket and pulled out a small black coin purse. "I've got my money from shelling peas," the darling boy said, blue eyes blinking as he looked down at her, jingling his coins.

"*Gut* for you!" Tessie said, unable to keep from smiling.

"Mamma gave us five cents a cup this summer."

"You saved it all this time?"

Levi spoke up. "This one's a penny pincher, let me tell ya. *Schpaarsam* —

frugal." He reached up and tousled Joey's twin's hair. "Ain't so, Jake?"

Both boys chuckled.

"Well, have yourself a *wunnerbaar-gut* mornin'," Levi said, a twinkle in his hazel eyes.

"Denki, and you, too."

Levi nodded and urged the horse onward.

For pity's sake, she thought, wondering how many more folks she'd encounter. Still, she had to smile at Levi's comical reaction to her nice dress and apron. He had always been one of the more amiable, easygoing young men at the Singings and other youth gatherings, yet work always found its way to his door — both attributes must have attracted Tessie's father's enthusiasm. Even so, Tessie didn't have an iota of regret about not letting Levi date her back when, though she had felt a bit sorry for him when she'd heard months ago that he was no longer courting Preacher Yoder's vivacious granddaughter.

The Lord will surely bring someone along for him. Without Dat's help!

Tessie hastened her steps, lest Marcus wonder if she was dawdling, having second thoughts.

As they walked up the courthouse steps in

West Chester, Tessie looked at Marcus for reassurance and welcomed his confident gaze. *We're actually doing this — we're going to be married!*

Pleased though she was, it was impossible later for her not to compare this so-called ceremony to the Amish wedding she was sacrificing. Nor could she stop thinking about the worry her parents and sisters would experience once the truth about this moment was known. *They'll come around,* she thought.

Providentially, they'd met another couple, *Englischers* at least several years older than Marcus and Tessie, who also needed witnesses to fulfill the legal requirement for the union. So they agreed to take turns with them, and presently this affectionate couple stood back behind a roped-off area as witnesses for her and Marcus while she and her soon-to-be husband sat with their right hands in the air and their left hands resting on Marcus's Bible, vowing that the information on the marriage license was indeed correct.

Marcus smiled endearingly at her, and she smiled back. Yet it wasn't until they were declared husband and wife and the appropriate papers were signed that Tessie began to feel somewhat relieved. All they lacked was the final prayer, which Marcus would surely offer later, after they left the courthouse. The tension concerning what she'd done without her parents' permission began to diminish, as well. She was thankful for the familiar sense of security she always felt with Marcus, who had attended to every detail. She wondered how he'd managed to line up the appointment with the judge, for instance, but it wasn't her place to ask. Nor to question.

The fact was, they were wed now in accordance with the law of the land. Yet what about the Lord God's approval? Oh, she so longed for that, too. Had Marcus been right that this was the answer to his many prayers?

They took time to politely thank the other newly married couple before heading outside to wait for the Mennonite van driver. "I love my beautiful bride," Marcus whispered in her ear once they were sitting behind the somewhat inquisitive driver who would drive them to the restaurant where Marcus wanted to treat her to their first meal as husband and wife. Though he remained close by her side, he did not lean over to kiss her, and Tessie wondered when they might seal their love.

Mandy laid out a blue-and-white-striped

tablecloth on the kitchen table, set it for two, and then stepped back to admire the corner where she and Sylvan would sit alone to eat this noon, a rarity. Sylvan's widowed great-aunt, Elaine Beiler, lived in the smaller of their two Dawdi Hauses, but she was under the weather and staying put today. It made this the ideal occasion for Mandy to seek out her husband's opinion on something she'd already gone ahead and discussed with Cousin Emmalyn, who was over the moon about Mandy's grand idea. *Surely he won't dismiss it out of hand,* she thought, going to the back door and seeing him coming this way across the yard.

"Hope you're *gut* and hungry," she said as she greeted him inside the back porch. "I think I've made enough for two families."

He removed his straw hat. "Maybe you can take leftovers to *Aendi* Elaine later . . . if she's up to eating."

"Jah, thought of that." She waited for Sylvan to roll up his shirt sleeves and scrub his big callused hands and sunburned arms in the large basin on the indoor porch.

"Mmm, smells *gut.*" He sniffed the air like a hungry hound, blue eyes wide.

"It's veal cutlet with mashed potatoes and gravy." She hoped that all the hours she'd put into their dinner and the delicious dessert of black raspberry pie might please him. She'd put up more berries last summer than usual, with help from her older sisters, Marta and Molly, along with Tessie and Mamma. Thinking now of her youngest sister, Mandy felt the urge to pray, not knowing what had been bothering Tessie the last two times they'd seen each other. Mandy knew from her own experience that prayer was vital.

Sylvan made small talk after they'd bowed their heads for the silent blessing. "I heard from your father that Marcus King moved into a rental house on the outskirts of the hollow. Seems mighty odd before getting hitched up, jah?"

Mandy recalled what she'd witnessed on the road between Marcus and Tessie. "Just maybe the place came up for lease before wedding season."

"He must be sweet on someone, then — planning to marry soon. Why else would he secure a place ahead of time? It'd make better financial sense to stay under his father's roof till it's needed." Sylvan took a large helping of potatoes, then dug in.

"Does seem peculiar." Mandy reached for the water pitcher and poured some in both their tumblers. "Hope ya don't mind just water at the meal," she said almost as an afterthought.

He glanced toward the fridge. "Is there any meadow tea left?"

She nodded her head. "Jah, sure, but —"

"Do ya mind?"

She rose quickly to get the desired drink. Sometimes it seemed Sylvan wanted altogether different things than what she'd planned — and not just at mealtimes. She wondered just then if it was such a good idea to bring up her idea, excited though she and Cousin Emmalyn were about it.

Sylvan seemed rather content presently, enjoying his meal. He said no more as he helped himself to seconds, then raised his glass of sweetened meadow tea and drank it straight down.

Mandy felt her courage dwindling. *Maybe it would be best for the conversation to wait.* Till just when, though, she wasn't sure.

Marcus held Tessie's hand across the table once they were seated at the restaurant. *Husband and wife!* Tessie thought. And as if to make up for the lack of a prayer of blessing at the courthouse, Marcus prayed over their union prior to eating, offering their lives as a married couple to God's bidding all the days of their lives. "We will look to Thee, O Lord, for every blessing."

"Denki," she said after his amen, fighting back tears. "That means a lot to me . . . to us."

Marcus nodded. "I also felt the absence of the church today."

She hoped he was not regretting the way they'd started their marriage, but his cheerful demeanor during the meal put her mind at ease.

Later, as they rode back to Hickory Hollow in the van, she enjoyed his sweet kiss. "We're married now, Tessie Ann," he said quietly as they passed his rental house with its graceful poplar trees lining the entire north side. She peered out the window at what would ultimately be her home, too, and he whispered, "Meet me there tomorrow, my love . . . after dusk."

She understood and happily agreed, smiling into his alluring eyes.

A few minutes later, when Tessie arrived home, she was relieved to find Mamma had not yet returned. In fact, she looked on it as providential as she hurried upstairs to change clothes. There must be no evidence of the highly unusual step she and Marcus had taken this day.

Chapter 6

"What sort of wares are you thinkin' of selling at our little gift shop?" Mandy asked when Emmalyn stopped by that afternoon.

"I say we should offer embroidered linens and other handiwork. My mother's aunt who lives in Mount Hope, Ohio, does this sort of thing, too — says those are hot items with tourists." Emmalyn's plump face had a liveliness to it today.

"Sounds like a great idea."

Emmalyn tilted her head. "Does Sylvan know yet?"

"I came that close to telling him but then changed my mind. I'd really just like to surprise him with some extra money, ya know." Oh, she wished she and Sylvan could talk more freely about things. *And not just this . . .* She glanced out the window toward the stable. "We sure could use another good road horse."

"Ach, you'll have enough money for that

soon enough, trust me."

"Trust ya?" Mandy laughed. "That's just what I'm doin'." She didn't say she needed to get out amongst other folk, rub shoulders with Amish and Mennonites alike. Oh, how wonderful it would be to have the opportunity to leave the house more, instead of being alone with her desperate waiting to find out if she was finally expecting a baby.

Later, when Cousin Emmalyn headed for home, Mandy felt melancholy, and she indulged herself by entertaining the exciting dream of setting up the little shop. *I need to figure out a way to talk to Sylvan about it . . . and soon!*

She stood in the doorway to the back porch, where she could see her husband over near the woodshed, talking with her father, who'd dropped by as he often did. Dat had gone over to help make homemade sauerkraut with the firefighters and their families at the Kinzer Fire Company firehouse, in preparation for the New Year's Day fundraiser, a pork-and-sauerkraut dinner featuring the homemade treat. Her mouth watered at the thought of the delicious meal.

Staring out at her father and Sylvan talking, she tried to imagine Dat making over her and Sylvan's firstborn son. Or baby daughter. Surely Dat — and Mamma — looked forward to that day almost as much as she and Sylvan did.

If and when almighty God sees fit to bless us with a child, Mandy thought, so discouraged she fought back tears.

The fragrant blend of fresh-cut hay and new silage permeated the Saturday evening air as Tessie Ann waited in the shadow of the small copse of trees along Hickory Lane. In the waning light, she spotted Marcus walking toward her and quickly stepped into view. It was his idea to meet there to escort her to the home that was to become theirs. She wished they could hold hands as they leisurely walked. Soon, though, they would be in each other's arms, and she felt the tingle of anticipation as they exchanged knowing smiles.

At the back door of the small home, her playful husband took her off guard and scooped her up to carry her across the threshold, where he kissed her soundly once he'd closed the door. She'd heard of Englischer newlyweds and some of her more progressive cousins in other parts of the country doing this, as well. Nevertheless, she felt a bit breathless, being held so close she could smell a hint of the cologne he must have dabbed on before meeting her.

Perhaps sensing her surprise, Marcus set her down and reached for her hand. "Let me show you around the place," he said. "Just think, very soon you'll be moving your things in here with me." He turned to look down into her face, smiling broadly. "I can hardly wait till we can declare our love to the whole world."

She laughed softly, taken by his enthusiasm. How she adored this darling man of hers! "Well, at least to Hickory Hollow, jah?"

He nodded and led her into the kitchen, where he suggested she decide where she wanted her dishes and utensils and whatnot. "I'm making do for now," he added casually. Tessie wondered how Marcus was managing to cook for himself and quickly discovered that he was mostly making sandwiches, and eating cold cereal and toast for breakfast.

He mentioned having borrowed some odds and ends of kitchenware from his mother and older sisters. "They're all so eager to help out." Marcus grinned. "Of course, they suspect somethin's up."

They sat together at his table and talked of the near future, how lovely it would be for Marcus to welcome her there for good. "We'll have to share our story with our children and grandchildren someday," Tessie said, noting their offspring might not believe what they'd had to do for love.

"Ain't that the truth." He moved her chair over next to his and cupped her face in his hands. "I love you more than I can put into words, dearest Tessie," he whispered, then leaned closer to kiss her. This time, his lips felt softer.

Can it be we're truly husband and wife? she thought, captured by his loving gaze.

Tessie felt truly strange staring at the back of Marcus's head during the first and second sermons at Preaching service Sunday. She was seated on the long bench between Mamma and Miriam, her oldest sister, who held her toddler son, Yonnie, on her lap. Right or wrong, Tessie could not erase the sweet memory of her husband's tenderness last evening . . . and the lovely things they'd said to each other, too.

They had been quite mindful of the hour, and in the end Marcus had managed to return her home before too late. They did not want her father to suspect anything, hoping he would just assume she was out on a date and not nestled away in her new husband's house.

Tessie could hardly wait to see Marcus

again as his loving bride, instead of this playacting. The pretense would encompass the entire morning and afternoon, even the shared meal where the young married couples sat together during the second seating. It was all Tessie could do to go along with it. She loved Marcus so and could not stop daydreaming during the final silent prayer, when the People knelt at their benches in contrition and respect before the Lord.

How many days before Marcus tells Dat our news? she wondered, and in turn asked God the selfsame thing.

Dat stayed behind to fellowship a bit longer, but Mamma decided not to wait around, delaying the trip home with Tessie. Three-year-old niece Anna, one of Miriam's girls, had asked to return home with them for the afternoon, and the little one sat on Tessie's lap, already droopy eyed well before the horse had taken them even a half mile.

"I wasn't goin' to bring this up," Mamma said quietly, glancing at petite Anna while holding the reins. "But I feel I ought to now that we're alone, Tessie, dear."

She bristled, sensing what was next.

"I presume you were out with Marcus King again last evening." Mamma frowned.

"He's still courting you against our wishes, ain't so?"

"We're no longer dating, Mamma."

We're married! she thought, her heart heavy at her mother's words.

"Well, 'tis *gut* to hear. You had me . . . well, *us,* mighty worried."

Tessie kept still. Thank goodness Mamma hadn't pressed in a different direction. *Best to just let things be.*

Even so, she was now deliberately misleading her mother, and this new deception piled on top of everything else. And looking down at lovable Anna, she yearned for things to be ever so different. Why couldn't Dat and Mamma accept Marcus, when Tessie herself loved him as she did?

A full week came and went, and Tessie slipped over to see Marcus twice, once for a short time the first Wednesday in October, when her chores were done and supper was in the oven, and then for another few hours the following Sunday evening, when the youth were expected to be out late anyway.

She felt nearly breathless to know if Marcus might be working alongside her father, or perhaps have some interaction with him over at Paul Hostetler's place, where Marcus helped out several times each week.

Anything at all to understand where things stood between the two men in her life. But Marcus was completely mum on the topic, and though it was ever so hard, Tessie held her peace, as well.

They waited till dark to sit out on the front porch, enjoying the starlight. Tessie said how happy she felt when she was with him. "I can hardly wait to sit here each and every night, till winter comes."

"Ain't the right time just yet," Marcus said, reaching for her hand. "Bear with me a bit longer, love."

She nodded and said she would while crickets chirped and courting buggies rolled up and down Hickory Lane.

St. Michael's Day came on October eleventh, and the People fasted and prayed prior to their communion Sunday, when they had their biannual foot washing service, followed by the common meal.

Truth be known, Tessie was weary of silently marking time and living at home. She also felt dreadfully convicted during the Sunday service, not sure she should have even attended. And then there was Mamma, who seemed to think Tessie had been going to youth activities here lately.

Tessie felt guilty at the remembrance of

the ecru-colored doily Mamma was crocheting for Tessie's hope chest. And there was talk of Dawdi Dave's interest in making her a corner cupboard, as well.

"Tell me what you love," Marcus had asked the last time she'd been with him in his house, a night of thunderstorms and torrential rain. She'd felt so out of sorts she hadn't said much. It wasn't at all like their courting days, when they'd ridden blissfully together under the moon for hours on end. Her patience was all but gone.

Marcus had sensed something amiss. She let him hold her while she cried, and he kissed her wet cheeks over and over again.

After Marcus saw Tessie home to her father's house, following yet another too brief visit, he pulled out his journal and began to write.

Monday, October 14

I fully understand Tessie's frustration, wanting to live here with me and wondering when I'll speak up to see where the chips fall. She is patient, though, and has not questioned my lead in this.

This afternoon, while at the blacksmith's shop, I tried again to speak with

Tessie's father, only to be rebuffed once more. I was so tempted to blurt out to him that I'm married to his daughter, but I refrained. And all Ammon would say to my request to work with him was that he has all the help he needs at his place. So that's that . . . for today, anyway.

If only I could work beside him, I believe I could gain his trust. If that's what he's looking for. With such a man, it's awful hard to know, really.

Truth is, I'm becoming as irritated with this peculiar situation as my precious bride is. I'm praying even more earnestly for the Lord God to make a way where there seems to be none . . . just a never-ending barricade.

CHAPTER 7

Mandy searched all over for Cousin Emmalyn before the work frolic got under way the following Thursday morning at the bishop's place. Twenty-five women from the church district had gathered there to tie colorful warm comforters to be sent to Christian Aid Ministries in Berlin, Ohio, which distributed items to the poor all over the world.

There was excited chatter about the big two-story barn that had burned to the ground just north of Harristown Road, struck by lightning during the recent storm. Plans were under way to raise a new barn before too long, once beams were cut and the foundation walls repaired.

At around eleven-thirty, after working diligently, Mandy spotted Cousin Emmalyn clear on the other side of the front room and waved at her, hoping she might join her for the dinnertime break. Mary Beiler offered up the most delicious Busy Day stew, along with homemade wheat rolls and rhubarb and strawberry jam. There was also the peanut-butter spread made with marshmallow cream, and Cousin Emmalyn had brought jars of mouthwatering homemade cheese spread to share. Naturally, there were desserts, too — shoofly pie and pumpkin torte, as well as various types of cookies: pineapple, pumpkin, and dropped sugar.

"I wondered if you've given any more thought to our, uh, joint project," Mandy whispered when they were seated at the long table.

"Interesting you asked — I just made a deposit on the rent for that space in Bird-in-Hand," said Emmalyn, her pale blue eyes shining. "The tiny shop we discussed, and perfect for what we need. Oh, and we can start setting up tomorrow, if you'd like."

"You moved on it awful quick." Mandy couldn't believe her ears. "And without me."

"I thought you were ready to move ahead. Besides, I have so many embroidered and quilted things to sell now. Time's a-wastin' — the fall tourist season is already in full swing, ya know."

Emmalyn was right. Still, Mandy hoped it was wise for her to have said yes to this venture without asking Sylvan first. What if he hit the roof about the news? Oh, she hoped Sylvan would come around eventually. *And I've never given Emmalyn any reason to think I can't.* "All right, then. Count me in."

Emmalyn squealed her glee. "I could just hug the stuffin' out of you!" And she attempted to do just that, right there at the table with many sets of eyes observing them. "Meet me at my house first thing tomorrow, and bring all of your own goods to sell."

Giddy as Mandy felt at the prospect of having their very own shop, she wondered how to transport all the dozens of quilted potholders and toaster covers, and embroidered linens, too, from the house without raising Sylvan's suspicions.

But then she had the perfect idea. Why not simply load up the buggy prior to hitching up tomorrow? Sylvan would be busy in the barns, and he didn't need to know, not just yet.

At the shop's opening, two days later, oodles of tourists seemed eager to plunk down money for Mandy's and Emmalyn's homemade items. Mandy had told Sylvan she was going visiting and that Tessie would be over to cook the noon meal that day. Mandy was fairly certain he understood her need to get away sometimes, possibly even felt sorry for her, if he stopped to think about it — her staying home alone all the time and all. And though he hadn't said as much, she assumed he was happy she was getting out.

But . . . going visiting. She felt wicked and knew she must come clean — and mighty soon, too.

Yet Mandy soon forgot her guilt in the day's busy pace. She loved working with her outgoing cousin and felt truly invigorated while talking with people from all over the country, as well as quite a number from England, some who made an annual trip to Lancaster County to enjoy the harvest. The customers were cordial and curious, eager to stop in and chat for a while and describe the local inns where they were staying or make over the goods, laughing here and there. Many guest homes were owned by Mennonites, and some by Amish families whose bishops allowed them to have electricity on the side of the house where their paying guests stayed. All of it was giving Mandy wonderful-*gut* ideas . . . ways not to feel so isolated at home. At least till her babies started coming. *O Lord, may it happen soon,* she thought, beginning to fear she might be infertile. She dreaded the thought as she took her time organizing a display of Cousin Emmalyn's crocheted baby booties in pale green, yellow, and pink.

"Ah, I see you've got your eye on something . . . for the future?" Emmalyn came over, smiling broadly, in a moment when there were no customers. She leaned her head close to Mandy's. "Are ya keepin' a secret, cousin?"

"Don't be silly. You'll be one of the first to know. After Sylvan, of course."

Emmalyn turned her around, holding on to her wrists. "Look me in the eye and say you don't want a whole batch of little ones." She waited, a frown creeping onto her face as she searched Mandy's face. "Honey? You all right?"

Mandy didn't feel the need to spill her heart out, especially not today, when she'd been enjoying herself so. "Sure, I want oodles of children, like every other young woman."

Her cousin nodded. "When *I'm* married I want at least eight, maybe more."

"See?" Mandy smiled, relieved. Far better for Emmalyn to talk about herself. "Girls or boys?"

"Oh, four or five boys to start with, then some little dishwashers, ya know."

"You must be thinkin' your husband will need workers." She considered that, wondering why she hadn't really pondered Sylvan's own need before.

"I honestly hope I marry a farmer." Emmalyn's face was all dreamy. "But there's so little farmland left round here."

"Is there someone special, maybe?"

"Oh, jah . . . but I'll let you know how that goes." Emmalyn's eyes twinkled.

"Okay, then."

And they both laughed as another cluster of patrons headed up the walkway into the shop.

Mandy had yet to ask Emmalyn about the rent amount, but when closing time rolled around, they were both exhausted. Hurrying off to catch her ride home with a paid driver, Mandy had a gnawing feeling in her stomach. Even though she'd managed to pull the wool over Sylvan's eyes, she felt uneasy, leading a double life. But after the fun she'd had today, she didn't want to give up the shop now.

Tessie was glad to cook for her brother-in-law and the handful of other workers at his and Mandy's place — it helped to keep her mind off missing Marcus. Yet how odd that Mandy had pleaded with her to cover for her, not saying where she was headed in such a big hurry that morning. It did seem peculiar, Tessie's own longing to be cooking and keeping house for Marcus while Mandy ran off to parts unknown, shirking her own duty.

Tessie hardly knew what to think of the situation her sister had placed her in. Besides that, now that the vineyard was dormant for the season, Marcus was kept busy at the Hostetler farm, and there were fewer opportunities for the two of them to be alone discreetly. She did not like feeling so cut off from her own husband, yet what could be done?

Lately she'd started to wonder if their wonderful-*gut* plan to force her father into accepting the marriage wasn't fraught with problems. What if she were to simply announce she was married and move in with Marcus? Would her father disown her?

Her discouraged state only served to compound her tetchiness, which made it hard for her to be as pleasant to her husband as she longed to be. Here it was already almost a month since they'd wed, and there was still no indication from Marcus of when they could openly be together. Could it be Marcus had come to realize the same thing . . . that they might have made a mistake in thinking they could force her father to accept their union?

Weary of pondering her discouraging

circumstance and glad to be back home once again, Tessie set about cleaning Mamma's sitting room, where they entertained Sunday afternoon visitors — mostly grandparents and cousins. She caught a whiff of her chocolate cake baking for dessert after supper — Midnight Cake, she liked to call it. Focused on the promise of the scrumptious dessert that evening, she moved toward her father's rolltop desk, which was especially dusty, though she'd given it a thorough going over just last week.

Sliding it open, she noticed a couple of sticky notes — reminders for the vet's visit to administer the horses' routine shots. There was also a black folder lying out with the words *Family Charts* written on a yellow tab. Curious, she opened it and found a listing of Hickory Hollow families: Stoltzfus, Fisher, and Beiler/Byler . . . She'd heard of such genetic charts being kept quietly by the older patriarchs and some ministers in other church districts, but never in Hickory Hollow, where Bishop John had forbidden it. The People believed the health of their children was up to God's will, when all was said and done. So she was shocked to see her own father kept such a list.

She looked more closely: The surname King seemed to jump off the page. Tessie read on and was stunned to discover that Marcus's father, Lloyd King, was actually a third cousin to her own father . . . which made her and Marcus third cousins once removed. Distant enough to marry legally, but a potentially alarming mix in their closely related community.

Scanning the charts, Tessie realized her father must have painstakingly created these lists of families that, for genetic reasons, he considered off-limits to his daughters — he'd taken care to note some of the diseases each family had encountered in recent generations. Clearly, his concern was for high-risk genetic disorders like mental retardation, dwarfism, autism, cerebral palsy, sudden infant death, and others.

Tessie had seen more than a handful of Lancaster County farmhouses glowing nightly with steady blue lights in the bedrooms of Amish and Mennonite children who suffered from Crigler-Najjar syndrome, a condition that resulted in severe jaundice and brain damage, even possible death. New genetic diseases due to close intermarriage were being identified all the time.

Tessie was horror-struck. To think *this* was likely the primary reason her parents opposed a marriage to Marcus.

Leaning heavily on the desk, she considered the implications.

What have we done?

She caught her breath as she recalled that one of Marcus's older sisters had given birth to a baby with a fatal genetic disorder just in the past year. And now that she thought of it, Marcus's aunt Suzy had lost a toddler boy to the same disease not long ago.

The bleak reality plagued her.

She moaned. "Could it be that Dat only wanted to spare me heartache?" Turning, Tessie stared out the window. From this distance, the meadow beyond the corncrib looked pea green and, in some places near the mule roads, almost as if a giant foot had flattened it.

The truth was more dreadful than she'd imagined, and her legs went as limp as slack ropes. She tumbled into the willow chair near the desk and raised her hands to her face, murmuring, "Why didn't they just tell me?" She began to weep. "Why?"

Chapter 8

The hues of Hickory Hollow were peacefully muted and fall-like that Sunday morning as daylight began to peek over the distant hills.

Marcus reached for his ledger as he rolled out of bed that no-Preaching day, exhausted in every way. A feeling of detachment from the People had begun to engulf him, all the more so since communion and foot washing last Sunday. He should not have participated in the Lord's Supper, but lest he call attention to himself, he'd gone ahead. Prior to the day, he'd fasted on Friday, beseeching God to forgive him for getting Tessie into such an excruciating mess. And for disobeying his unwitting father-in-law.

Filled with turmoil, he began to write.

Sunday, October 20

My beloved Tessie is troubled. If only I could remedy that! Her father continues to be a roadblock. I've tried several times to work with Ammon, to somehow get into his good graces. Yet I don't trust what he might say or do — it might hurt Tessie further, and my first priority is to protect my bride. It rankles me no end, not being able to bring her home with me. That is all I want. When, O Lord?

I've decided it isn't prudent to keep our marriage quiet any longer. The upcoming wedding season may be the best time to reveal the truth, preferably at one of Tessie's cousins' weddings, where I'm sure Ammon will be respectful, or at least not fly at me like a hornet. Any large gathering would be ideal.

It's a shame our joy has been squelched so, when I am anxious to share it with my family . . . and with all the People. This secrecy is cause for unhappiness in my Tessie's heart, as well. It pains me to see the sorrow in her eyes each time we're together.

In thinking back to our marriage at the courthouse, I'm mighty glad I took my Bible along . . . and later prayed over

Tessie and me, in place of the bishop. Not that I presume to have offered the kind of blessing he would've prayed over the two of us in a church wedding. Still, it's a comfort that we did everything as right as we possibly could, given the circumstances.

Marcus tucked their marriage license into his daily journal; then he decided to write a brief note to Tessie. He said he couldn't stand living apart from her much longer, and that he planned to talk with her father at the first of her relatives' weddings.

Please be praying for wisdom for me as I speak to your Dat . . . and that he might receive the news with some measure of grace.

Honestly, Tessie Ann, I have been so lonely without you. Some nights I stay up late and write in my journal instead of trying to fall asleep. I've told you about my journal before, haven't I? I've been recording the story of our marriage there — never want to forget all we've gone through to be together. Of course I don't dare keep such a record out in the open, at least for now. I've got a concealed compartment in the top middle drawer of my bureau, which should suffice.

I'm looking forward to growing a beard very soon — the all-important symbol of a married man. I can hardly wait, my dearest love!

He signed off, *Yours always, Marcus,* then slipped the note into an envelope to mail in the morning.

Tessie had the jitters on the ride to the barn raising early Tuesday morning, anxious to tell Marcus about the folder in her father's desk. She'd missed seeing him this past Sunday, having no choice but to visit relatives with her parents. Then, yesterday's washing took up much of the day. To think today was the first time she could share Dat's reason for being so set against Marcus as her husband.

Such terrible news, she thought miserably. *Marcus and I should never risk having children!*

She wondered how they might solve this . . . somehow. Should they go to the bishop and confess their private deed, perhaps? What would Bishop John suggest? Their marriage could not be undone; she knew that much. And as for birth control measures, those were forbidden, as well.

Today Mandy had joined Tessie and Mamma in the family buggy, since Dat had left the house before dawn with the bishop, who'd come for him on the way to the site. Tessie had seen her father hang his nail apron and leather tool belt on one of the wooden pegs in the outer room beyond the kitchen just last evening. She'd wondered, at the time, what job Marcus might have at this barn raising. He was so lean and limber — the many experienced foremen typically liked to have such young men work as nailers high on the rafters.

"Too bad 'bout the perty white barn that burned down," Mandy said from where she and Mamma sat in front of Tessie Ann.

"Jah, and to think the phone at the nearest shanty was out on the very day it was so needed," Mamma said, melancholy in her voice.

"Somethin' awful." Mandy glanced over her shoulder at Tessie.

"Can you imagine if the *house* had caught fire?" Mamma added.

Tessie and Mandy gasped in unison, and Mandy shook her head.

"*Gut* thing the community comes together like this."

Tessie agreed and was glad to be able to

spend a good part of the day setting up the serving tables for more than four hundred men and dozens of younger boys. Some families would come from as far away as Strasburg and Nickel Mines. She quickly settled into the work, enjoying the fun-loving banter and talk among the women-folk.

"I hear there's a local Amish farmer who's raisin' camels for their milk," Rebecca Lapp said presently, catching Tessie's attention.

"Jah, Miller's Organic Farm is shipping it all over the country," Rhoda Kurtz answered. "Ten dollars a pint."

"Guess it tastes like skim milk, only a little saltier," Rebecca said. "S'posed to be mighty *gut* for folks with diabetes and other illnesses."

"Word has it, it's even helped some of the autistic children round Bird-in-Hand," Lillianne Hostetler chimed in.

"Well, not so quick," Rebecca said. "No one's stating outright that camel's milk will cure anything. Let's just be real clear on that."

Tessie smiled, wondering about all this camel talk as she, Mamma, and Mandy set out three dozen snitz pies. By midafternoon, the new barn would be pretty much closed in, if all went as usual. A good number of folk would stay on till closer to supper, making vents to place in the eaves, and taking time to build grain bins, too. She envisioned sledgehammers and long ropes, chalk lines and measuring tapes, and pry bars. A head carpenter had been appointed days before. The eight-by-eight timbers had already arrived, and sill planks were laid out on the vast foundation. The older men would build the animal stalls inside the towering barn walls, amidst what might seem to an outsider like mass disorder, yet was anything but.

With everything Tessie Ann had to do to help with the meals for the male workers, she didn't know exactly when she might whisper her startling discovery to Marcus. How might he respond? Still, it was only fair that she told him the probable source of the lingering tension between him and Dat, even though it would add a new burden to their young marriage.

Perhaps they could take a short walk after the noon meal, right before Marcus returned to his high perch on the barn's roof. She prayed the Lord might make it possible to do so privately.

Marcus paused to wipe his brow with the back of his arm, there high on the rafters.

He squinted into the sunlight, thankful for this near-perfect weather. A number of men had commented earlier on it, saying the Lord God had seen fit to give them a fine day to raise this barn. As was usual at such gatherings, the atmosphere was abuzz with the camaraderie of all the workers — men and womenfolk alike.

He scanned the area below, searching for sweet Tessie. And then he spotted her, clear over near the large tent erected off to the left of the field, no doubt helping to spread out the food.

Even at this distance, she was mighty pretty. And more than that, helpful and kind, possessing all the worthy character traits a man would ever desire in a wife. At the thought, he glanced over at Ammon Miller, working several tiers below him. Marcus had high hopes for the Lord's intervention for a conversation with Tessie's father, possibly even today.

I trust in Thy will, O Lord, he prayed, watching Ammon hammer nails with the force of a young man. *A man with strength in many areas,* Marcus thought. *A man who surely has his daughter's best interest at heart.*

One of Tessie's Amish neighbors, Maryanna Esh, who owned a greenhouse, was chattering about an old upright piano her elderly aunt had seen at a German Brethren meetinghouse. The young man who'd played it had explained to her that such instruments needed exceptional care. "A *gut* piano like that reminded my aunt of some people, I guess." Maryanna continued, "You just can't let them be for too long without tending to them. They'll break down and weaken . . . and, in the case of a piano, lose their ability to stay in tune." Maryanna glanced up from cutting squares of strawberry Jell-O in a large pan.

"Lookin' after each other *is* important," Tessie agreed softly, saying the words more to herself than to anyone.

Other women had interesting anecdotes, too, including Rebecca Lapp, known all over the hollow as a storyteller. Oh, could she ever grab your interest, particularly with hilarious childhood tales, which soon had the women cutting up and laughing.

Tessie looked over at the already raised wooden walls of the barn, trying her best to locate Marcus. There were so many men, most wearing their black work jackets because the day was chilly, although some of the younger fellows had shed theirs.

She sighed. There was no way to pick out which of the menfolk might be Marcus. And in that moment, she felt farther from him than ever.

Tessie was counting out plastic utensils with Mandy in the large dinner tent when she heard a collective gasp. She looked up to see men scrambling down from their locations on the beamed barn walls.

"What's happened?" Mandy glanced toward the rush of men.

Tessie held her breath. The atmosphere was hushed . . . too still.

O Lord, don't let any of the men be hurt, she prayed, recalling other times when injuries had occurred.

Cousin Emmalyn rushed to them suddenly. "It's Marcus King. He's fallen!"

Tessie's legs locked, and she felt she might faint. Oh, but she couldn't let herself do that when she wanted to dash across the field to go to him. But no one knew of their intimate relationship. "Is he hurt?" she whispered as fear gripped her heart, but Emmalyn didn't know.

Mandy turned to wrap her arms around Tessie Ann, holding on to her or holding her together — Tessie wasn't sure which. She saw two young boys race toward the phone shed.

I should be with Marcus. . . .

Terror overwhelmed her, yet she could not turn and weep in Mandy's arms — could not, *would not* cause a scene. Marcus himself had refused to allow their marriage to be known till the time was right, so she must try to honor him even now.

The knot of men in black suspenders and work trousers crowded in closer, the swarm ever increasing as more workers rushed to gather near fallen Marcus. As she watched, incapable of breath, every muscle in Tessie's body felt stiff . . . hard as the nails Marcus had used this day.

Then, one by one, the men respectfully removed their straw hats. A siren wailed in the distance.

No, no, no! Tessie screamed silently. And she broke free of her sister and dashed across the wide green field, running and crying, not caring who saw her as she burst through the throng of men, hurrying to her husband's side.

CHAPTER 9

Mandy gasped as Tessie dashed off in the direction of Marcus and the workmen.

Emmalyn and her mother stood near Mandy, watching . . . waiting. Mamm wrung her hands as she stepped closer to Mandy. Her sweet face had turned bright pink, and though Mandy offered soothing words, she was unable to settle her mother down. "What's Tessie doin' over yonder?" Mamm asked, then babbled something in Deitsch about Tessie Ann and Marcus's recent breakup. None of it made sense.

"There, there," Mandy said, unable to grasp her mother's concern over that at such a fragile time. Yet, as beside herself as Mamm seemed to be, it wasn't Mandy's place to explain that Tessie did indeed love Marcus King. She'd seen the evidence weeks ago, and her sister's bold action now reconfirmed it.

"He's going to be okay, isn't he?" Mamm

craned her neck to see.

Mandy touched her mother's back. "Let's be in prayer . . . not say more."

"Jah." Mamm's frown was etched on her brow, and her chin quivered as the ambulance pulled up and paramedics emerged with a long stretcher. The Amishmen parted to make room.

In a few short moments, Marcus was carried off the field to the waiting emergency vehicle, covered with a stark white sheet. Tessie's head bowed low as she walked next to the stretcher.

Mandy clenched her jaw, trying not to cry as she watched her poor, dear sister place a hand on Marcus's heart for a moment, then step back as he was carried into the ambulance and the doors were closed. The vehicle pulled out onto the road, but the siren was as still as the young Amishman inside.

By the time Tessie arrived home with her sister and mother, she felt not only stunned but sick. Neither Mandy nor Mamma had posed a single question about her behavior on the hushed ride back from the barn raising, and for this she was thankful, not knowing what she would have said anyway.

When they pulled up to the stable, Mandy kindly offered to unhitch the horse for

Mamma and urged Tessie inside. Tessie went into the house and up the stairs, going to her room to lie facedown on her bed, inconsolable. Oh, she wished her tears might come now that she was alone! But they remained locked away inside her as she helplessly replayed her last precious, loving hours with Marcus. She had to cling to those memories, for they were all she had.

Eventually, Mandy came into her room, closed the door, and lay down on the bed. When she felt her sister's arm slip around her, Tessie's tears finally began to flow, mingling with Mandy's own.

"How can I ever live through this?" Tessie whispered, sobbing. "How?"

"You must have cared for him very much." Mandy's voice was soft and soothing.

"More than anyone knows." *More than anyone will ever know,* Tessie thought.

Mandy stroked her back until, sometime later, Tessie gave in to deep and numbing sleep.

"After supper, let's talk a bit," Sylvan said to Mandy when he came into the house to change out of his work clothes soon after her return from her parents'. He stood in the doorway of the downstairs washroom and indicated he'd heard some surprising things at the barn raising today prior to Marcus King's fatal fall. "I wouldn't have said anything, considering, but it seems like everyone but your husband knows 'bout your boldness," he said before closing the door. "How can that be, love?"

I worried it might come to this, Mandy thought, her conscience pricked.

"Honestly, I tried to tell ya," she whispered. "I don't want to turn back now." Hot tears rolled down her cheeks. It had been enough today to witness the aftermath of Marcus's shocking fall from the pinnacle of the barn rafters . . . and Tessie's devastation. *And now this.*

When Tessie awakened to a knock, she called out sleepily. "Come in, Mamma," she said, seeing Mandy was gone. Her whole body ached as she attempted to rise from her snug spot on the bed.

"Sorry to bother ya, but this just came in the mail . . . for you," Mamma said, looking at her apprehensively.

"Denki."

Her mother was quiet as she paused at the door. She stood there, eyeing Tessie, as if she wanted to say something more.

Tessie Ann wished for a consoling embrace that would not come, because her mother did not know the terrible truth that Tessie had just lost her husband. "I'll be down to help with supper soon," she finally offered, wishing she could lie down for the rest of the day. *Or month.*

"All right, then." Mamma closed the door.

Tessie looked down at the envelope. "From Marcus," she murmured, tears springing to her eyes again. Her hands shook as she quickly opened it. She savored his final words to her, then was suddenly befuddled. Had he intended for her to retrieve the journal someday?

Did my darling think he was about to die?

Moving to the window, she raised the letter to her lips and stared out, looking up the long road toward the house, just out of view, where they'd planned to live together. The thought ripped her heart anew.

"Mandy knows I love him," she said softly, then considered the crowd of men surrounding Marcus as he lay dead on the ground. All of them knew she loved him now, too.

If she felt up to going, she wanted to run over to the rental house later tonight and look for Marcus's journal, once her parents were asleep. What a treasure that would be! After that, she must pack up her beloved memories and store them in her mind and heart, sealing them away for the rest of her life. Especially now, given the alarming information she possessed, something her husband would never come to know this side of heaven. It would take everything she had to do this, but she must. How else could she survive, knowing what she did?

No one needed to know what she and Marcus had truly been to each other. Not even Mandy. The secret of their brief marriage could simply go to his grave.

First thing tomorrow, Tessie would start sewing her black dress for the funeral. Even though she would not reveal that she was, in fact, his widow, the dark color would stand for something.

Mandy considered Sylvan's earlier remark as she raked the side yard, waiting for supper to bake. Couldn't she have *some* say about what she did during her daylight hours? How frustrated she felt just now, with all the many emotions scrambling inside of her. *I should have tried harder to talk to him about it.*

Refusing to be put out at Sylvan, she used her energy to gather up the scattered gold, red, and orange leaves that were falling even now, showering her head and shoulders. The linden leaves had turned a soft yellow, and the oaks an inviting bronze, yet as much as she loved the changing palette of color, Mandy also relished how warm the air still felt — warm enough to keep the windows in the house wide open.

All the happy autumn days, raking and piling up leaves with my sisters. At times like this, she missed her siblings terribly, missed being absorbed in their shared work and play. And, oh, the pleasant chatter.

She saw two school-age girls out on the road, riding their bikes like scooters, pushing with their right foot as she and her sisters always had. As required by the bishop, there were no pedals, so they couldn't go too fast.

Thinking again of Sylvan, Mandy realized that he was her family now. He was a good and decent man, after all, and Mamm had once suggested that, if respect came first, sometimes love would flower in time. *But without children, where does that leave us?* She sighed, knowing full well that a marriage without *Kinner* was a blight on any Amish home.

She finished her raking chore and headed for the house, making her way into the back door. Supper would be later than usual because of the barn raising and Marcus King's horrific accident. *Ach, poor Tessie*

Ann. Her heart ached yet again.

She personally could not imagine losing a beloved to death — it pained her to ponder such a thing. Although she'd felt something similar to that when her first beau left Hickory Hollow so unexpectedly.

Glancing outside, she saw her father and Bishop John Beiler pulling into the lane. Dat hopped out and went calling to Sylvan, hurrying toward him near the barn while the bishop tied the horse to the hitching post.

Men talk, she thought, hoping that her father didn't know about the shop . . . or that she'd kept it from Sylvan. Mandy felt embarrassed. What would things be like once supper was over and Sylvan was ready to voice his full displeasure? Despite their rocky start, Mandy hoped against hope that Sylvan might be okay with her plans even now.

A strong breeze rustled the leaves outside below the window, which slammed shut. Mandy startled and pressed her hand to her heart, willing it to slow.

Tessie stepped away from helping Mamma make supper to answer the knock at the back porch door. There stood Marcus's golden-haired fourteen-year-old nephew,

Enos, evidently one of the several young men — *leicht-ah-sager* — going house to house to invite the relatives and friends of the deceased to the funeral. Haltingly, the freckle-faced lad stated, "Marcus King's funeral will take place this Friday at Lloyd and Hannah King's . . . at eight-thirty in the morning."

"Denki" was all Tessie could manage to say at the sight of his youthful, tear-stained face.

"Viewing starts first thing Thursday mornin'," added Enos before he turned to run down the driveway toward the road.

Overcome once more with the cruel reality of her loss, she suddenly felt anxious to run to his house and get Marcus's journal. Had he written private words there for her eyes only? She longed to grasp everything — anything — related to him, needing to hold on to even the smallest shreds. Her life with dear Marcus was gone like wildflower blossoms in the wind.

She poked her head into the kitchen and told her mother, "I'll be back in time to set the table."

"Can't it wait, Tessie?" asked Mamma, her expression worried.

"I'm sorry. I won't be long." She didn't wait for her mother to comment further as she reached for her short black coat and hurried out the door.

When Tessie arrived at Marcus's, she was relieved to see no one around. She rushed to the back door and let herself in, avoiding the inclination to look too closely at the trappings of this precious place, to memorize them.

But time was short, so she moved on to the bedroom where Marcus slept. There, she pulled open the top middle bureau drawer and felt all around, even in the back, as the letter had described. But she found nothing. Trying again, she could not locate the space Marcus had written about in his note.

Discouraged now, and wanting to retrieve his journal nearly more than anything on earth, Tessie made the mistake of turning to look about the room. *Our room . . . our refuge.*

Her strength sapped, she went to sit on the bed, her lip quivering.

Suddenly, there were voices at the back door — relatives must be coming, as was their way. *Puh, I've waited too long!*

The last thing she wanted was to be discovered there, so she quickly slipped into the smaller adjoining room. She and Marcus had decided one evening that it would be the perfect little sewing room or nursery someday. There was a good-sized empty closet there, and Tessie opened the door and stepped inside.

She held her breath and left the door parted just enough to overhear what might be said, there in her hiding place. But the sounds she heard were mournful — his parents' soft murmurings, snippets of conversation here and there. Too distressed, no doubt, to speak in full sentences.

Soon, there were additional male voices, measured and low, and the thuds of the bed frame being dismantled and the movement of other furniture.

Tessie groaned inwardly and racked her brain — had she left any of her possessions in the occasionally shared room? The thought that they had wed before a justice of the peace seemed strange now, even impulsive, yet given Marcus's death, she was glad they had done so. Besides, no one would ever have to know of their reckless decision now.

Including Mamma and Dat, she thought as the many footsteps subsided and shifted to the back of the house. Quickly, she saw her opportunity and crept to Marcus's bedroom, still praying not to be discovered. But the oak dresser was gone, along with the wooden cane chair and double bed.

Sighing, Tessie did not know what to do. The journal was out of reach, and for her to press the issue with Marcus's parents would only serve to raise eyebrows. She didn't dare do that.

Dejected and feeling terribly alone, Tessie crept to the front door and down the porch steps, then made her way swiftly through the yard, not looking back.

CHAPTER 10

"Ach, Mandy, I wish you'd discussed this with me first," her husband stated as they lingered at the supper table. "Why would ya go behind my back?"

"I *need* this shop," she pleaded, looking away. "I really *do.*"

"But . . . to be deceitful, dear?"

"It was wrong, I know that." She wanted to tell him how nervous she was around him at times. How she longed to feel comfortable talking with him.

Sylvan drew a deep sigh and rose to go and stand at the sink, his back to her. For the longest time he stood there, as if staring down at the faucet, then up at the wall clock. "If I'd known this was so important to you, I could've set up something real nice for ya right here, at home."

She nodded reluctantly. "Guess I just wanted to surprise ya."

Slowly, he turned and leaned against the

counter. "There's something else." His face was painfully solemn. "I'd rather your sister Tessie didn't come over here, cookin' in your stead. 'Least not often." He went to stand behind his chair at the head of the table. "Would ya honestly rather keep the store than keep house for your husband?"

She wouldn't say. She just couldn't.

"Is somethin' troubling you, Mandy? Something you're not telling me?"

Pausing, she chose her next words carefully, lest she upset him further. "What if Tessie worked at the gift shop part of the time — say, a day or two a week — in my place?" Her sister would surely need something now to occupy her mind.

"How often would *you* go to town?" The indignation had faded from his voice.

"I'll have to talk to Tessie Ann . . . see what she says 'bout this."

"It'd make better sense, really. Two single women over there, runnin' things, ya know."

"Maybe so." Mandy paused and glanced toward the window. "Still, I'd like to keep workin' there some . . . if ya don't mind too awful much."

"Well, jah, I do. But we'll see how things go." Sylvan unfolded his arms and gripped the back of his chair. "First, we've got a funeral to attend in a few days."

"So hard to imagine someone that young . . . gone already," Mandy whispered.

"An awful shame," Sylvan said, head bowed. "Seems he was engaged, too. No doubt a promising future just ahead."

"I can't imagine how his family must feel tonight."

"Dark hours, for certain." Sylvan looked at her then and said more tenderly, "Each day is a gift from the Father's hand, ya know."

She agreed, wondering if she shouldn't go over and check in on Tessie Ann yet again.

Mandy watched Sylvan take the horse and buggy to offer assistance at Lloyd King's farm, in preparation for the viewing. Numerous other families would already be there, helping so that Marcus's parents wouldn't have to focus on chores like cooking and cleaning and caring for the farm animals.

She slipped on her coat and went to sit on the back porch, needing time alone in the fragrant night air. It was hard to shake off the memory of Tessie's earlier reaction to the horrid accident. Yet she felt helpless to offer the kind of support her sister surely needed. Mandy wished Sylvan had left the discussion about the shop alone. Couldn't that have waited for another day . . . or week, even?

Moonbeams fell on the backyard, spotlighting her plentiful mums of all colors on either side of the walkway. Oh, she was so glad the hard frost hadn't come to nip them. *Not just yet.* How she dreaded the gray winter months.

Yawning, she raised her arms to stretch. And if she hadn't looked up just then, she wouldn't have noticed Tessie's long legs dangling from the oak tree.

"Tessie Ann . . . sister?" Mandy rose to stand on the porch step, leaning to see better. "Why don't ya come down and sit with me a spell?"

A muffled sob. Then Tessie's sad, sad voice: "You weren't s'posed to notice me up here."

"Well, I did, and I do," she said, knowing Tessie would eventually emerge. It wasn't clear to her what her sister did up there, but it really didn't matter. Tonight especially she must feel utterly bewildered, realizing she'd never see her beau again on earth. "I'll just sit an' wait for ya . . . till you're ready," Mandy said softly and headed back to the chair on the porch.

How long has Tessie been climbing that tree? The old oak must feel like a home away from home, Mandy guessed, and she wondered if her mournful sister would open up about Marcus King.

She assumed that if the two of them had planned to marry come fall, her sister would have shared the news with Mamm. But then, on such a wretched day, that was neither here nor there.

Mandy decided it wasn't sensible to ask Tessie about working at her new shop with Cousin Emmalyn. Not till after the funeral and maybe a few more days following. Surely Sylvan would understand, though he certainly had his opinions about most things, as did nearly all the men she'd ever known.

At that moment, Tessie came down out of the tree to sit on one of the porch chairs with an audible sigh. "I wasn't ignoring ya," she said, blowing her nose with her hankie. "I hope ya know."

"You needed time," Mandy said, reaching across to touch her shoulder.

"I honestly wish I could just get away for a while. Far away from here." She sniffled. "I feel just awful."

Mandy nodded and remembered how alone she'd felt right after Norm's departure. "Do Dat and Mamma know you loved Marcus?"

"They know."

"So they'll be a *gut* comfort to you, then."

Tessie fell silent.

"They will," Mandy urged. "I'm sure of it."

Still Tessie said nothing.

Mandy found this to be downright peculiar, but she let things be.

"I was thinkin' of you and Sylvan just now . . . how you've made such a nice, happy home for him, even though you loved, well, someone else before you married."

Mandy understood.

"It gives me hope, now that I'm alone without Marcus, ya know."

Not responding, Mandy let the words float off. And the two of them sat side by side, immersed in the night sounds till Tessie said much later that she'd best be going on home. She got up from the chair with the effort of an older person and meandered down the few steps, nearly losing her balance on the final one, catching herself at the last moment.

"You all right?" Mandy rose, alarmed.

The poor thing just stood there, her head bowed low, like she was close to fainting. Then she glanced back at Mandy with her big, sorrowful eyes.

"I'll come see ya tomorrow, all right?" Mandy held her breath, hoping Tessie might wave or say something. Anything at all.

"I've got a funeral dress to sew," Tessie said so softly Mandy strained to hear. "A black one."

Like a widow's, thought Mandy. Something was terribly wrong with her sister, and it wasn't just Marcus's sudden passing, although that alone was enough to cause a girl to lose her equilibrium — and then some.

Chapter 11

The late October sun shimmered on the tops of maple trees still boasting patches of orange as Tessie and her mother took the team over to the general store the next morning for a few baking ingredients — some of the items they didn't grow or have stored in their cold cellar.

Tessie was lost in thought, pondering how to privately say good-bye to Marcus at the viewing tomorrow. Meanwhile, she had completely given up the idea of trying to locate his journal. Perhaps it was providential not to have found it, since their secret might somehow be discovered later.

On the way up the steps to the store, they encountered Levi Smucker and his mother, Sarah, coming out with a large box of groceries, which Levi was carrying on his shoulder. He smiled immediately when he saw Tessie, and Sarah Smucker exchanged a pleasant "hullo" with Mamma.

Levi managed to hold the door as he balanced the cumbersome box, letting his mother pass ahead of him. "This must be a difficult time for you and your family," he said quietly, his focus on Tessie. "We'll keep yous in our prayers."

"Denki," she whispered, glancing at Levi's mother.

Once Mamma and Tessie were inside the well-organized store, her mother said, "Such a thoughtful young man."

Was Mamma really going to make a point of drawing attention to Levi now? Tessie made no response as she walked the aisles just in case there was something Mamma had forgotten to put on her list. The store offered everything from teakettles and cake pans to spring-clip wooden clothespins and Swiss cheese cut fresh from the block, but today Tessie could scarcely keep her mind on her surroundings, let alone shopping . . . not with the loss of Marcus still so new.

Tessie's heart leaped up as a shock of thick blond hair appeared over on the other side of the aisle. *Marcus?* Everything stopped for a second, but it was not her darling, and she realized anew this was the terrible way things would always be. She had to find a way to live with this gaping hole in her life even if it meant doing so one minute at a time.

Mamma stopped in front of the olives, suddenly looking miserable. "Tessie Ann, I want you to know I'm awful sorry Marcus fell . . . and . . ." She paused, her gaze on her hands. "I feel so blue for Lloyd and Hannah King and their family." There was a catch in her throat. "I honestly can't imagine what they're goin' through. Or you, honey-girl."

Tessie nodded, thankful for at least that much. She pondered what she ought to say next and what she truly *wanted* to say. Glancing about, she was relieved there was no one within earshot. "Mamma, I've been wanting to mention somethin' to ya."

Mamma's head came up. "What is it, dear?"

"I stumbled upon some genetic listings for local families while I was dusting the old rolltop desk. In Dat's handwriting," Tessie ventured, lowering her voice further. "I wish he'd told me — or that you had. It was just so hard, not knowin' why you were both so against us."

"*Nee,* not against." Mamma pushed her words out. "Not that a'tall. Your father had his reasons for keepin' it mum."

She waited, ready for more.

"He hoped you might obey without questioning."

For once, Tessie thought unhappily. It wasn't the first time she had been known to push against her father's wisdom. She'd struggled with surrender to her elders her whole life. *The yielded spirit is the blessed spirit.*

But when it came to something as important as giving birth to healthy children, Tessie honestly did not understand why her parents had kept her in the dark.

At least there was nothing to worry about now. There would be no babies.

"Black's the best color for this funeral," Tessie told her mother when it came up Thursday morning, after breakfast. She threaded the needle for hand stitching on her dress's facing, finding it necessary to keep her hands, and mind, ever busy. The pain had been nearly insufferable upon awakening that morning — oh, the devastating realization all over again that Marcus was gone.

"My dear girl, you're not thinkin' straight," Mamma insisted. "Ain't customary for a girl to wear black to a beau's funeral."

"But my heart belongs to Marcus." *And always will . . .* "So black's the truest color for *me,*" Tessie stated bravely.

Mamma didn't seem to know what to say to that, so she shook her head and kept busy with her own sewing, her thimble poised on her plump middle finger.

Tessie was tempted to declare the truth: *I'm Marcus King's wife!* But she reached instead for a hanger, hurrying to press her funeral dress, not wanting to mar the new fabric with her tears.

Tessie Ann waited till her parents had long since retired for the night to walk over to Lloyd King's for the viewing. She planned to wait outdoors, near the side bushes, till there was no one inside tending the body, then slip inside.

A gray tabby cat lay asleep on the top step, reminding her of an early date she'd had with Marcus. He'd leaned down to pick up a tiny kitten and held it so gently it took Tessie's breath away. Then he'd handed the adorable kitty to her. *Marcus was always like that. . . .*

When all was quiet in the front room, Tessie crept inside toward the open casket. Standing there in loving reverence, she felt something of herself wither and die. Her youthful husband looked very much the same as he had in life, other than the gash on his temple. And his dear face was so terribly white as he lay without a speck of breath in him. "Good-bye, my love," she whispered, tears coming quickly.

Even now, she could picture Marcus healthy and alive, listening to her with his head ducked forward, or his strong hand clasping another man's in a firm handshake as he walked toward the temporary house of worship on a Preaching Sunday morning. She remembered, too, the warmth of his lips on hers. Oh, goodness, how she would miss this wonderful man!

She reached out to touch his waxy-looking hand but drew hers back quickly, marveling at how very handsome he still looked in his black vest and frock coat. She couldn't help recalling that he'd worn the selfsame suit to the courthouse, and she faltered for a second before placing her hand lightly over his heart to let it rest there, thankful no one was around to see.

Eventually, she pulled back, struggling to accept his unexpected death. *Too soon.* She tried not to cry again.

The real Marcus — her darling — was gone far from her, out of her loving reach. She hoped with everything in her that the dear heavenly Father would not count it against him, their marrying outside the church. *Marcus was so sure we were following God's will in all that. . . .*

Suddenly, Tessie heard the sound of quiet conversation in the kitchen, just around the corner, and her knees quaked, lest she be discovered. She turned to leave by way of the front door, disturbing the slumbering cat there. A pair of yellow-green eyes stared at her as the feline thumped its tail against the white banister.

Tessie Ann hurried down the steps and toward the narrow road where she and her sisters and their hardworking neighbor, Levi Smucker, had taken their ponies and carts years before she'd ever dated Marcus. So long ago now, it seemed, when life was far less complicated.

Sometimes we do what our heart instructs us, and sometimes that's the right thing, she thought, aware of the babbling of a small creek near the road. *But sometimes it's not.*

"I love you, Marcus King." She flung the words to the stars, thankful for a bright moon on such a sorrowful night. "I'll never forget you . . . or *us.*"

Perhaps it was her vulnerable mood — she didn't know exactly — but Tessie felt almost certain that Marcus's presence was right there with her on the long and lonely walk home.

■ ■ ■ ■

The next day, a good many eyes widened and the ministers' eyebrows lifted nearly to the edge of their straight bangs when Tessie arrived at the funeral with her parents in her all-black attire. The deacon's teen granddaughters whispered to one another, and Marcus's own mother looked askance at her. The somber Friday was a blur all around, the hardest hours of Tessie's life.

And as the days plodded forward, Tessie continued to wear a black dress and apron, as did her mother, who by marriage was a distant cousin to the Kings. Tessie sewed two more black dresses so she wouldn't have to wash them so often.

Her mother brought no more attention to her clothing, even though Dat continued to look at her suspiciously at nearly every meal, muttering such things as, "How long are ya gonna be in mournin', daughter?" She wondered if he was afraid she might scare away potential suitors.

Tessie tried to ignore it and refrained from letting anyone see her tears, keeping them locked up until bedtime. In those private hours, she let them fall freely as she talked tenderly to the Lord Jesus, her only solace.

The Friday after the funeral, Tessie agreed to help Mandy at the shop in Bird-in-Hand, something Mandy had recently requested of her. Tessie actually welcomed the opportunity to work with Cousin Emmalyn, impressed with her consistent compassion and care. Emmalyn never asked any uncomfortable questions, but Tessie sensed she was there if needed, ready to listen.

It was Ella Mae Zook who was the one to probe while browsing in the Amish gift shop. The petite woman gazed up at the clothesline Emmalyn had strung up from one corner to another to display colorful quilted potholders, like they did with Christmas cards each year. Ella Mae remarked how pretty everything looked, then she went straight to Tessie Ann, eyes shimmering. "Pity's sake, dearie, your dress is as gloomy as your countenance. Might we do something 'bout that?" the elderly woman said. Her words may have sounded pointed, but her demeanor was sweet, a combination Tessie found heartening.

"Years ago, when my husband passed away, my house died, too," said Ella Mae ever so quietly, fixed on Tessie's gaze. "There was absolutely no life left in the place — too quiet, I'll say. Even so, I went through the motions of keepin' the place clean an' redded up, but it was like lookin' after a grave."

Cousin Emmalyn intervened with a thin smile as she stood behind the counter. "Ain't like Tessie's mournin' a husband, though."

Ella Mae tilted her little white head and reached to take Tessie's hand. "Widows carry the selfsame sorrow I see on your face, my dear," she said.

Gently tugging Tessie's hand, Ella Mae whispered to her, "I've been known to make some tasty peppermint tea. 'Tis *gut* for the soul . . . when the heart needs a listening ear."

"Denki," whispered Tessie, tears welling up at the feel of the older woman's cool little hand in hers. "I'll keep that in mind."

Chapter 12

The first hard frost came, nipping the hardy hosta leaves and hushing the locusts, katydids, and crickets for the season. Morning glory vines and other formerly thriving greenery withdrew into curled creepers and turned into cracked brown leaves. And the wind howled at night, making it hard to sleep.

Three weeks dragged like they were thirty years. Tessie helped Mamma cook and clean, their usual daily schedule. Occasionally, she went walking out along the road, especially grateful for the late autumn haze that allowed her to fall into the depths of her sadness and seemingly blend in with the bleak landscape. And on nights when she did not relive her darling's terrible fall and subsequent death, she escaped her sorrow in sleep.

Tessie went through the motions of attending quilting bees and charity functions, where they made various items to donate to the Mennonite Disaster Service, as well as the Disaster Response Services, an organization created by an alliance of Amish and conservative Mennonites. She went over to help her expectant sister Molly scour the house for an upcoming Preaching service a month away. But her heart was all bound up in her memories of Marcus.

When she had a spare moment, she visited the Amish cemetery just up the road. Unlike some folks who'd lost spouses and shied away from going to the grave after the burial service, Tessie actually felt closer to her husband there. Once, before the ground had gotten so cold, she'd even sat in the yellowing grass near his feet and vowed her constant love, crying and wishing . . . hoping she'd wake up from this dreadful dream and find that Marcus hadn't gone to the barn raising that fateful day after all.

His headstone was small and white, consistent with all the other simple markers in the square-shaped cemetery. The only real difference between his grave and the others was the uneven raised patch of grass that had been cut away to lay his body to rest.

Time tramped forward and people's lives seemed to resume to normal. Tessie marveled at how swiftly their world seemed to right itself when she still felt nearly oblivious to everything around her, even toward herself. But her ongoing fatigue troubled her, and one solemn December day, she realized she had missed her second menstrual cycle. *Can it simply be the stress of my great loss?* she wondered, willing her suspicion away.

But it only intensified the following week, when a wave of severe nausea caught her by surprise one morning . . . then the next. Until Tessie could no longer dismiss what she suspected.

I must be pregnant.

Such mixed emotions came with this realization. Oh, the blessing of carrying her beloved's baby, yet the awful anxiety that she might deliver a disabled or deformed child — even stillborn. And she fretted, torn between terror and love for her child . . . and what the bishop and the People would do to her when they learned of her condition.

Mamma was kind and helpful, assuring Tessie the stomach upset was merely due to something she'd eaten, "that's all." But Tessie assumed differently, and the reality of this new and shocking predicament kept her awake at night. Was she bearing the punishment for her willful behavior, eloping as she had with Marcus? Not only had her husband died, but now, if what she suspected was true, she could very well be carrying his impaired child, too. *A special child.*

She felt sad that she could no longer keep her legal union with Marcus private in this precious and secret world she'd created from her lovely memories of their few weeks as a married couple. Eventually, it would be impossible to deny that she'd conceived. *And unless I admit to our elopement, everyone will assume it was out of wedlock.* Both were sinful in the sight of the church.

I should have told the bishop right after Marcus's death, she thought, dismayed. Wouldn't admitting the marriage now seem like an attempt at an excuse? Yet it still behooved her to come clean before the bishop.

Tears veiled her eyes as she stood before her wall calendar, counting the weeks. As best as she could calculate before consulting a doctor, her baby would come sometime between early to mid-July of next year.

Panic-stricken though she was, Tessie wondered how soon she should see a doctor, especially to share what she'd seen in her father's file. Or should she slip off to Mattie Beiler, the hollow's midwife, and confide in her?

Tessie muttered her woes to the chickens while she tossed feed to them, especially to Obadiah and Strawberry, the two with the most personality. “Have ya ever heard the expression ‘Your goose is cooked’?” she found herself asking.

I’ll have to continue living under Dat’s roof . . . become an alt Maidel, she mused, knowing Amishwomen were born to marry and have children, lots of them. She wondered if she’d be ousted by her father once he found out she was expecting a baby, and trembled at the thought.

Each night, Tessie placed her hands on her stomach, praying the Lord’s Prayer, repeating the phrase “Thy will be done on earth as it is in heaven.”

Yet, as hard as her shame would be in the months ahead — unmarried as she was in the eyes of the People — Tessie felt somewhat cheered by the knowledge that Marcus’s tiny babe nestled beneath her heart. She could only hope this child would be strong and healthy and kind and fun loving . . . like Marcus always was.

Or were her father’s charts a frightful prediction? she wondered more times than she could count. *Will our little one be born deformed or suffer a terrible disease? Will he or she even live past birth?*

The nights were the worst, Mandy thought, or so they were becoming. Was her working at the shop still a problem for Sylvan? But Mandy guessed there was more to the distance between them — her little shop merely a symbol of what was really wrong.

When will I ever be with child?

It was a week before Christmas Day, and Mandy lay very still in bed next to Sylvan, his back to her. She could hear him breathing deeply and realized he must be asleep already, although it was scarcely nine o'clock. Both were tired from the long day's work. Tessie had come over to cook the noon meal, making it possible for Mandy to hurry off to Bird-in-Hand right after breakfast and stay late, closing up for Cousin Emmalyn. She'd pled with Sylvan to understand her need to get away from the too-quiet house. Even though she knew it went against the teachings of the church to engage in outside work while hoping for a family.

Sylvan had been kind and listened, encouraging her, or so it seemed, to enjoy the one day a week at the shop. *But only one?* She wondered if he shared her growing disappointment at their empty nest. Sylvan was working longer hours than ever before, caught up in his own doings with winter imminent. He rarely referred to his duties or to the partnership with her father, hinting once, when she attempted to ask, that she would find such conversation tedious, even uninteresting. He must prefer she not be in the know about the family business.

One more thing we don't talk about.

Several days later, on Christmas Eve morning, Sylvan surprised Mandy at breakfast by being almost talkative as they sat there, the kitchen filled with momentary sunlight. He mentioned casually that some of the men traded to the Indiana church district were coming home to Hickory Hollow for the season. "Norman Byler is one of them."

"Who told ya?" she asked, surprised.

"Norm's father. Saw James over at the Fishers' auction a few days ago."

She wondered why Sylvan hadn't told her till now and wished he hadn't brought it up at all; they'd never really discussed her former beau.

"Norm may be comin' to work for his sister Hallie's husband."

Her heart sank. "He's movin' back to stay, then?"

"Guess he wants to introduce his fiancée

to the family, have her stay round for the holidays — see if she likes it here enough to settle down."

"Oh." She let the woeful word slip before thinking.

"You all right, love?" He narrowed his gaze. "Mandy?"

"It's just strange to hear he's returning."

He looked at her kindly. "But none of it matters now, does it?"

She shook her head. "Not at all." She thought suddenly of the box of Norm's letters and cards she'd saved from their courtship and wondered why she'd kept them even this long. For what purpose?

Sylvan was silent for a time and then pushed back from the table. "So we'll leave it right there." He headed across the kitchen to the back door. "I'll be in the barn workin' late," he said over his shoulder and left.

Surely Sylvan's not jealous, she thought, leaning her face into her hands. *O Lord, grant us Thy great wisdom,* she prayed silently.

Chapter 13

Tessie dutifully helped her mother extend the kitchen table with three wide leaves following breakfast on Christmas morning. Earlier, while drying dishes, she'd caught Mamma studying her surreptitiously. Tessie cringed at what a shambles this special day might become — and their upcoming family gathering — if Mamma were to inquire about Tessie's sudden food aversions and nausea. In just a few hours, her sisters Marta and Molly and their respective husbands, Seth and Ben, were expected to arrive with their children. Tessie's nephews and nieces, three-year-old identical twin boys, Manny and Matthew, and one-year-old Mimi, named after Tessie's oldest sister, Miriam, would keep her very busy, as would Molly's two angel-haired girls, Mae and Marian, four and two. Molly was expecting her third child after the first of the year.

She'd once overheard Miriam, in hushed

tones, telling Ella Mae Zook that Mamma had been surprised to discover that she was expecting another baby. *Was that why I wasn't given an M name like Mamma and my sisters?* she wondered. Tessie had been named for her father's favorite aunt, Tessie Ann, who passed away unexpectedly back when Dat was only seventeen and counting the days till he could make his baptismal vow and join church.

"I was hopin' you'd wear something more colorful today," Mamma said as they went to get the best china from the sitting-room hutch. "It's been two months now. . . ."

Tessie felt ill again at this mention.

Mamma glanced at her, handing down a pile of sparkling white dessert plates first, and suddenly backpedaled. "But, of course, you and Marcus were . . . close friends."

If she only knew, Tessie thought, loath to spoil their family celebration. Despite that, she was fairly sure Mamma suspected something.

They carried stacks of plates into the kitchen, and eventually, Mamma changed the subject, asking Tessie which set of glassware she liked better for the table — the clear glass tumblers or the golden-tinted set passed down from Mamma's own grandmother years before.

One way for Mamma to recover the conversation, most likely, she thought, choosing the gold-tinted ones.

Mandy and Sylvan walked single file on the pebbled path that led next door to his great-aunt's, taking with them a gift of dark almond bark, Great-Aunt Elaine's very favorite. The stooped woman welcomed them inside from the cold, beaming with delight, and they sat and visited with her for more than an hour that Christmas morning. Earlier they had invited her to come along with them for the day, but Elaine had declined and insisted she was expecting some of her immediate family members to drop by around noon for the meal. "Well, if you're sure you'll have some company," Mandy said with a glance at Sylvan.

"We don't want you alone on Christmas Day," he added.

Aunt Elaine nodded, looking a bit peaked despite her pretty burgundy dress and matching apron, and assured them she'd be just fine. Then she said, "I ain't cookin' a big meal for just myself, ya know . . . yous go on an' have yourselves a real nice time at your folks', Sylvan. Don't ya worry none, hear?"

Mandy gave the independent little woman

a gentle hug before they left, and declined accepting one of the chocolates for the second time. "Denki, but they're all for you," she said, smiling.

Later, after hitching up, they rode up Hickory Lane, Mandy sitting on Sylvan's left on the way to his parents' home. The peaceful rural landscape with its dusting of snow relaxed her, making her forget time and space — and the undertow of tension between them.

When they drove past the deacon's herd of dairy cattle, Mandy recalled hearing that the deacon's wife had insisted on naming three of their cows — Polly, Gentle, and Frieda — just as Tessie Ann had named her two favorite chickens. This made Mandy smile. *Such a playful sister.*

A while later, they passed one of Marcus King's married sisters, Arie Ann Esh, and her husband, Noah, nephew to the late Benuel Esh, and their three little tykes all piled in the back of the buggy. Arie Ann was Marcus's only brunette sister out of his blond siblings. She looked as somber as Tessie had all this time, dressed completely in black, including her outer bonnet.

Waving and waiting till the buggy passed, Sylvan asked Mandy, "Why on earth do ya think Tessie's still in mourning?"

"I don't know."

"Does it wonder you?"

"Sometimes."

Sylvan was quiet for a while. Then he said more firmly, "Seems mighty strange she should wear black garb for this long. Or at all."

"She must have her reasons," Mandy said quietly. Surely Sylvan guessed at Tessie's love for Marcus. Few among the People hadn't witnessed her reaction the day of his death and the change in her afterward.

Mandy was relieved when nothing more was said about Tessie's dreary clothing. Neither was anything else shared on the way to her in-laws' place. Mandy didn't actually dread the day ahead, but given a say, she'd much preferred to have gone to her parents' home for Christmas dinner, to be near Tessie Ann. Two of their married sisters were also going over there to fellowship around Mamm's bountiful table. Thus far, she and Sylvan had taken turns with her parents and his, going every other Christmas, as most couples did.

When Sylvan pulled into the tree-lined drive, four enclosed gray buggies were already parked in the side yard. Mandy wondered who else might be coming for dinner, very glad she'd made extra helpings of everything — especially her cherry and pecan pies.

Sylvan helped her carry the food into the big farmhouse, where they greeted his cordial gray-haired mother before Mandy hurried back out to their carriage to get the box of small gifts she'd brought for Sylvan's parents and the youngest nieces and nephews.

Looking up just then, she was shocked to see Norman Byler walking this way. She thought she must be seeing things as he made the turn into the driveway, his long stride ever so familiar.

Unable to budge, she just stood and gawked. What was he doing there?

"Guder Mariye, Mandy Miller," he called, apparently forgetting her married name as he quickened his pace.

"En hallicher Grischtdaag," she said, wishing him a happy Christmas.

Seeing his determined countenance — the glow of winter's sun on his vibrant face, his wavy wheat-colored hair — felt utterly wrong in every way. She was thoroughly married now.

He reached her side and offered to help with her box.

"Ain't heavy, really," she insisted.

"Well, I'm here, so let me do this for ya."

She couldn't imagine the looks from everyone in the house if she walked into her mother-in-law's kitchen side by side with Norman. It was not the best way to start this Christmas gathering. "Are ya . . ." She stopped, unable to go on.

"Jah, my parents are comin' in the buggy with Glenice in a few minutes," Norm said, perceiving her thoughts as he took the box.

What sort of fancy name is that?

"There wasn't room for all of us in Dat's single-seater."

"Oh . . . well, I'm sure."

"I'm awful glad you and Sylvan will be at the meal, too," Norm said so casually it stunned her. How could he just show up like this and nearly take up where they'd left off, at least with his informal manner?

"Well, we're *related* to the hosts," she reminded him.

He laughed nervously, or so it seemed. She really wanted to ask why he and his family, and Glenice from Indiana, were intruding on *their* family feast, but she knew it would be ungracious.

Yet Norman must have guessed what was winding around in her head, since he began to explain that Sylvan's parents knew he was in town. "They invited my parents and me and Glenice to spend part of the day here when they found out most of my married siblings are in Mount Hope, Ohio, for Christmas, visiting cousins."

They must not know Norm and I were once practically engaged, she thought, flabbergasted that she and Sylvan would have to spend a good portion of the holiday together with Norm and his bride-to-be.

Norm glanced at the sky, beautifully free of clouds. "I forgot how much I've missed Hickory Hollow."

She pondered his nearness, his remarkable friendliness. *Like always.*

"What is it, Mandy?"

"Nothin'." She sighed. "I'm just surprised to see ya. And on Christmas, yet."

He smiled down at her as he carried the lightweight box, his black felt hat tilted off center, like he'd always worn it during Rumschpringe. He glanced into the box and said, "Unfortunately, we have no gifts for you and your family. Glenice isn't accustomed to gift givin' at Christmas, being from out in the Midwest, ya know. She comes from a mighty strict *Gmay.*"

"Understandable," Mandy said, thinking how awkward this conversation was.

Glenice . . .

He matched his stride to hers. "Seein' you, well, like this, is mighty unexpected," he admitted. "But it's nice for two old friends to get caught up a little."

She made no reply.

"Glenice Lehman and I will be wed the Tuesday after New Year's," he said just then. "Her family will come here for the wedding."

Mandy found this ever so peculiar; a bride always got married in her parents' home. "Why here?" she couldn't help asking.

"She agreed to honor my family. My elderly grandparents want to be at the wedding, and there's no way they could make the trip to Indiana."

"Oh." Mandy could understand that.

"And we'll be livin' here in Hickory Hollow with my parents till we can get our own place."

"That's real nice of them."

"Jah. And you'll like Glenice. I just know it."

She forced a smile. "I don't have to like her, Norm. But *you* do."

He chuckled and they walked for a few seconds without saying more. Then Norm mentioned Marcus King's untimely death, startling her. "He wrote not many months ago, askin' if I'd consider returning home if he was to marry."

Does Tessie know?

"He never said who his sweetheart-girl was, so I guess he wanted to follow the more traditional way and keep it quiet till —"

"Marcus is gone, so what's it matter?" she interrupted, peeved at this personal talk. She reached for the storm door and held it for him. Nodding, he headed into the enclosed porch-like room with the box as she deliberately stood there, lingering to thwart the notion that she'd actually go in with him.

Thankfully, Sylvan was nowhere to be seen, undoubtedly having gone to the front room to visit with his father and the other men. *Lord, have mercy on this day!* Mandy prayed in earnest, relieved when Norman grimaced at her and turned to head back outside to wait for his parents — and his Glenice.

Have mercy, indeed!

Chapter 14

Tessie sat on the floor in the front room with her young nephews and nieces, entertaining them near the heater stove. Giggling and babbling in Deitsch, the children helped her carefully place the colorful wooden blocks to build a four-sided tower. Although she loved hearing the little ones burst into happy squeals, she had to be mindful not to let first Manny, then Matthew, knock the tower down too quickly, before they had a chance to get it all the way up.

"Dawdi Ammon made these blocks," she told them. "Before I was born."

After the simple festivities of visiting, eating desserts, and singing hymns related to Jesus' birth, the adults exchanged greeting cards — many homemade. Later, Manny, Matthew, Mae, and Marian opened their small gifts of hard candies, coloring books, and crayons. Towheaded and curly-haired Mimi primly pulled the wrapping off her cloth baby doll with a pink blanket sleeper sewn onto it. Bringing the dolly with her, she toddled over to Tessie and raised her dimpled arms, apparently wanting to sit on her lap.

It wasn't long, though, till restless Mimi wanted down. She promptly waddled over to Dawdi Ammon, who was more than willing to set her on his knee. "*Hup-die-dudendu!* — Upsy-daisy!" he said again and again, grinning.

And for this moment in time — this special day of days — Tessie felt a little less sad, as if the sweetness of the children offered a comfort she hadn't known since Marcus's death.

Oh, my dear, dear Marcus, we're going to have a baby, she thought while the extended family joined in silent prayer after Bible reading.

The minute her sisters and their families departed, Tessie set about helping Mamma redd up once again. After a while, she suddenly felt tired and made the mistake of telling Mamma.

"Well, you've looked flushed all day, Tessie Ann."

"Overeating has made me weary, I think." She shrugged and tried to smile.

Mamma pushed up her small glasses.

Then, frowning, she reached to pat her hand. "Ach, if I didn't know better, I'd say you were with child, my dear girl."

Tessie kept her face straight and relaxed, not daring to respond in any way. Yet her heart was hammering so hard, she wondered if her mother could hear it.

Not expecting the conversation to progress further, Tessie was chagrined when Mamma suggested she see a doctor. "You must be ill, daughter. I'd be glad to go with ya, in fact."

"No need . . . I'll be fine."

"You sure don't look it."

Tessie wondered if some days her fatigue had more to do with her grief than her pregnancy — if she was indeed expecting a baby.

"I won't mention anything to your father 'bout you bein' under the weather," Mamma added.

This admission confounded Tessie. Did her mother suspect what she wasn't saying, and was she trying to pull Tessie out of her shell, to get her to talk?

"Why should Dat care?"

"You oughta be ashamed to talk so!" Mamma snapped.

"I'm sorry . . . just all in." She longed to head to her room. *Please don't talk to Dat about this!* she pleaded with her eyes. The strain between them had so quickly grown to odd proportions.

"I suggest getting yourself a *gut* night of sleep for a change, jah?" Mamma said pointedly.

How did her mother know Tessie suffered occasional insomnia, unless she, too, struggled to sleep through the night and was up? "Denki, Mamma," Tessie said meekly. "I'll do my best."

Her mother's expression softened. "Come here." She held out her ample arms. "You're out of sorts today, ain't so? Let me give you a Christmas hug." Mamma held her near and kissed her cheek. "I love ya dearly, Tessie Ann."

"Happy Christmas, Mamma. I love you, too." With that, Tessie trudged upstairs to dress for bed, embracing the stillness of the house never more so than now.

Mandy awakened early the next morning, Second Christmas, aware that Sylvan's side of the bed was already empty. Rising, she pushed on the new white slippers she'd received from her mother-in-law for Christmas before lighting the nearby gas lamp. Immediately, a small circle of light filled the room, leaving the rest in lingering darkness.

She opened her devotional book and read the day's selection, then bowed her head to pray the Lord's Prayer. When she'd said amen, she reached for her Bible, all the while aware of a nudging within. She strongly believed she was supposed to locate all of Norman's old cards and letters and dispose of them — the last remnants of a failed courtship. She'd been thinking about this for some time, and seeing Norm again yesterday had reminded her of it.

So, after breakfast dishes were washed, dried, and put away, Mandy gathered up all the letters and such, tossed them into a paper bag, and then put on her warmest coat and gloves. She carried the paper bag out to the barn, took the old shovel off its nail, and hurried to a secluded spot behind the woodshed. She made a sizable hole, though it wasn't at all easy to dig, the ground was so hard. Nevertheless, she made a small pit and lit a match to the stack of correspondence before standing back to watch it burn.

In a few minutes, Sylvan rushed over and asked what on earth she was doing. She briefly told him, but he seemed more concerned about the fire than its contents. "What if an unexpected wind comes up and catches the woodshed ablaze?" he asked, obviously displeased with her for being careless.

"So sorry, Sylvan . . . hadn't thought about that," she said.

"Are you feelin' all right, Mandy?"

She nodded, fighting back tears. "I'm destroying my past, every bit of it." *At last.*

He ran his fingers sideways through his short beard, clearly speechless.

She felt terrible about having saved Norman's courting correspondence. "I should've done this before we got married," she muttered, watching the fire flame up for a moment before sinking some. "I'm truly sorry, Sylvan."

He looked at her, his eyes softening. "Maybe you'd like to work with Cousin Emmalyn at your little shop tomorrow," he suggested. "Would that make you happier?"

She looked at him, surprised and pleased.

"Might just do ya some *gut.*"

"All right, then. Denki," she said.

He folded his arms and stood there on the opposite side of the dying fire, looking at her through a thin veil of smoke. She felt overwhelmed and wanted to run over there and wrap her arms around him. But she stayed put. Sylvan preferred to be the pursuer, she knew.

"Since you're here, I've been wonderin'

something," she said slowly, getting up the nerve. "Why were you so welcoming to Norman and his fiancée yesterday at the dinner table?"

He frowned. "She has a name."

"Sure," she said. "It's Glenice Lehman."

He smiled faintly and continued. "Thought it was a *gut* idea to extend the right hand of fellowship, since they'll be our neighbors." Sylvan shook his head. "Didja know?"

"Jah, I heard."

"A right nice couple," he added. "Don't you think so?"

She nodded.

"Well, I've got work to do." He headed back toward the barn. "Be sure an' shovel a bunch of dirt on that fire!" Sylvan called over his shoulder.

Mandy didn't answer as she watched the smoldering fire. It was as if the letters and cards had been the flimsy cord that attached her to what had been her former life. Now they, too, were gone.

Second Christmas was spent visiting two of Tessie's sisters who hadn't been able to join them yesterday. First, Miriam and her family at their farm. And, later in the afternoon, Dat and Mamma decided to stop in at

Mandy and Sylvan's on the way home. There, they all sat and talked about the big, healthy twin heifer calves recently birthed at the next farm over, as well as the half dozen camels over in Bird-in-Hand. It seemed to Tessie that these unusual farm animals were getting plenty of attention — they'd even made it into the Lancaster newspapers.

After a time, Mandy began to look mighty fidgety, as if itching to take a walk. She asked Tessie to go with her while Dat and Mamma continued chatting with Sylvan.

When they reached the end of snowy Cattail Road to the north, over by the Hickory Hollow schoolhouse, Mandy said, "Ach, we should've included Mamma, ain't so?"

"Well, she seemed content to sit and visit," Tessie replied, glad for this time alone with her sister.

"Maybe you're right." Mandy nodded, then mentioned she was planning to work at the Bird-in-Hand shop tomorrow. "So surprising, really. It's actually Sylvan's suggestion."

"I had the impression he was opposed to it."

"Oh, you're quite right. He really is."

"So why are ya goin' tomorrow, then?"

Mandy was quiet for a moment, then,

"Maybe because he's feeling guilty at bein' put out with me."

"Mandy . . ."

"We've had a few words lately. Nothin' to worry about."

Tessie cringed. She'd never heard such talk before from her sister. "A lover's quarrel?"

"Oh, jah . . . nothin' more." Mandy went on to ask if Tessie would mind cooking for Sylvan and the workmen tomorrow. "Just dinner at noon. Could ya help me out in a pinch?"

"Sorry, but I can't tomorrow. It'd suit me better another time."

"Oh." Mandy sounded miffed now.

"Maybe you should ask Sylvan's mother or one of our sisters."

"I couldn't, Tessie Ann. Not on such short notice."

"It's just that I might be goin' into town." Tessie didn't say where or why.

Mandy sparked a frown. "Well, are ya goin' or not?"

"I really can't commit for tomorrow."

Mandy's shoulders slumped, and she didn't seem to regain her cheer as they turned back to the house. She looked as glum as Tessie felt.

Entering the backyard, Tessie craned her

neck to look at the majestic oak, struck with the notion that in a few more weeks, it wouldn't be wise to climb so high. *Especially now that winter has come.* Sighing, she wondered how long she could keep her pregnancy from her sisters, especially Mandy.

Then, of all things, Tessie was shocked to witness a transformation in her sister, who walked into the kitchen wearing a broad smile. Was it for Dat and Mamma's benefit . . . and Sylvan's, too? This apparent cheerfulness was hard to overlook as Mandy prepared a few refreshments, including leftover pie and a selection of cookies. How could she change so quickly?

Tessie remembered what her sister had shared briefly during the walk. *Is Mandy's seeming happiness merely an act?* She turned the question around in her brain as she helped pour hot coffee for her parents and Sylvan. Always before, Mandy's steadfast resolve to be a devoted and kind wife to Sylvan had been an inspiration to Tessie, despite their awkward initial stages as a couple.

Tessie chose hot cocoa for herself, wanting less caffeine in case she was correct about her condition. *By tomorrow at this time, I'll know for sure,* she thought with a shudder.

Chapter 15

Mamma had planned all along to accompany Tessie to their family physician at the nearby Bird-in-Hand health clinic the next morning. But at the last minute, Mandy's pleas for their mother to cook Sylvan's dinner left Tessie alone in the Mennonite driver's van. Given what was at stake, Tessie believed it was for the better.

The sun sparkled on the crusty snow during the drive to the small medical practice. The days were short on daylight and long on cold, and Tessie disliked going out on the roads even in a warm van.

At the doctor's office, she quickly realized she was the only Amish patient in the waiting room, and, as was fairly typical, several Englischers looked at her inquisitively. It didn't bother Tessie, though; she was accustomed to it.

She glanced at the pile of magazines, surprised to have gotten right in to see the doctor today, following yesterday's call from the phone shanty. Tessie sat close to the entrance and thumbed through a harmless-looking magazine that featured springtime gardens of wild flowers and potted plants. How her heart yearned to turn back the pages of time and return to the wonderful-*gut* spring and summer. Life was not a meager existence then but a joyful one, filled with Marcus's infectious smiles and their love.

Oh, the silence where there had been Marcus's familiar voice, his longed-for presence, his fine plans for their future. Being around other couples, such as the one sitting across from her and holding hands as they looked so fondly at each other, was a painful reminder of Marcus's absence.

Sighing, she noticed a brochure for a health center in nearby Strasburg, and her heart beat faster when she saw that it was for the well-known Clinic for Special Children. Reading every word carefully, Tessie saw that only several surnames accounted for over ten percent of all Amish families. They were King, Fisher, and Beiler or Byler.

King, she thought, realizing this meant there was an even higher risk for her unborn babe than she'd supposed. *No wonder Dat was so concerned. . . .*

When the nurse appeared from behind a door and called her name, Tessie winced, wondering what Marcus might suggest she tell the doctor during this first checkup. She knew one thing for sure: She wouldn't hold back the truth — she would tell him she had been secretly married and was now a widow. There was no reason not to.

Yet, as she took her seat in the examination room off the hall, the latter made her heart sink. *A widow?* The unpleasant label was meant for a much older woman, not for young Tessie Miller King. Alas, she did not feel young anymore in body or spirit.

"What brings you in today?" dark-haired Dr. Landis asked, his stethoscope encircling his neck. Beneath his white doctor's coat, he wore a tie striped in blue, gray, and white over a crisp white shirt.

"I might be pregnant. . . ."

Mandy pondered Sylvan's early morning remarks, surprising as they were. Evidently he'd changed his mind after all about her going to work today. *Why?* she'd thought, irritated. The truth was, it had been too late to alter plans, and she'd tried to explain this to him. She was befuddled, however, at his implication that it wasn't right for her to expect her mother to rush over there to cook for him when Mamma should be keeping Mandy's father happy with something hot for *his* noontime meal.

Why the last-minute switch?

Busy now with waiting on customers and surrounded by all the pretty homemade items, Mandy still felt frustrated and confused.

"Are you all right?" Cousin Emmalyn asked as the last woman of a group left the shop.

Mandy covered her mouth with her hand. "I'm doin' the best I can."

"Well, maybe you're takin' on some of your sister's burden," Emmalyn suggested, leaning her head close. "Tessie Ann's takin' Marcus's death exceptionally hard, don't ya think?"

"We're distant cousins." Mandy didn't want to say more.

Emmalyn shook her head and went to the window to watch the snow as it fell. She wore her pretty mint green dress and black cape and apron today. "When I look at Tessie, I see far more sadness in her eyes than that of a cousin for a deceased relative. They must've been engaged or close to it, since she's still wearin' black."

"They were . . . deeply in love."

"I wondered, although they must've kept their courtship real private."

Mandy felt sadder with the talk of Tessie and Marcus. "Some of us still hold to the Old Ways. Or try to."

"If I could just get *my* beau to commit to marriage, that'd be real nice," Emmalyn said, turning away from the window, a slow smile coming. "Some men aren't too eager to get hitched."

"Is your beau baptized yet?"

"No, and that's part of the problem. He needs to get Rumschpringe out of his system."

Understanding, Mandy smiled now.

"You must know there are a-plenty fellas who *are* ready to settle down." Mandy was aware of several, and she wondered how long Tessie Ann would stay away from the Sunday night Singings and other youth gatherings.

"Levi Smucker's one great catch," Cousin Emmalyn said, nodding. "He's had his eye on your sister for plenty of years, if she doesn't already know. But bein' a gentleman, he never pursued her."

"He had to have known about Marcus King's interest in her, then." Mandy considered this, wondering suddenly why Sylvan had pushed so hard for *her* when Norman was already seriously courting her back when. Quickly, she brushed off the parallel — no need rethinking any of it.

"If Tessie would simply put on a colorful dress, someone like Levi just might have the chance to make her smile again." Emmalyn strolled over to a shelf half filled with pillowcases and pointed out the diminishing inventory to Mandy. "How fast can ya embroider more?" she asked, eyes wide.

"What if we both do a few over the weekend?"

Her cousin gave a soft laugh. "Well, I don't have a husband to fuss with, so I'll see what I can do."

Mandy wasn't about to say she'd have ample time on her hands, too, since she was mostly caught up on her housework. And Sylvan wasn't one to require much of her time. *Not these days.*

The whole of the landscape was embedded in snowy white all the way to the horizon, obscuring the brown of late autumn in one wintry blast. Low gray clouds crisscrossed the sky in every direction.

Tessie sat with folded hands as she rode back toward Hickory Hollow with their regular paid driver, Thomas Flory, shaken with the positive results of her pregnancy test. Yet she was also pleased. How could a person feel so anxious, even fretful, yet so happy?

As for Mamma, she would surely ask about the doctor's findings. Tessie shifted in her seat and wondered if it was time to reveal the truth. If so, the bishop was the first person she'd have to speak with, even though the thought of revealing her situation to John Beiler and his wife, Mary, made her stomach wrench. Without a doubt, no matter what she did or didn't do, her father's wrath was waiting in the wings, and she was just too frail emotionally to bear it.

On New Year's Eve morning, a wedding was scheduled to take place at Jerome Smucker's place. His daughter Fannie Sue was betrothed to marry Jerome's longtime dairy hand, Jonas Lee Kurtz, neighbor Nate Kurtz's nephew. Tessie and her parents had been invited some weeks earlier, although Mamma hadn't known for sure if Dat was even interested in going. So Tessie was surprised to hear just last evening that they were, in fact, attending.

In a few short hours, Mamma had crocheted two identical white doilies to take as her wedding gift for the bride. Empty-handed, Tessie had robbed her own hope chest, deciding on a sparkling white tablecloth, brand-new and still in its packaging. She'd wrapped it in yellow-and-white-striped paper and made a bouncy white bow out of some medium-width ribbon from the sewing room. She assumed her father would take a newly purchased set of pliers from the Hickory Hollow General Store as his usual gift to the groom.

The day was windy and dreadfully cold, with heavy snow falling, making it difficult for Amish guests coming from within horse-and-buggy driving distances in and around Lancaster County. On such a frosty morning, Tessie was glad for the extra-thick woolen lap blankets Dat had placed in the buggy.

They passed by the harness shop and the smithy's, and Tessie wondered what Marcus's family had done with the beautiful black courting buggy she and Marcus had ridden around in for years. *That's neither here nor there,* she thought.

After the three-hour Preaching service, the five-minute wedding followed. Later, with the start of the traditional feast, Tessie happened to see tall Levi Smucker, his light brown bangs trimmed just so, and a handful of his male cousins waiting outdoors near the stable. The young men were rubbing their bare hands together and tugging on their black frock coats, all in a huddle. Were they planning a prank on the new couple, perhaps — sprinkling flour between the sheets on their wedding bed, maybe, or taking their horse's harness? Or worse, hoisting their carriage on top of the woodshed.

She waited patiently with other single young women, including several of her own cousins, there in the warm enclosed summer kitchen built onto the back of the house. She was certainly glad to be inside on such a day. Naturally Levi would be in attendance today — he was, after all, a first cousin to the timid bride . . . and quite unhitched himself.

Glancing about her at the other girls, Tessie wondered which of them might be paired up with the easygoing fellow who'd seemed so happy to see her the day she'd snuck off to marry. *Same bright smile at the general store, too,* she recalled.

In her awkward state of limbo, she wished she had not been included with the other young women present. A young pregnant widow; how out of place was she? Still, Fannie Sue couldn't have guessed at any of that, when no one else knew. Tessie trembled at her own deception, but it seemed too late to reveal the secret of her marriage now. She'd waited far too long.

Observing her dejected sister over with many of their girl cousins, Mandy recalled the day she'd gone to her last wedding as a single girl, prior to marrying Sylvan the following year. She had been especially excited for the late-night Singing that was to take place in the barn at the bride's parents' home. She and Norm had stayed for the whole hour of structured singing, though with little patience, and the minute they could justify slipping away, they certainly had. That night, across the vast meadow in a grove of willows, she'd let him kiss her for the first time ever. And not only once.

Maybe that's why I kept his letters, she reasoned, mortified at the thought. She moved away from the window and headed back to help in the kitchen. She wished she could talk frankly with Sylvan about all of this — get it out in the open. Wasn't honesty the best approach?

Mandy worked alongside her sister Miriam, who was describing the many sewing projects she had lined up for the winter. Mandy tuned her out, thinking instead of her own earlier matchmaking with Fannie Sue. Oh, goodness, Mandy hoped she had done Tessie a favor by seating her with one of the bride's most sought-after cousins. After all, the wedding feast and activities following were for the purpose of choosing potential partners for the courting-age young men and women present.

Mandy glanced over her shoulder at Tessie Ann once again. Her reddish blond hair looked so pretty, shiny and clean. Even so, Mandy wished her youngest sister might raise the corners of her mouth a smidgen and try to look more cheerful. Otherwise, how was the dear girl *ever* going to get a fellow to notice her again?

CHAPTER 16

It seemed *zweifelhaft* — doubtful — to Tessie that she should end up beside Levi Smucker at the wedding feast for Jonas Lee and Fannie Sue by pure chance. It was truly cause for suspicion, even though Tessie was having a pleasant enough time.

Who matched us up? she wondered.

The white linen tablecloth and other lovely trappings caught her eye at the *Eck* — the special corner of the bride and groom's table. Self-conscious, she occupied her thoughts and tried to pretend to herself as she and Levi ate together that she was anywhere but there. And she wondered if those who'd gone on before could ever look down and see what their loved ones were doing. If so, what on earth would Marcus think of this surprising howdy-do?

"Do ya plan to attend the Singing tonight?" Levi asked later, during the in-house hymn sing, when the young folk — *die*

Youngie — and older adults sat in the front room and sang from the *Ausbund* hymnal. The livelier songs were saved for the Singing, which could last till midnight.

"Not this time," she said, keeping her eyes on her folded hands.

"Well, if ya change your mind, *I'm* goin'."

She wondered what her parents and Mandy might be thinking just now if they happened to observe the strange circumstance Tessie found herself in. But then, maybe they weren't watching her at all. *Maybe I'm just imagining things, feeling so embarrassed.*

Later, while she ate white wedding cake and strawberry ice cream, Levi talked enthusiastically about having accompanied his father's parents to Pinecraft, an Amish retreat in the suburbs of Sarasota, Florida. "Ever hear of it, Tessie Ann?"

It seemed odd to her ears, hearing another young man say her name so eagerly. "Oh jah," she said, suddenly shy. "I've heard that some of the Amishmen there don't bother wearing their suspenders and hats during the winter months."

Levi chuckled. "Snowbirds, they call themselves." His smile was contagious, and she was captured by his enthusiasm. "It seems the place is a sort of no-man's land when it comes to following a particular church ordinance. Makes things downright interesting, 'least according to my grandfather."

"No church rules?"

"Jah. Some say it ain't for folks with a strict Ordnung back home, if ya know what I mean." He seemed to note her puzzlement. "It's just that things happen there that would be looked upon as transgressions up here."

Very curious, she asked, "Like what?"

"For one thing, many of the Pinecraft cottages have electricity . . . in fact, most do."

"Interesting."

"So what goes on there is kept hush-hush. Evidently the bishops don't even want to know about it."

"Because they can't enforce anything so far from home?"

He nodded, and she wondered just then if any of that non-compliance was comparable to what she'd done — going against her parents' wishes to marry. "Maybe we should all just move to this no-rules life in Pinecraft," she mumbled.

"Sorry?"

"Oh, just thinkin' out loud."

"So I heard." Levi wore an interested frown. "Why would you want to go there, anyway, Tessie Ann?"

"Ach, don't mind me . . . really."

He continued to study her as he drank his coffee, and she knew she must be more careful not to mutter her thoughts again.

Mandy went out of her way to prepare a hot, hearty breakfast for Sylvan on New Year's Day. Though a little tired upon awakening, she'd gotten up earlier than usual and made scrambled eggs with bits of ham and cheese mixed in, mush made from cornmeal and sausage, and fried potatoes. To top things off, there was snitz pie and hot coffee, too.

Sylvan surprised her by remaining awhile at the table after the final prayer. He took time to read aloud to her from the Bible — a passage from the New Testament — which gave her pause. Pleased at the extra attention, she waved at him from the window when he headed outdoors to tend to the steers.

She redded up things right quick in the kitchen, then sat down to make a list of chores. When she heard the knock at the back door, she turned to look, puzzled why the person hadn't just walked in, like her sisters and Mamma always did. "Door's open!" she called.

Oddly, there was another set of light taps, and she frowned, wondering who this could be. She got up, and when she opened the door, she gave a little inward gasp at the sight of Norm's fiancée, Glenice Lehman, standing there.

"Hope I'm not disturbing you," the young woman said, her light brown hair peeking out beneath a navy blue woolen scarf. "It's New Year's, after all."

Mandy noticed her red, swollen eyes, like she'd been crying, and opened the door wider. "Would ya like to come in?"

"Denki." Norman's soon-to-be bride stepped inside and removed her black coat. "I won't stay long."

Mandy felt like a flibbertigibbet, hardly knowing what to do first. "You can hang your coat up there, if you'd like." She pointed to an available peg in the outer room, then went to the stove to find a pan for heating up milk. "I'll make us some hot cocoa. How's that?"

Glenice nodded and took a seat at the table where Mandy invited her. "I wanted to talk to you, since you knew Norman best. Well . . . as a former beau, that is."

Mandy sloshed some of the milk she was pouring into the pan onto the counter, feeling even more uncomfortable. Quickly, she reached for the dishrag and wiped up the spill, then turned on the gas burner.

"I doubt anyone suspects, but I've really been struggling here in your little hollow," Glenice confided.

Not accustomed to such intimate conversations with a near stranger, Mandy only nodded her head slightly. She certainly felt sorry for her, especially if the young woman had been crying this close to her wedding day.

Mandy was on edge as Glenice recited a list of problems between her and Norman. According to Glenice, Norm had been dismissive of her concerns when she asked him to zero in on holding down one good job rather than a few, worried they'd end up having to live in his bedroom upstairs at his parents' house for years on end. "Norman also seems uninterested in allowing me to continue my Indiana Amish traditions. Fact is, he's resistant to nearly everything I've grown up with — the way I was raised." Glenice dabbed at her pretty brown eyes. "I really don't know what to do."

Mandy was appalled. How could *she* advise her? "Have you discussed these things with Norman?"

"Believe me, I've tried. But he says he prefers to hold down three or four part-time jobs. Those don't bring in much money. And as for the rest of it . . . he just shakes his head, is all."

She really wanted to ask Glenice if she loved Norman, and if so, then shouldn't she be willing to overlook some of this? But Mandy knew she was not the best counselor for Norm's fiancée. *Not in the least.*

Glenice smoothed her peach-colored dress, a bit loud for Mandy's tastes. She wasn't finished, though. "Was Norman ever standoffish when he was courting you, Mandy? Stubborn too?"

Mandy was taken aback. It could serve no purpose to share the good dating rapport she'd had with Norm. "Ach, I'd rather not discuss my courting years, if ya don't mind. I'm sure you understand." Mandy poured the homemade cocoa mix into the warmed milk, then reached for two large mugs from the cupboard and set them on the counter.

"Maybe things were just fine 'tween you two," Glenice said, making that leap. "Maybe I'm the problem." She reached for a hankie from beneath her sleeve and dabbed at her face.

"I really doubt that," Mandy said.

Glenice looked away and stared now forlornly out the window as she blinked back tears.

Then, lest she press further, Mandy gently reminded her, "I'm married to Sylvan now." She carried the mugs of cocoa over to the table. "Would you care for some?" she asked, her words stuck in her throat. Never in her life had she been confronted so.

Glenice nodded and accepted the cocoa, holding the base of the mug with both her hands, as if she were cold. Mandy sat next to her, thinking better of sitting across from her, not wanting to have to look into the young woman's eyes.

"Ach, I've upset you, haven't I? I'm so sorry," Glenice said, her voice cracking.

Mandy's heart went out to her, and before she thought twice, she touched Glenice's wrist. "I hope things work out for you and Norman, Lord willing." Then she suggested Glenice might want to go to one of the preachers or the bishop. "Or better yet, talk to Ella Mae Zook."

"I've heard of the Wise Woman." Glenice sighed audibly. "Unfortunately, there are only a few days left before the wedding, so I'm not sure much can or will change before then."

"Seein' eye to eye can take time," Mandy said, surprised she'd revealed that. Was she talking about herself and Sylvan?

"I'll have to decide right quick if I'm willing to marry someone with such character flaws." Glenice rubbed her forehead. She repeated her frustration with Norman's evident lack of interest in getting a good, steady job. Then she added, " 'Tween you and me, I have no desire to relocate here . . . so far from home."

"Ach, then ya must tell Norman. And soon, too."

Glenice hung her head. And by the time they'd drained their cocoa mugs, Mandy said she hoped Glenice felt some better for having made the trek there in the snowstorm. "May the Lord send you forth in His will," she said, recalling what the bishop said at weddings.

Glenice nodded and waved briefly, then hurried to put on her coat and scarf over her bright dress, which lacked a cape or apron. She slipped out the back door.

Watching the tall young woman make her way toward the road in the thickly falling snow, Mandy was beginning to think she'd been spared from marrying a man with little interest in working hard and providing well for his family. *Or in listening to the desires of his wife's heart.*

Character flaws.

Glenice had used those exact words.

■ ■ ■ ■

Tessie braved the snowstorm to get the mail for Mamma and was very surprised, shocked even, to receive a card from Levi Smucker, wishing her a happy New Year. She hardly knew how to react; the more she considered it, she sensed he wished she had stayed for the barn Singing after the wedding. Still, her heart belonged to Marcus, and she could not release his memory and their love — especially with his child growing inside her. It just seemed so disloyal . . . and far too soon.

On Friday afternoon, Mandy smiled when she looked up from behind the cash register in her shop and saw her sister Marta coming in the door, carrying chubby Mimi.

"I'm in need of two weddin' gifts — don't have time to do up anything right quick," Marta announced.

Cousin Emmalyn had stepped out to get some hot cocoa up the snowy street, so Mandy showed Marta around the place herself, truly happy for the chance to do so. "Whose weddings are ya goin' to?" she asked.

"Oh, two of Seth's cousins on his mother's

side," she said, shifting curly-haired Mimi in her arms. But the little girl began to squirm, and Mandy took her so Marta had the freedom to look around. "I'd thought of picking up something for Norman Byler and his bride-to-be, too," Marta said, "but word has it she's up and left."

"Wha-at?" Mandy wasn't sure she'd heard correctly.

"Apparently made a beeline back to Indiana. Any later, and Glenice would've stood up her groom on the wedding day."

"Like Katie Lapp did," whispered Mandy.

"Funny, I thought of that, too."

"Wonder if Norm will stay around, then." Mandy didn't think she ought to make a big deal of this, not wanting to give her sister the wrong idea. Even so, in spite of Glenice's impromptu visit, she was astounded at this bizarre turn of events.

"Evidently Norman's movin' ahead with his plans to work part-time with his brother-in-law. Seth says Norm plans to purchase some of Marcus King's old furniture for his room at Lloyd and Maggie's house. For the time being, though, he'll stay on with his parents." Marta shook her head and reached for a couple tatted doilies. "Now, these here are awful perty." She held them up to inspect them.

"Made 'em myself." Mandy laughed a little.

"Well then, I must have a *gut* eye for quality, ain't so?"

"I guess I couldn't agree with you more." Mandy felt a little funny, boasting so.

They both laughed. Then Marta said, "Don't get a big head, now, ya hear?"

"I promise not to." Mandy's thoughts were full of Marta's astonishing news, and she wondered if Glenice's visit might have been the turning point for the poor young woman. "Are ya sure 'bout all this business with Norm's fiancée?"

"Sorry?" Marta turned to look at her.

"You're not mistaken, are ya, 'bout Glenice leavin'?"

"Oh, I heard it from two reliable sources."

"It must've just happened."

"Jah, early this morning." Marta looked at her with kindness and compassion in her eyes. Then she slipped her arm around Mandy, encircling dimpled Mimi, as well, and held Mandy's gaze. It was as if she were trying to say, *"I'm sorry I brought this up."*

"Must be for the best, then."

Marta nodded, then releasing her, she asked, "How's Tessie Ann doin'?" She carried her chosen items to the cash register.

"Well, her color's better."

"Didn't know she was ailin'." Marta reached to take Mimi from Mandy.

"Tessie misses Marcus," she replied, wondering what Marta knew of their sister's courtship.

"Ah, so that's why she wore black to Fannie Sue's wedding. It gave me pause — thought I'd missed something."

"Jah, s'pose so."

"And, Mandy . . . I hope you aren't upset by what I said 'bout Norman Byler. Didn't mean to —"

"Not at all," Mandy said right quick. "It's not like we were ever meant to be together . . . that's for certain."

"Sometimes we're given precisely what we need no matter what we think at the time," Marta said, her blue eyes sober. "The Good Lord knows exactly who that person is, as you surely know by now."

Mandy nodded. She couldn't agree more.

Marta opened her purse to pay the bill.

"Nee . . . no." Mandy refused the money. "Consider it a gift."

"Are ya sure, sister?"

"I insist." She hurried around to the other side of the counter and kissed Marta's freckled cheek, then cupped Mimi's round dumpling of a face in her hands. "It's ever so nice seein' ya both."

"You really have a lovely place here to sell your things," Marta said and opened the door to leave.

Watching her sister stroll down the little shoveled walkway, Mandy recalled her words. *"Sometimes we're given precisely what we need."* She contemplated them long after, telling Emmalyn, when she returned, that she would not be at work for another week.

Chapter 17

By early February, Tessie's morning sickness had dissipated. Thankfully, there were no more probing remarks from Mamma, who'd accepted the rather cryptic explanation that Tessie had anemia. Tessie was taking some iron tablets to remedy that, as well as the prenatal vitamins her doctor had prescribed. She'd discussed with the doctor the possibility of acquiring a certified midwife, such as their own Mattie Beiler, Ella Mae's daughter. Tessie was still considering that, though she wanted to wait until she told Mamma her news. The Amish grapevine would have a heyday with it.

Her mother had no idea Tessie had seen the doctor twice now or that he'd already spoken with one of the specialists at the Clinic for Special Children. She'd quickly learned that the ability to predict genetic diseases among the Plain community was complicated. And since aborting high-risk babies was not at all the Amish way, no prenatal testing would take place — only a preliminary consultation before the baby's birth.

Tessie Ann spent most of her days cooking at home in her mother's absence, since Molly needed Mamma's help with her infant son, Michael Abram. As for herself, Tessie was needed more at the shop than at Sylvan and Mandy's, since Mandy had quite suddenly decided to stay at home more often now. Sylvan had sketched out a blueprint for a small addition to the back of the family home to be built in early spring. This would make it possible to move Mandy and Emmalyn's store when the short-term lease expired in April.

Mandy had told Mamma at a recent quilting frolic that the Amish bishops in the country, one hundred and eighty in all, had met at a conference not long ago, and the biggest issue of concern was the use of cell phones. Apparently Mandy had asked Sylvan if she could have an iPhone for her business, since Emmalyn used one quite often. Sylvan, however, was opposed to it and assumed Bishop John Beiler would be, too, so Mandy dropped the idea.

Tessie thought it was considerate of Sylvan to provide a spot for her sister and Emmalyn's shop goods on the back of the house. Did that mean their marriage was back on an even keel? *If Mandy's not confiding in me, then all must be better,* thought Tessie.

"So . . . all's well," she whispered while gathering ingredients for a pumpkin chiffon pie. She'd heard others repeat such words when there was no way to know how things might turn out. Or worse, when intuitively they knew that *nothing* would ever be well again. But she wouldn't reflect her own worries onto Mandy. No, it seemed that even with her sister's former beau back and living in Hickory Hollow, things were going along just fine for Mandy and Sylvan. Tessie certainly hoped so.

On the day before Valentine's Day, Tessie received another card from Levi Smucker and was thankful she'd opened it in private, because Levi had written a dinner invitation at the bottom. *If you're willing,* he'd added.

She appreciated that he hadn't pressed her for a date after his initial indication of interest at Fannie Sue's wedding feast. She'd saved that previous card, unsure why, because if Levi had any knowledge of her condition, she was certain that both the correspondence and his interest would vanish instantly.

She pondered Levi's dinner request for a couple days, feeling hesitant to accept. Soon, very soon, she would no longer be able to conceal her growing babe, and then what?

But she needed a friend, and perhaps Levi could be just that. So she got up and wrote a note, deciding to hand it to him discreetly after the shared meal following Preaching tomorrow. *If it works out,* she thought as she reached for her black dress from the wooden pegs to inspect it.

Thinking of his kind attention, Tessie changed her mind about what to wear tomorrow. "I've looked dismal long enough." She pulled out her best blue dress and white cape and apron, then went to the sewing room to let out the seams a bit.

During the Sunday common meal of cold cuts and snitz pie, Mandy overheard Sylvan talking with Norman Byler. Earlier, Norm had seated himself directly across the table from Sylvan and Mandy, and she had spent most of the meal recalling the things poor Glenice had privately shared. Presently, though, Mandy heard Levi Smucker's name mentioned — from the bits and pieces she was gathering, Sylvan and Norm had started to volunteer at the local fire company where

Levi Smucker was assistant fire chief. Evidently Levi had given both of them beepers to alert them to a fire.

"Some Amish from more progressive churches are allowed to receive texts on their cell phones instead," Norm informed Sylvan.

She hadn't meant to snoop, although it was difficult to tune out all of their excitement over plans to raise money for the fire company at the April running marathon in Bird-in-Hand.

Deliberately, Mandy turned her attention to Tessie, who had sat down with their mother and Dawdi Dave near the end of another row of tables. Mandy was suddenly struck by her sister's altered attire. *When did this happen? And how did I miss it during Preaching?*

Mandy wondered what had precipitated the surprising turn and found joy in the prospect that Tessie was emerging from her grieving time.

After enduring as much talk between Sylvan and Norm as she could possibly manage, Mandy excused herself and strolled to the kitchen to offer some help, even though it wasn't her turn. She had to get some breathing space, somewhere as far from Norm as possible.

When her help was graciously rejected, Mandy wandered out to the large utility room and located her coat, outer bonnet, and gloves. Donning them, she decided to venture out to the back porch for some air. It was there she noticed Tessie outside now, as well, and standing near the thick clump of trees that formed a windbreak on the northeast side of the property. Mandy was surprised to see her sister had ventured out with little more than a shawl and gloves.

Then, out of the blue, Levi Smucker appeared, and if Mandy wasn't mistaken, it looked like Tessie handed him something. They stood together for a moment; then Levi skedaddled off to join the other young men his age over near the corncrib. Mandy's curiosity was piqued to high heaven as she watched him go.

Ah, so Levi's the reason for Tessie's blue dress today, Mandy thought, grinning at the discovery.

She moved down the steps and wandered across the yard, breathing in the crisp air while observing her youngest sister. Presently, a *ferhoodled* look appeared on Tessie's pretty face, and Tessie began to weave in and out of the trees before she finally stopped to lean against one of the larger trunks. She stared up at the branches.

Is she honestly thinking of climbing up there on the Lord's Day? Mandy choked back a chuckle.

Still focused on Tessie Ann, she watched her sister slide her hands beneath her white Sunday apron and turn to face the north. The slightly rounded silhouette of Tessie's belly was alarming at first. Then Mandy wondered if she was just getting a little chubby like some of the girls Tessie's age who loved their mashed potatoes and gravy, and many sweet desserts.

But, no, the way Tessie held herself just now made Mandy wilt. For the life of her, it looked like Tessie was pregnant. Oh, she wanted to reject the notion, but it was impossible not to wonder if Tessie and Marcus King had slipped up and made a mistake in a weak moment.

Tessie bowed her head just then and looked like she was struggling. Or was she praying? Her shoulders rose and fell as her upper body heaved.

Saddened and terribly perplexed, Mandy lifted her skirt and rushed across the yard. "Tessie Ann," she called to her. "Schwe-schder!"

"Mandy, please keep your voice low," Tessie pleaded, still shocked that her sister had confronted her in this way — and on the heels of Tessie's short conversation with Levi, too.

"What'll happen when Mamma and Dat put together that you're expecting a baby? What then?" asked Mandy, looking altogether forlorn.

Tessie shook her head, scarcely able to take it all in. "Dat will hit the roof and then some."

"Well, you'd better go to the bishop and confess to him first — and right away. He'll find out sooner or later." Mandy was staring at Tessie's middle now.

"You don't know what I'm goin' through."

"Nee, I don't." Mandy's face fell. "I assume Marcus was the baby's father."

"Jah," Tessie admitted, "but you daresn't tell a soul."

"Sister, you can't hide this forever."

Tessie sighed. "I'm just askin' you to keep this quiet . . . for now."

"Well, if you don't go to the bishop yourself, someone has to!"

"It's not your place, Mandy!"

Her sister exhaled loudly. "Whose, then?"

"Certainly not yours!" Tears began to spill down Tessie's face. Oh, she wished Mandy hadn't discovered her secret already. Yet she wasn't surprised at her sister's accusation, really. She should have known it was just a matter of time before all of this came to light. *But why today?*

"Listen, I won't be askin' you questions 'bout what took place an' all — mistakes can happen sometimes," Mandy said, her tone softer now. "I'm not excusing it, mind you — not whatsoever. But ya can't just wait till a baby comes to confess your sin."

Tessie couldn't stop the tears. "Ach, this isn't what you're thinkin', I assure you." Her heart thudded in her chest, and a wave of nausea threatened to overtake her.

"Well then, I don't understand. Why wait?"

Tessie folded her arms. "You just keep it to yourself, ya hear?" With that, she headed for the east side of the barn, away from the stable, though she'd gone only a few steps when she turned back and called over her shoulder, "I mean it!"

Chapter 18

Tessie received a follow-up note from Levi on Tuesday, saying where to meet and the restaurant he'd chosen to treat her to supper Saturday evening. She turned sideways and looked in the dresser mirror, shaking her head. Who next might realize the truth about her? It pained her that Mandy had reacted so, yet if the tables were turned, she, too, would have urged her sister to confess her situation to the man of God.

Tessie also worried that Mandy might spill the beans, given the right circumstance. *Or the wrong one.* What Tessie really wanted was to talk privately with her sister Molly to find out what things she would face in the months ahead before the baby came. Tessie had stopped in at the library and looked through a book on such matters, but she hadn't dared to check it out. Molly would know very well, as would Miriam, Marta . . . and Mamma. But it was unfeasible to share with any of them, not just yet.

She placed Levi's note in her dresser along with the cards and decided to make the best of the proposed date. She couldn't deny that she felt remarkably peaceful around Levi, so that was something, at least.

I'll go with him only once, she promised herself, adjusting her soft blue apron against her matching dress.

Friday noon, while they waited for Great-Aunt Elaine to arrive for the meal, Mandy listened as Sylvan told her about his busy morning getting the family buggy wheels reset.

"I ran into a hole on the road and bent an axle," Sylvan said, scowling.

"Good thing you weren't hurt when the carriage hit it."

"No chance of that," he replied quickly, still glowering at his misfortune. "But it's all fixed now . . . just more money out of the budget than I wanted to spend."

She considered that and wondered why he wasn't more pleased for the extra money she was bringing in, although it wasn't terribly much.

Before she could say more, Sylvan added that it was mighty good to see Tessie *finally* wearing normal clothes again. "It's time she was out of mourning attire, that's for certain."

Mandy shifted in her chair, suddenly uncomfortable. Even though she had *not* promised to keep to herself what she knew, she felt a responsibility to stay quiet about it.

After his aunt Elaine came over and they'd enjoyed their meal, Sylvan offered the silent table blessing, then left to go outdoors. Mandy walked Elaine back to the Dawdi Haus, then returned to make two big batches of hot dish, trying her best to get over her grouchy attitude. Knowing yet another sister was in the family way — *and Tessie, no less* — was another blow to Mandy's own hopes.

When at last the task was complete and she was ready to head out, Mandy led their most reliable horse from the stable and hitched up the carriage by herself, frustrated that Sylvan hadn't noticed or bothered to help.

She loaded the food into the buggy and headed to their English neighbors' three miles up the road, where they rented space in one of their big freezers. And all the way, Mandy fumed and fretted, knowing her feelings were not at all pleasing to God.

■ ■ ■ ■

Later that afternoon, Tessie Ann dropped by Mandy's on foot, wearing her snow boots and heaviest coat. Mandy greeted her, looking her right in the eye, not letting her gaze wander to Tessie's middle. "Glad you came by, sister," she said with a hug.

"Needed some air, cold as it is." Tessie looked downright miserable. "But I'm really here because of Mamma . . . she's starting to look at me funny."

"Well, I wonder whether she suspects."

"What would it hurt if I just came right out and told her?" asked Tessie, following Mandy into the kitchen. "Bring an end to the questions in her eyes."

"That's up to you."

Tessie shook her head, quiet for a moment. "No, I don't think I'm ready for all of that yet. I'm really not."

"Just wait till you are, then."

Tessie sat at the table on the wooden bench while Mandy brought over two mugs of hot cocoa. Tessie took her time stirring her cocoa. "Do ya have marshmallows, maybe?"

"How many?"

Tessie smiled a little, then laughed. It was

an outright giggle.

"What's so funny?"

"Nothin', I guess. I'm just every which way with my emotions nowadays. Maybe that's normal . . . for my situation."

Mandy made no comment. She really didn't want to hear about any of that, perturbed as she was with her own inability to conceive.

They had been drinking their cocoa for only a few minutes when here came Ella Mae Zook, riding into the driveway, alone in her gray carriage.

"I'd never expect her out on such a frosty day," Tessie said, appearing surprised. "I've actually wanted to go and visit her. Ella Mae invited me over to see her a while back. I just never got around to goin'."

"Ah, for some of her wonderful-*gut* peppermint tea?"

Tessie nodded as she stared out the window. "That's just what she offered."

Mandy knew full well what could happen if you sat long enough at the Wise Woman's cottage sipping her famous tea. Oh, she knew, all right. "Well, it might be providential that you're both here today."

Tessie blinked and looked at her, not speaking what her eyes implied.

"Don't worry none." Mandy meant it; she

had no intention of saying anything about the baby Tessie was carrying.

Her sister looked relieved. "I'm so weary of all the grief. I even cry in my sleep — ever hear of such a thing?" She paused and fingered the handle on the mug.

Mandy was at a loss to know how to cheer her up. "Want some sugar cookies to nibble on? I've got a big batch."

"Sugar's helpful, sure, but I'm getting *fett.*"

Mandy decided to let that comment be and excused herself, going to the back door to welcome the elderly woman.

"Guess who just arrived a few minutes ago," she said as Ella Mae came up the walkway, all bundled up.

"Ain't Cupid, is it?" The old woman's eyes were full of mischief.

Mandy frowned a little. *What on earth?*

"Well, wasn't Valentine's Day just last week?" Ella Mae grinned, showing her teeth. "Or don't you two lovebirds celebrate such Englisch holidays?"

Mandy couldn't help but smile. Ella Mae sure had an uncanny way of being able to see right to the heart of things.

When the dear woman was safely inside, Mandy helped hang up her woolen coat and scarf. Ella Mae went straight to the heater stove in the corner of the kitchen and stood there, rubbing her wrinkled hands together. She glanced over at Tessie. "Awful nice to see ya, dearie."

"You, too, Ella Mae." Tessie started to get up but sat back down right quick, which surprised Mandy. The Wise Woman didn't seem to notice.

" 'Tis a real cold snap," she said. "Oh, and I brought along a German sweet chocolate cake to share, but it's still in the carriage. Maybe one of yous can go out and bring it in when you're ready."

Mandy volunteered, leaving Tessie and the Wise Woman alone as she put on her wrap and headed outdoors. She hoped her sister might share her burdens with Ella Mae, at least for a few minutes.

So she dallied, admiring the now white pastureland laden with layers of snow. She could see tiny footprints of squirrels and the larger ones of deer, tracks that led out to the windmill and others that traveled in circular patterns rather than straight lines. *Like our lives,* she mused, remembering how, when she married Sylvan, everything had seemed so clear-cut — according to her father, anyway.

Out near the stable, she spotted Sylvan conversing with another man, his hands clasped behind his back. *Always talking to everyone else . . .*

With a sigh, Mandy glanced toward the kitchen windows and saw that Ella Mae was sitting right next to Tessie. *Des gut,* she thought. *If anyone can give my sister the help she needs, it's the Wise Woman.*

Chapter 19

Tessie figured something was peculiar for Mandy to jump at the chance to run outside and get the German chocolate cake from Ella Mae's buggy. *But what's keeping her now?*

Waiting, she engaged in small talk with Ella Mae. Yet Tessie knew this commonplace chatter would not continue for long. Ella Mae liked to get down to brass tacks, as anyone who'd spent any time with her over tea in the woman's charming little cottage knew very well.

"Are ya goin' to the hog butcherin' over at Smuckers' place in a few weeks?" Ella Mae asked casually. She'd already refused Tessie's offer of hot cocoa and sat empty-handed at the table.

"First I've heard of it," Tessie replied.

"It'll be a big doin's. Five families butchering together, I hear."

Tessie found it interesting that the

Smucker name had been dropped right off the bat. Did Ella Mae already have knowledge of Levi's interest in her?

"You ain't so chatty today, Tessie Ann."

"Feelin' a bit weary, is all."

"Well, that's to be expected when someone mourns so awful hard."

She nodded. "Time to move on past all of that, I'm thinkin'." She said it, but she didn't mean it for a second. Putting aside her mourning clothes hadn't changed that.

"Ain't always the easiest thing — keep that in mind, honey-girl."

She agreed and asked if Ella Mae might like some hot tea now. "It won't taste near as *gut* as yours, though." Tessie smiled.

"Oh, I'll wait for some fresh milk with my cake." Ella Mae craned her neck to look out the window. "What's become of your sister, I wonder?"

"Maybe she's helped herself to a chunk of your delicious treat. Who knows?"

Ella Mae chuckled. "That's the spirit!" She patted Tessie on the hand. "I've been worried you lost your sense of humor."

"Guess I did . . . for a while there."

"Grieving takes near everything out of a person." Ella Mae sighed audibly. "I do understand that."

"Marcus wasn't just anyone to me," Tessie

confided.

"And that's mighty clear." Ella Mae leaned her head a bit, studying her. "You loved him very much, ain't so?"

"But he's gone now, and there isn't anything I can do to change that."

Ella Mae gave her a faint smile. "You'll see him again, don't forget. One sweet day over in Gloryland."

Tessie really wished Mandy would hurry and get herself back inside, or she might start to cry and divulge far too much about herself . . . and then feel sorry later.

Well, if this isn't turning out to be a busy place, Mandy thought, seeing the bishop's wife, Mary, pulling into the driveway. Because Ella Mae's horse and carriage were already parked there, Mary Beiler's team could only get so far up the lane.

Mandy waved and went to meet her, then invited her inside, forgetting all about the chocolate cake. "Ella Mae's here, too . . . and Tessie Ann," she said.

"Ach, your little sister? How's she doin'?" Mary asked, looking pretty and prim in her black outer bonnet and white knit scarf and matching mittens.

"Oh . . . you know. Losin' a beau to death has been difficult."

"To tell ya the truth, I've been concerned over her . . . 'specially here lately." Mary stayed in the buggy, not making a move to get out.

"Why don't ya come in and warm up some?" Mandy urged.

"Honestly, it might be better to just talk out here," confided the minister's thoughtful wife. "Private-like."

Mandy held her breath. What was on her mind?

"Is everything all right with Tessie?" asked Mary, her big blue eyes penetrating Mandy's.

"She's been in deep mourning, ya know." Mandy felt like she was repeating herself.

"Jah, the whole community's seen how hard she's taken Marcus's passing." Mary paused, twiddling her gloved fingers and staring down at them. "Sure hope there's nothing amiss with all of that."

Mandy stiffened. *Please don't ask!*

"What I mean is, did they, well . . . get the cart before the horse?"

Stunned now, Mandy wasn't sure how to respond.

Mary looked at her hard. "*Is* there something the bishop should know, Mandy?"

"Really ain't my place to say."

Mary's eyes narrowed. "So then, there

must be."

"I never said that."

Shaking her head, Mary pushed air through her lips. "You wouldn't lie, would ya, now?"

Mandy hung her head.

"We really can't stand for this sort of thing to happen amongst our courting-age couples."

"Nee . . ."

They looked awkwardly at each other before Mary added, "I believe Tessie needs to talk with the bishop, and right quick."

Mandy wanted to say in the worst way that she'd encouraged her sister to do just that but to no avail. She felt as trapped as a mouse in a tight corner.

"Will you please relay this to her, Mandy?"

"I'll see what I can do."

"Guess I won't be comin' in after all." Mary squinted at her from the buggy seat. "You won't forget now, will ya?"

Mandy dreaded having to pass on news of this uncomfortable conversation to her sister. "Will she have to go through a shaming?" It was difficult to speak the words.

"That's all up to the ministers." Mary glanced toward the house. "But the sooner Tessie confesses, the better."

Mandy tried to swallow the lump in her

throat. She mustn't let herself cry; the tears would freeze on her face.

"Well, I'll stop by another time. I think 'tis best."

"Maybe so."

Mary Beiler signaled the horse to back out of the driveway, and Mandy stood there watching, shivering uncontrollably. And not just from the bitter cold.

"I enjoyed stopping in at your sister's shop," Ella Mae said as she and Tessie continued to chat while awaiting Mandy's return.

"It's a cozy spot, for sure," Tessie replied. "And Mandy and Emmalyn have done it up so nice, too."

"The grapevine has it that you're over there quite a lot, too."

"More than Mandy is these days."

"Seems like a smart thing for two young gals to look after it."

Tessie nodded and hoped she wasn't speaking out of turn. "Mandy's content to be at home here lately."

"Waiting to start her family, no doubt." Ella Mae's silvery blue eyes fixed Tessie with a stare.

" 'Spect so."

Mandy burst in the back door just then. Tessie could feel the cold penetrate the kitchen and wondered why she'd stayed out there so long.

"Mary Beiler just stopped by for a moment," Mandy told them as she came in and went right to the stove to heat up some more water for coffee or tea, Tessie wasn't sure which.

Ella Mae turned to smile at Mandy. " 'Tis strange she didn't come in and visit."

Tessie could tell by her sister's quiet demeanor that something was up.

"She said what she came by to tell me." Mandy went to the cupboard and took out another mug. Tessie noticed her hand was shaking as she set it down.

"All right, then," Ella Mae said with a curious glance at Tessie. "Sure doesn't seem like our Mary, though."

"Oh no! I forgot the cake!" With that, Mandy hurried back outside, this time not bothering with her coat and scarf.

"Well, that, too, is mighty odd," Ella Mae murmured. "How does one forget a mouth-watering cake, anyway?"

Tessie could not suppress her smile, and when Mandy hurried back inside, she set the lovely cake dish and cover directly in front of Ella Mae.

To distract her, no doubt. Tessie found this interesting, and observing Mandy further, she realized there had been much more to the outdoor discussion than her sister was willing to share at the moment. But Tessie intended to find out before she left here. For certain!

Chapter 20

"You *must've* told her!" Tessie said. "How else would she know, Mandy? *How?*"

It was a good thing Ella Mae had already taken her leave, because Mandy would have dreaded having the dear woman witness her sister's anger. "Evidently the bishop's wife isn't blind," Mandy replied calmly. "You're starting to show, after all."

Tessie slumped down at the table, chewing on her lip. "I should've known." She pressed her hands to her temples and moaned.

"Mary Beiler seemed to already know . . . honestly."

Tessie rose abruptly, leaving her mug on the table. "I guess I have no one to blame but myself," she said as she made her way out to the mud room to put on her coat and scarf.

Mandy heard the door between the kitchen and the outer room close. A few moments later, there was muffled weeping, and then a familiar squeak as her sister left through the exterior door.

Feeling like a bird in a locked cage the next morning, Tessie took the long way to the bishop's farm after breakfast. She'd slept on it, as her mother might've said, and after much contemplation, she had decided that Mandy and Mary were right. She must go and bare her soul to the bishop.

Tessie had put on extra layers of clothes to keep warm, not wanting to ask Dat for the horse and carriage. Not really wanting to involve her parents at all, having so disgraced them. And she hadn't told Mamma where she was going.

The bishop's place was a sweeping spread of tranquil pastureland and fields, with three majestic mulberry trees beautifying the front yard. During the warmer months, purple impatiens nestled near the base of each tree.

Twelve-year-old Jacob Beiler opened the door and let her in, his deep-set eyes innocent. "Hullo, Tessie Ann," he said, his voice as respectful as usual. Tessie remembered it was Saturday, and Jacob and his younger siblings were home from school.

Mary ushered Tessie inside the toasty

kitchen, offering some hot tea while she asked Jacob to go and fetch Bishop John from the barn, "Right quick, son. Tell him Tessie Miller's here," Mary said, jarring Tessie's nerves.

"Hope I didn't come over too early," she murmured as she took a seat near the heater stove at Mary's suggestion.

"Ach, you're fine . . . just fine." Mary made small talk by saying, "Looks like more snow is on the way."

"Already it's startin' to spit." Tessie glanced at the low, gray sky through the window near the big table, where two of the younger girls sat playing with paper dolls.

"The bishop should be right in," Mary said, sounding as nervous as Tessie felt.

"Denki." She so wished now she'd told the truth right away, after Marcus died. She should have told the bishop what they'd decided to do, going off to the world to marry. Thinking of Marcus buried in the cold, hard ground, Tessie inhaled deeply. The loss still broke her heart.

"Life's got a way of workin' out," Ella Mae often said, but as Tessie sat there anxious and forlorn, it was hard to believe.

Eventually, the bishop came in behind Jacob, who led the way, and then the lad disappeared upstairs. Without saying much, the man of God and his wife motioned for Tessie to follow them into the front room, where they offered her a seat on the only upholstered chair. The two of them sat on a large settee opposite, and Mary reached for one of its pillows and held it in front of her. *Like a shield,* Tessie thought.

She shifted her gaze to the bishop. His eyes rarely smiled, and they were certainly serious now.

"Tessie Miller, have you come to confess?"

"Jah." She nodded. "I was disobedient to my parents," she said. "And now I'm expecting a baby."

Bishop's face was motionless. "I see." He did not ask if Marcus King was the father. Like all the People, John Beiler must be aware that she and Marcus had courted at length.

"Are you repentant before the Lord Gott?" he asked solemnly.

Expected though she was to demonstrate the meek spirit of submission — *Gelassenheit* — to the bishop's authority, Tessie was unprepared to answer directly. Did the Lord expect her to renounce her marriage? True, it had taken place outside the church, but she and Marcus had prayed that God would use it and bless it.

"I'm here to ask your forgiveness for

disobeying my parents, bishop," she said at last, thinking again of her father's refusal of Marcus. She felt compelled to walk a fence with the bishop, because it was unfitting to say she was sorry about having conceived her husband's child. Wasn't it?

Oh, she felt so awfully confused just now, yet she wanted to do the right thing as a church member — one who used to be in good standing.

"You must certainly be ashamed, then," the bishop said, folding his hands in his lap.

"I am."

"It is also the father's responsibility to confess his sin, and I pray that Marcus King made that known to the Lord God before his passing."

Before his passing.

The ominous words hung in the room.

"On our next Preaching Sunday, one week from tomorrow, you will confess your sin before the church membership, following the final hymn."

She nodded and waited for him to say how long she would be shamed, similar to an excommunication. But he quickly moved on to add that he and the two ministers, including Preacher Yoder, would meet later today to discuss her disgrace and the length of her discipline.

"Most women in your situation request to withdraw their church membership, offering their own short-term excommunication," Bishop John added. "But I'm not hearin' that from you, Tessie."

She waited for a moment, then said softly, "Nee."

"And why is that?"

The bishop couldn't possibly understand what she was feeling. Yet she could not complicate things by letting her tears fall. She thought of telling them outright that she had married Marcus King, but she had no proof — she had no idea where Marcus had put their marriage license, for one thing. And revealing their elopement might just create more troubles for everyone.

"Honestly, I crave the fellowship of the membership," she finally managed. "I truly do. I couldn't bear to be shamed and kept away from the church."

Mary Beiler rose just then and came to stand next to Tessie's chair. She placed a hand on Tessie's shoulder. "We care about ya, dear. All the People do. You mustn't forget that."

"Denki, Mary," she whispered.

The bishop got up and nodded at the two of them. Tessie thought for sure he was on his way out, but he lingered in the doorway.

"May the Lord go before you, Tessie Miller." He sounded almost sympathetic.

She could not speak; things were so jumbled in her heart . . . her head. *Have I done the right thing?* she wondered.

Chapter 21

Tessie Ann halfheartedly decided to keep her appointed date with Levi Smucker that evening, since she couldn't get word to him in time to cancel. As she dressed, she did not count the brushstrokes through her strawberry-hued blond hair like she frequently did, her mind elsewhere. She redid the thick bun and smoothed her apron, too, all second nature.

The more she considered her visit with the bishop and Mary, the more uneasy Tessie felt. If only tomorrow were the next Preaching Sunday, her confession would be over sooner.

She sighed deeply. *I'll be ousted from the church . . . and for how long?* She would miss attending Preaching service and the wintertime activities for the womenfolk. Fellowship with her sisters might be scarce, as well. And Mamma? How would things be at home once the shaming began?

Placing a freshly washed Kapp on her head, she turned from the mirror and glanced out the window, noting the fading sunlight. The day had brightened mid-afternoon, the gloom and drear of heavy snow clouds clearing away and making the prospects for the evening much colder. Tessie was thankful Levi was taking her directly to the restaurant, where she would be warm. Thankfully, she could easily conceal her condition with her coat. Soon, though, word would trickle out, then rapidly rush down Hickory Lane like a swollen creek after torrential rains — a flash flood of gossip.

Tessie Miller's with child!

"That'll nix Levi's interest in me right quick," she muttered. At least she wouldn't have to be the one to refuse potential future dates.

Tessie moved from the window, going to sit on the bed. There, she placed her hands on her stomach, pleading with the sovereign Lord, once more, for the health of her unborn child. *Thou hast written this baby's name on Thy heart, O Lord,* she prayed silently.

Tessie quickly discovered how very likeable Levi Smucker was, which she should have remembered from going to Singings during her midteens. Smart and pleasant, Levi wasn't one to shy away from discussing any topic, it seemed. In fact, he carried the conversation between them in the hired van, especially eager to tell her about an upcoming trip to Florida to visit his grandparents, who were struggling health-wise.

"They're becoming enamored with the place, I think." His eyes were thoughtful. "It's their second winter there." He seemed pleased when she showed interest, then happy to tell her more fascinating stories of the retired folk who frequented the area called Pinecraft. "I'll be leavin' next Thursday to help out, but I'll be back as soon as I can line up further care for them, my grandmother in particular."

"They must miss Lancaster County," she said.

He laughed softly. "Well, they've had some wonderful-*gut* times down there." He paused a moment, head down briefly. "Till now." He told her of some of the retired People's fishing trips at South Lido Beach, of playing shuffleboard for hours — with prizes for winning, no less. "Bocce too. Some of their friends take a short bus ride to Siesta Key and spend the day swimming in the ocean or walking along the shoreline."

"Sounds nice." She sighed. "I hope your

grandmother gets well quickly."

He said he hoped so, too. "Would ya mind if I wrote to you while I'm there?"

"I s'pose that'd be all right," she said, immediately rejecting the idea of having any sort of courting relationship with him or anyone. Her heart belonged to Marcus King, forever and always.

Levi glanced at her, smiling. "I don't mean to press ya, I hope you understand," he added.

Nodding absently, she recalled sitting in this very van, heading somewhere on a cold evening with Marcus. So many lovely late-night trips spent riding around Hickory Hollow and sometimes down to Strasburg, to the creamery, and the long walks along country roads, too, holding hands in the midst of a perfect, pure silence — the most comfortable kind of all.

Levi's anything but quiet, she thought. It was as if he didn't mind whether the Mennonite driver overheard them, for surely Thomas Flory could understand bits and pieces of their Deitsch.

Later, when they were seated across from each other at a candlelit table, Levi did not seem troubled by being gawked at by a whole roomful of Englischers as he leaned forward, engaging her in animated conversation. Being with Levi made her feel as if they were in a small bubble made for two, and she felt bewildered. This was not at all what her heart needed.

Truth be told, she was having a nice time. But halfway through her veal tenderloin and mashed potatoes, the bishop's remarks about her upcoming confession and possible excommunication repeated in her thoughts. Surely the prospect of additional dates with Levi — or anyone — would come to a swift end once the grapevine had its way with the People.

How soon? Next week?

Her fleeting contentment was merely that.

Winter clouds, splendid in their dappled darkness, swirled apart in patches the next morning. Shafts of sunlight broke through them and shone onto the countryside.

While the quiet house was sweet with the residual smell of cinnamon, Tessie took the opportunity to sit down with Mamma over some hot cocoa after breakfast, this being a no-Preaching Sunday. In that moment, she found herself wishing for a visit to see soft-spoken Ella Mae and have a taste of her tea at last. But it was impractical to postpone the inevitable conversation with her mother any longer. Tessie was glad they were alone and began simply by saying, “I went to see the bishop yesterday.”

“Oh?”

“I’m going to have a baby . . . and the father is Marcus.” The words spilled out.

Her mother’s round, pink face did not fall, nor did she gasp. “I s’pose Bishop John had some admonition for you?” Mamma’s blue eyes were moist in the corners. She did not reach for Tessie’s hand as she might have.

Tessie filled her in quickly.

Mamma removed her glasses and puffed a breath on each lens before rubbing them on the hem of her apron. “Will ya raise your child alone, as a single mother, then?”

“Well, I won’t hurry up and marry. I just couldn’t.”

Mamma sucked in some air and coughed. “Ach, I’d think you’d want to give your babe a father. A last name, too.”

“Jah . . .”

Thankfully, the possibility the baby could be born with a rare and serious disease did not come up. Yet it was all she could do to sit there and talk about this with her mother. The very act stretched her thin, and Tessie was starting to believe things were almost better when she was the only one aware of the baby, aside from the doctor and the bishop.

And Mandy. How she missed her sister just up the road!

"Someone's got to break this to your father," Mamma said suddenly. "It's not going to be me; I can tell you that."

Tessie nodded. Telling Dat would not be easy — he'd have himself a rant. She expected her mother to get up right then and start pacing between there and the front room, as she sometimes did when pondering *Druwwel* — trouble. If it were summer, Mamma might have promptly headed outdoors to drag a hose around the yard, giving her flowers a drink.

But Mamma, bless her heart, just sat there and drank her cocoa, the plate of leftover sticky buns sitting untouched before them. Mother and daughter glanced shyly at each other while the wind bent the poplar trees in the distance and brittle brown leaves spun across the cold white ground.

Chapter 22

Tuesday morning, both Tessie and Mandy showed up at the shop in Bird-in-Hand, a half hour apart. Emmalyn greeted them with a big smile, eyes laughing, and Tessie sensed that their cousin was about to remark on their both being there by mistake.

But Mandy acted strange . . . even somewhat standoffish. Or perhaps she just had her mind on something else. It had been a while since she'd taken a day to work at the shop.

The three young women worked side by side to straighten the piles of homespun offerings — counting the frilly and not-so-frilly doilies, refolding some of the quilted aprons, and spacing out the potholders on the line above them, saying not a word.

As the hour progressed, Tessie felt certain Mandy was miffed for some reason. Everyone knew practically everything about anyone in the hollow, so what had Tessie missed? Was she hurt by Tessie's accusation last week?

When customers were few and far between, Mandy suddenly announced, "I got my wires crossed somehow. I need to get home and start cooking the noon meal for Sylvan." She cast a look at Tessie.

"Oh . . . well, goodness, were ya expecting me over there today?" Tessie asked, suddenly uncertain.

"Like I said, I'm just ferhoodled." Mandy went to get her black coat and gray scarf. "Maybe I'll see ya tomorrow, Cousin Emmalyn." And out the door she went.

"Wonder what's got her so mixed up?" Cousin Emmalyn said, going to the door and peering out into the sunshine, her hands clasped behind her back. The light was nearly blinding against the heavy snow; a good five inches or more had fallen in the night.

Tessie went to sit on the chair in the corner. She sighed, gazing about her at the lovely shop. "My sister's upset, is all." She said nothing for a moment, and then surprised herself by adding, "I'm expecting a baby, cousin."

Emmalyn's plump face changed just then; her eyes seemed smaller and less bright. "I didn't know," she said, coming this way, all serious. "And after Marcus . . . well, this has to be the hardest thing you've ever experienced."

Tessie nodded.

"Oh, honey-girl . . . I care deeply for ya. And for your baby, too."

"Denki, Emmalyn."

"You all right?" Emmalyn crouched down next to her, putting folded hands on Tessie's knee. "This doesn't change anything by me. Not one iota."

Tessie struggled not to cry.

"You're gonna need a caring heart round here." Emmalyn looked up at her. "Ain't so?"

"You can't know how much this means to me." Tessie ducked her head near Emmalyn's. "I'm glad you felt you could say this . . . considering."

"Well, and let's not judge Mandy, either," Emmalyn said softly. "Just as I don't judge you." Emmalyn made a few more kind remarks about Mandy, and Tessie took it all in. This was the type of girl to have in her corner.

The ebb and flow of Tessie's sisterly relationship with Mandy remained unpredictable. Tessie couldn't have guessed Mandy would react the way she had. Now she wondered if she shouldn't have told her sister straight out, instead of making her figure it out for herself.

"Jah, no sense judging," Tessie finally said. "No one knows anyone, really, till they've walked in their shoes." *Or bare feet . . .*

She sighed, thinking of her own penchant for having her way. "We all have our cross to bear."

The last thing Tessie would do was feel sorry for herself as she approached the stable before supper. She was terribly nervous — oh, was she ever. But Mamma was right: It shouldn't fall on anyone's shoulders but Tessie's to reveal this news to Dat.

She found him in the small, dank room just to the left of the barn door. How many times had she made this short trek between the house and the barn to ask her father to forgive her? How many times had she failed him due to her own determined will? She could see his many lists posted on bulletin boards — rainfall charts, hay yields, breeding records, and scheduled vet appointments. She still wondered why he hadn't kept his office over at the original farm, where Sylvan had all the steers, but there was no need to ponder that just now.

His back to her as she crept in, Dat

reached for the clear dish filled with paper clips. "Dat, I need to talk to you," she said softly.

Her father turned and waved her over to sit on a stool in the corner, near a tall file cabinet. "Rarely do I see ya out here, Tessie Ann — well, lately, anyhow. What's on your mind?"

She drew a breath, wishing she were still back at the little shop in Bird-in-Hand. Anywhere but here. "I'm going to have a baby, Dat . . . come July."

His jaw tightened and he turned away for a moment. He shook his head before returning his gaze. "Marcus King's?"

Tessie couldn't bear the disappointment etched on his suntanned face. "It's not what ya think. Honestly."

"Well, Tessie, what else *can* I think?"

She had to tell him, even though she was afraid this, too, would make things worse, if that were possible. "Marcus and I were married, Dat."

The stain of red on his neck rose to his face. "Do not compound your sin with a lie, daughter!"

She bowed her head — without proof, it was pointless to argue the fact. In that terrible moment, Tessie realized that others would react in much the same way, and she shuddered, longing to return to the house. Alas, she felt like a scolded little girl again, recalling the many times she'd brought pain to her father's heart.

But this was different. Wasn't it? She'd followed what she and Marcus had believed . . . had hoped was God's will for them.

"Don't be goin' round sayin' such ridiculous things, daughter . . . hear me? I want you to hush up 'bout whatever you're bablin'." He rose now and glared at her. "Understood?"

Finally Dat dismissed her. Feeling bewildered and shaken as she crossed the wide backyard to the house, Tessie sadly resolved to remain silent about her marriage to Marcus. *Unless I can find the marriage license.* But with all his things gone from the rental house, where to look?

Tessie's father was quiet, if not sullen, at suppertime. His prickliness had not softened in the least — there would be no table games of checkers or Dutch Blitz tonight. Dat's silence reminded her of Marcus's way of handling tension. He hadn't always been like that, not as a boy, but then, most young men never faced his and Tessie's kinds of struggles. What couple had they ever known who was forbidden to marry?

Recalling Dat's legitimate grounds for putting his foot down, though, she guessed his silence also had to do with concern and distress. Would his newest grandchild live for a few weeks or months, only to die? Surely that's why he would not even raise his head to look at Tessie during the meal. Along with his displeasure, he must be worried sick.

If that wasn't enough for Tessie, the next few days were filled with one suspicious thing after another — the sudden absence of any of her sisters dropping by, for one thing. Not even Dawdi Dave made an appearance from next door, so unlike him — especially around dessert time. She had not expected this palpable hush in the house. Even Mamma seemed far busier and more preoccupied than usual.

So, considering all this, when Saturday arrived, Tessie went upstairs and pulled on various underlayers, then hurried down to the outer room to don her tallest boots. She was thankful for a measure of sunshine as she took to the snow-packed road. It would be a lengthy trek in the cold, but she *had* to know the truth. Would Ella Mae Zook ignore her, too?

■ ■ ■ ■

Poor girl.

Mandy watched through her front room window as Tessie leaned into the wind, out there in the dreary weather. Feeling altogether sick at heart, Mandy rested her fingers against her lips. She knew from Mamm that her sister had at last talked to Bishop Beiler. Mamm and Dat, too. Yet now the reality of what lay ahead for them all loomed life-size in her mind. "What will this do to our family?" she whispered, inching closer to the window, stalking Tessie with her eyes. "She must be goin' to see the Wise Woman, as well she ought." Time spent with Ella Mae Zook would be a balm, Mandy knew. If only every older woman could be as reassuring.

Presently, Mandy returned to baking bread in the kitchen, where she'd first spotted her sister walking on the snowy road. Oh, it was next to impossible to shake off the thought of her youngest sister having to kneel to confess such a sin before the congregation.

Sitting now at the table, Mandy pressed her hand to her chest. She wondered if she might not be too ill to attend church tomorrow, just maybe.

Winded and her cheeks numb from the cold, Tessie stood next to Ella Mae's old-fashioned cookstove and shivered for more than a few minutes, trying to get warm. She wondered if her being so cold could harm the baby.

"Thought you might've given up on comin'," Ella Mae said with a playful look.

"It *has* been a while since you mentioned it." Tessie rubbed her icy hands together.

"Clear back in November." Ella Mae glanced at her, then back at the pretty blue teapot, its lid off and fresh peppermint tea steeping. "But I knew you'd come when you were ready. Prayed so . . ."

"What smells so *gut,* besides the tea?" Tessie breathed in the welcoming aroma.

"My newfangled cake's still in the oven." Ella Mae bobbed her head toward it. "The reason the kitchen's so cozy an' warm."

So she anticipated a visitor today. Tessie knew from other folk that this had happened before, and she had no idea how the Wise Woman managed such things. Each morning before Ella Mae's feet hit the floor, she said she liked to pray a blessing for the folk who might cross the threshold of her little house. She sometimes went so far as to ask the Good Lord to send the most hurting soul to her door. Tessie wasn't about to ask if she might have been one of those souls this morning. Still, she was awful curious.

Tessie was finally warm enough to shed her scarf and open her coat. Then, glancing down at the swell of her middle, she thought better of it.

Ella Mae looked at her, bobbing her little head. "I know you're in the family way. Guessed as much."

Feeling suddenly much freer, Tessie took off her coat and went to hang it and the scarf on the wooden pegs near the back door.

"And . . . I'm hopin' there's more to the story here than anyone knows," said Ella Mae.

Tessie nodded, then turned and offered to help put the teacups and saucers on the table.

Ella Mae cheerfully waved her away. "Go, sit an' relax some. I 'spect you're *mied* — weary, jah?"

"Not so much that as cold clear to the bone."

"Does your Mamma know you're here?"

Tessie shook her head. "I think she'll be glad, though, once I get home and tell her."

Smiling now, Ella Mae nodded.

Tessie took the seat across from Ella Mae's usual spot. "Your table's so perty." She noticed the placemats — a lavish purple and blue quilted set of two. "Did ya make these?"

"Mattie did. Said she was tired of seein' the same old yellow rose ones."

Tessie remembered from some time ago. "They were nice, too."

Ella Mae looked over at her. "You're full of compliments today, dearie. Honestly, you can chust relax."

She sighed, realizing she *was* a bit wound up.

"Just think on the dear Lord Jesus, won't ya? He loves you so, Tessie . . . your wee babe, too."

Tears sprang to her eyes, and she brushed them away. "I just needed to talk to someone."

"I'm awful glad you picked me." Ella Mae brought the teacups over, balancing them on their delicate saucers, then turned to get the blue teapot. "You're gonna like this. It'll warm ya clear down to your toes."

Tessie really smiled then. She leaned back in the chair and watched Ella Mae. Despite being somewhat shaky, the elderly woman poured her favorite tea without spilling a drop.

"Now, about that cake, would ya like to try some, once it's done?"

"Might have to wait awhile till it cools, jah?" Tessie wasn't sure how long she ought to stay.

"Oh, that's no problem. We have all day, ain't?"

For some reason, Ella Mae's response brought more tears, and this time when Tessie blinked, they rolled down her cheeks. *Ever so healing,* she thought, glad Ella Mae had turned to go back to the counter to get the sugar dish. By the time she'd returned and sat down, Tessie had wiped her face dry.

All of a sudden, she felt a strange flutter in her stomach, like a kernel of corn had just popped. "Oh," she said softly, clutching her middle. "What's that?"

"A quickening, maybe?" Ella Mae said, her face brightening. " 'Tis a mighty *gut* sign of life. Is this the first time you've felt it?"

Tessie hardly knew what else to say. But she didn't have to, because Ella Mae had bowed her head to pray and began to quote a verse from the Psalms — *"Lo, children are an heritage of the Lord."*

Tessie had heard that verse before, but it

hadn't ever held the meaning it did now. "Denki, Ella Mae," she said after the dear woman said amen.

"Don't thank me; thank the psalmist."

"Well, you know what I mean."

Ella Mae nodded, eyes serious now. "I certainly do . . . and let me tell you 'bout that." She began to tell a story about her own life while a blanket of heavier clouds covered the sky. "My first little one was born terribly ill. Back then no one seemed to know just what was wrong with him." She looked away, toward the light. "Our wee Joseph. I called him Joey."

Ella Mae fingered the edge of the place-mat near her spoon, her slight shoulders rising and falling as she drew a breath. Then she continued, more slowly now. Her frail son had lived only a few days on this earth. She had been nearly inconsolable at the funeral . . . the tiny custom-made coffin a grim reminder to the four hundred mourners of just how short little Joseph Zook's life had been. "Oh, I dearly loved that wee babe," she told Tessie. "Loved him and nurtured him as best I could, given his size . . . and his near constant pain." She paused. "We were ever so sad when he passed, and I craved aloneness for months on end. I felt like I was crippled, missing him so."

Tessie's heart broke for Ella Mae. "I've never heard about this."

" 'Twas before your mother was born." Ella Mae sighed. "In time, though, my husband and I opened our hearts and trusted the dear Lord for the health of our future children, and by faith, we went on to have more."

Tessie could not imagine suffering what Ella Mae had — losing her first baby! And what courage in being able to grasp the divine hope. Hearing the story touched her, and she felt heartened. "I pray over my baby often," she confided. "It's possible he or she will be born impaired."

"Prayer is the best thing, dearie. The most important of all." Ella Mae kissed her cheek before Tessie put on her coat and said goodbye. She opened the back door to head out with one last look at the Wise Woman. Lo and behold, a small dove flew in right past her, bumped the windowed doorway with a muffled thud, then fell to the floor.

Tessie closed the door quickly, and both she and Ella Mae rushed to the bird and hovered near it. "Looks like the poor thing is stunned," Tessie said, watching the dove lie there, then begin to twitch a bit, trying to stand before teetering over and collapsing again.

"I know just what to do," said Ella Mae. She made her way over to the nearby pantry and poured the contents of a box of cornflakes into a canister she brought down from the cupboard. Quickly, she began to tear and bend, forming a bed out of the cardboard box. Muttering a little, she placed a soft towel on the bottom and returned to Tessie and to the dove. "Here we are, little birdie." Gently, she picked it up in her fragile fingers and laid its body in the box, moving it closer to the heater stove.

Just then, the bird tried again to flap its wings, but it fell back, too weak.

"See there? Its wings still work fine." Ella Mae leaned near, watching the dove with gentle eyes. "You'll be all right in time," she whispered. "You will."

Tessie watched Ella Mae and the delicate bird with great wonder — it was hard to pull herself away from the scene. Still, Mamma would start to worry, and the snow was coming harder again.

Ella Mae's eyes glistened as she said goodbye again. "Hope is the silver cord that connects us to heaven," she said. "Never forget."

"Gott be with ya, Ella Mae."

"You, too, dearie."

All the way home, Tessie cherished her

visit to the warm little Dawdi Haus with the sweetest woman.

A safe haven for the wounded.

Chapter 23

"I think I might need something to help me sleep," Mamma told Mandy as they sat together that afternoon in Mandy's gloomy kitchen. They had been watching the snow pile up on the sidewalk to the back of the house for some time now.

Mandy was tempted to go out and sweep things off before it got too deep, but Mamma was out of sorts. "Have ya tried warm milk and some sugar cookies before bedtime? That relaxes Sylvan when he's all wound up."

"Jah, that, and chamomile tea, too."

"Bananas also help," Mandy added.

Mamma fiddled with her teacup.

"Tessie's confession is no doubt weighing on ya," Mandy said.

Mamma laughed softly, but it ended sounding more like a sob. "That's certain."

"Sorry, Mamma, I —"

"Ain't your fault, daughter." Mamma

looked at her over her cup. "Really, it's not."

"Well, I do have some mild sleeping pills if you want to try one."

"Or two?"

"I'd better check the expiration date, though."

Mandy rose and went to the medicine cabinet in the small bathroom off the sitting room, close enough to hear her mother praying or muttering something at the table. Quickly, she found the small bottle. "Here, take what's left of it," she said, returning to the kitchen.

"Don't ya need them?" Mamma rotated the bottle in her hand, frowning at the label.

"Not anymore."

Mamma set the bottle down in front of her. "It must have been awful for Tessie to have kept her secret all tucked away like that. Not sure how she managed to keep it from all of us for this long."

Mandy had heard of other young women who didn't show till the fifth or sixth month, depending on the position of the baby. *Especially with a first pregnancy . . .* Getting up, she went to open the fridge, needing to think of something besides Tessie's baby. She poked her head inside, hoping to find some leftovers she might warm up for supper. She just wasn't up to cooking tonight.

"Tessie left the house earlier." Mamma's voice was flat. "Never said where she was goin'."

"Well, I saw her heading up the way. Might have been off to Ella Mae's."

"What was she thinkin', steppin' out in this weather?"

"She has to be dyin' inside, Mamma. She's lost her first-ever love, and now there's all this talk of shaming and excommunication."

"Ain't like it'll last forever, like *die Meinding.*"

"Thank the dear Lord for that." Mandy meant it. They'd had enough of shunning with Katie Lapp all those years ago.

Tessie wandered downstairs Sunday morning, still in a daze. She'd washed and dressed earlier, and presently, she overheard her parents talking in the kitchen. Hanging back, she wasn't sure what to do.

"You seem anxious, dear," Dat was saying.

"Might be the pills I got from Mandy."

"Those are for sleepin', though. I doubt they cause anxiety."

Mamma went silent just then.

"We'll get through this, May, with plenty-a wisdom from above."

"Jah," Mamma finally agreed. Then she asked, "Any idea how long Tessie's temporary excommunication might last?"

"It's all up in the air, is what I heard. Could be as short as two weeks, depending on what happens when she confesses today."

Two weeks? Tessie leaned on the banister, waiting for more conversation, but none came. She breathed a sigh of relief at her father's answer, more hopeful now, and was aware of the sound of the wide drawer beneath the oven opening. She pictured Mamma setting the black griddle on the range.

Tessie tiptoed back up a few stairs and then came back down, hoping to make enough noise to alert her parents, sorry for eavesdropping.

Mandy couldn't stop fidgeting at the table that morning as she observed Sylvan while he ate his toast and hot oatmeal sprinkled with brown sugar and slivered almonds.

"I'm worried 'bout Tessie . . . what will become of her." She paused, wanting to tell her husband about her sister's pregnancy before church, since he'd hear it there soon enough. "She's expecting Marcus King's baby."

"Goodness, really?" Sylvan frowned and

had a sudden air of impatience about him, as if uncomfortable. He looked out the window, clearly pondering this revelation. "She'll want to marry, and soon." He peered at Mandy. "Don't you agree?"

She thought of Levi Smucker, who'd left Thursday for Florida. In a way, it was probably good he was to be gone for a while, considering Tessie's difficult confession today. Hopefully the precise details of what Tessie might say wouldn't find their way to Levi's ears too quick. Mandy still had some faith in the People's ability to nix the desire to gossip. *Well, I can hope, at least.* "Tessie's a sweet girl. Perty too," she said softly.

"Honestly, though, I doubt many men will look her way . . . now."

"You're probably right." Mandy knew that Tessie would still be desirable to the other young men in Hickory Hollow and surrounding areas had she and Marcus just waited till they'd married to consummate their love. "I don't know what to think 'bout my sister's situation, really," Mandy admitted. "It's shocking, to say the least." She rose to make another piece of toast for Sylvan. She should have made two to start with.

"I never would've guessed."

"And me neither." Mandy sighed. "Maybe

she'll develop a bit of backbone through all this." Oh, she prayed so. It was awful hard watching her sister flounder without Marcus. It would be even harder watching Tessie kneel up there before all the People in only a few more hours, hearing her say what she and Marcus had done together . . . unmarried and all. Goodness, but it was too late for Mandy to feign sickness now. She'd just have to go and keep her head bowed, like Tessie would do up there before the congregation.

I'll hold my breath till it's all over. . . .

Tessie Ann was all in knots in the back of the family carriage as she rode to church with her parents and Dawdi Dave, who had felt strong enough to attend Preaching service today, too. *Of all days.* He sat behind Tessie's parents with his blue-plaid muffler wrapped around his thin neck. Oh, Tessie could scarcely abide the thought of her precious grandfather hearing the things she was required to say to the bishop and to the membership this day!

If it hadn't been so terribly cold, the morning might have been a right pretty one, considering how very blue the sky was . . . the sun bright on her face as she peered out the back of her father's old buggy.

If I can just get through this, she thought as she saw various families come out of their lanes, the horses waiting patiently for their turn onto Hickory Lane. David and Mattie Beiler waved and smiled as Tessie's parents passed them, and she wondered how this upstanding couple would view her confession. David Beiler was the bishop's elder brother and highly regarded in the community. *As are Marcus's parents,* she thought, cringing at their likely reaction to her words following the three-hour service. Could she even sit that long, dreading what was ahead?

She was relieved on some level, knowing Levi Smucker was already gone. What a real blessing that was, at least for now.

It still seemed very odd just how well Tessie and Levi had clicked on their first and only date — getting along like close friends. They'd so lost track of time, they'd nearly closed down the restaurant. Tessie still could hardly believe he wanted to write to her.

If he only knew . . .

None of that was important, though, with her impending discipline to be meted out today. *Lord, please give me the grace to bear what's coming,* she prayed, pleading for courage.

Chapter 24

Mandy held her breath during the spoken benediction as the People rose together at last. Then, in unison, they bent their knees at the sacred words, "*Yesus Grischdus* — Jesus Christ," before sitting back down on the wooden benches for the closing hymn.

She really just wanted to sneak out of the service with the unbaptized teenagers and children who were presently filing out of the deacon's large front room — the temporary house of worship for this Preaching service. A holy hush fell over the place as the youngsters wearing their for-*gut* clothing made their way outdoors without a sound during the final song.

On the opposite side of the large room, the men's section faced the women's, and Mandy could see plainly that Sylvan had already bowed his head, along with the other men in his row, including Norm Byler, who was sandwiched in between Sylvan and her father. She would not let herself think much at all about Norm's association with either man — it just felt odd, considering everything.

Turning her attention to the matter at hand, Mandy prayed silently, *O Lord, help my sister as she offers up her repentance to Thee.*

The bishop, tall and solemn in his black frock coat, asked Tessie to step forward. Quickly, as if eager to do so, Tessie rose from the wooden bench where she'd sat with Mandy and Molly, her eyes downcast as she walked reverently toward the front. Bishop John took his seat with the other ministers, signifying their unity.

Mandy knew from past disciplinary meetings that, immediately upon the admission of sin of any kind, the People were swift to offer pardon, along with the blessing of the Lord God. Anything shared during the confession was to be kept mum and not discussed with others after the service.

Tessie knelt before the gathered body of believers, near the ministerial brethren, taking the position of contrition expected for the most severe transgressions, those violating biblical standards.

The bishop then asked Tessie to describe her sin.

In that moment, waiting for Tessie Ann to deliver up her admission of guilt, Mandy felt like she might faint right off the bench.

"Do you, our sister in the Lord, want to make peace and continue in the faith with God and the church?" Bishop John asked in Deitsch. "Do you want to confess your sin?"

Tessie said she did.

Unable to watch, Mandy bowed her head. Even so, she could picture Tessie up there, her hands folded, eyes squeezed shut. How it pained her to think of her sister like this — expecting a baby without a husband — when she herself had not yet conceived a child. Mandy struggled not to cry, and her sister Molly reached for her hand.

Tessie was plunged into a great conflict, remembering Marcus's decision not to reveal their marriage till the time was right. That time had never come while Marcus was living, and she wasn't absolutely certain now was the right time, either. Oh, she wished she could tell the People about her precious marriage to Marcus, but wouldn't they react like her father had, questioning her word? After all, it did seem awfully convenient to say she had been secretly married now that she'd turned up pregnant.

Visions of her sweet, yet few, times with

Marcus raced through her mind. Silently, she asked God for help and found the strength in that moment to rise to her feet. Heart hammering, Tessie opened her mouth, but it was as if she had been struck dumb. She simply could not speak.

"Our sister, do you have a question?" Bishop John asked, frowning as Tessie stood there. His eyes were as large and somber as a calf's.

Hastily, she shook her head. "Bishop, I'm here to confess my sin . . . of disobedience," she said, finding her voice. "Even so, my situation is not what everyone must suppose. Not at all."

Then, lifting her head further, Tessie met her father's eyes. She assumed he must be thinking, *Why hasn't she confessed to being with child?*

He'll say I'm defiant, she realized. Yet without proof of her marriage, she couldn't risk the bishop's — nor the membership's — disbelieving her, denying she was ever married to her darling. *I already have enough shame on my head. . . .*

Instead, Tessie turned and walked past the rows of womenfolk, momentarily locking eyes with softhearted Ella Mae Zook. When Tessie located her mother on the benches, she felt sad for Mamma, her eyes red, her bottom lip quivering. Then she looked at each of her four sisters — Mandy's head was down. Among the young women, only Cousin Emmalyn Lapp's expression exhibited no hint of shock or aversion. This somehow comforted Tessie, and she recalled Emmalyn's heartfelt declaration of loyalty, come what may.

But it was Mary Beiler, the bishop's wife, who held Tessie's gaze the longest, a somber curve to her mouth as she sat in the back with her youngest child, tiny Anna. Sighing, Tessie could only imagine what must be going through the woman's mind. Was she reliving the day her former best friend, Katie Lapp, had rushed out of the church service, refusing to marry the then-widowed Bishop John? Was dear Mary wondering why Tessie hadn't confessed more?

Of course she is, Tessie thought as she continued toward the kitchen and beyond. Her steps must not falter. And once she found her coat and scarf in the enclosed porch, she exited alone by way of the back door out into the crisp, cold air.

She refused to let anxiety overtake her as she walked briskly toward home. The wintertime sun sliced across snow-packed Hickory Lane, across the white rooftops of neighbors' homes and their tall silos. She didn't have to wonder if the bishop would recommend to impose a temporary excommunication — the *Bann* — for her apparent lack of sincerity today.

All the same, Tessie felt she'd done the right thing by her love for Marcus. And their baby.

Bishop John announced there would be a short meeting of the ministers in a room upstairs, urging the membership to wait there "for the will of the Lord to be done in this matter."

Mandy did not budge nor even look about her; none of the other women sharing her bench so much as whispered. She remembered Tessie's bold walk past them as she left the house of worship. What had happened to keep her from confessing all?

Is she mixed-up, confused?

The rows of benches in front of Mandy — seven, she'd counted earlier — supported the older women, their white organdy Kapps like small translucent moons floating on the back of their graying heads. Her heart went out to them; Tessie's peculiar behavior had extended the already long meeting. *Their backs must be aching,* she thought, remembering the years she'd spent as a teenager, prior to baptism, leaning against the wall on the last row of benches. The welcome resting spot had nearly been a deterrent to formally joining church.

When the ministers returned, the bishop firmly declared, "We are in agreement to cast a vote of the membership on the suggested remedy for Tessie's rebellious action this day."

Mandy froze. Were they going to put the Bann on her sister?

"Have you lost your mind, Tessie Ann? You made no sense whatsoever today at church," her father stated as he sat at the head of the table, hours later. The silence in the house reached into every room as he paused. "It's plainly clear that you sinned and did not confess it! 'Speak ye every man the truth . . .' " he said, quoting the Old Testament verse from Zechariah.

Just as she hadn't revealed her elopement at her confession, Tessie would not defend herself now. She had already told her father the truth, and it had done her no good. Now she felt sure it was her place to carry this love burden.

"The membership has voted," Dat continued. "You are required to return in two weeks to the next church gathering to hear the decision for yourself . . . to take your discipline." He sighed loudly and shook his head. "You never should've left for home after church without waiting for the membership to have their say. What were ya thinkin'?"

"She simply wasn't," Mamma said softly, shame for Tessie on her face.

Tessie nodded, knowing better than to press this. "I'll be there, next Preaching service . . . to take my discipline."

"Des *gut,* then." Dat pushed his callused hand through his thin hair. "And, while ya wait, it'd be right schmaert to beseech the Lord God for wisdom. That's all I'll say on this for now."

Feeling drained of emotion and needing to lie down, Tessie waited till her father had gone to rest in the guest room before she rose and headed upstairs.

No matter what she did — drinking warm milk, taking aspirin — nothing brought sleep to Mandy's weary eyes that night. And to think she'd given away all of her sleeping pills to Mamma, who on a night like this undoubtedly needed one, as well.

So, giving up on getting any rest, Mandy put on her slippers and bathrobe and trudged downstairs, where she sat at the table, feeling ill. For a girl who had always been well thought of, and whose giving spirit had reached out to the whole of the community . . . well, Tessie had certainly fooled everyone.

Mandy leaned her face into her hands. She felt as if her insides were giving way along with her heart. Despite that, she offered up a prayer for Tessie Ann, realizing their relationship was about to change drastically, unless a confession was forthcoming in two weeks. Would Tessie manage to repent sooner rather than later? And if not, what on earth was holding her back?

CHAPTER 25

Monday morning, Tessie and Mamma were up at four-thirty to get the washing, including Dawdi Dave's, through the wringer washer and out on the line early. They said very little to each other as they worked side by side. Now and then, Tessie noticed her mother looking at her askance, as if attempting to understand what had happened yesterday at church.

Finally Mamma said, "Declaring guilt is *gut* for the soul."

"I believe that, too," Tessie replied, but that was all she could manage.

Mamma looked ever so tired.

"Maybe you should try an' rest sometime this afternoon, once dinner's over," Tessie suggested kindly.

"Ain't so easy to sleep these days."

The words stung Tessie. She, too, struggled with regular insomnia more now than before, and she remembered that her sister Miriam had once shared about her wakefulness while she was pregnant. Yet knowing that Mamma was troubled and that it pointed to Tessie made her feel all the worse.

At the noon meal, Dat read from the Bible prior to the silent table prayer, though he usually only read the Scriptures in the evenings, after supper. Less surprising was the passage her father had chosen today. " 'Confess your faults one to another, and pray one for another, that ye may be healed. The effectual fervent prayer of a righteous man availeth much,' " Dat read from the epistle of James. The way her father leaned hard on the words *confess* and *healed* made Tessie take notice.

Even her dour-looking Dawdi Dave, his salt-and-pepper beard touching the table's surface across from her, captured Tessie's gaze with his quizzical eyes. Again, she felt regret that the rest of her family hadn't been told about her marriage. But she did not dare risk her father's anger and bring it up a second time.

The talk at the table was limited to casual asides about the cold weather, the delicious baked ham and mashed potatoes, and the sweet pumpkin bread Mamma had put on the table before serving up the lemon pound cake with whipped cream topping as a surprise.

"Why don't ya come over and visit me sometime soon, Tessie Ann," her grandfather said before leaving to go next door.

Tessie said she would, feeling low in spirit. No doubt he planned to say more of the things she'd already heard today from Mamma . . . and from Scripture.

Tuesday night arrived, twinkling with more snow and with the growing realization that Tessie's family life was definitely changing. Her mother, especially, seemed anxious to encourage Tessie to follow through with the confession she'd set out to give. She spoke of little else.

Since yesterday noon, each of Tessie's sisters had dropped in, as well, every one of them seeming to echo Mamma's words. Tessie Ann felt weary of all the advice. Oh, how she simply wished she could return to the past.

Wednesday afternoon, a letter arrived from Levi Smucker, postmarked Sarasota, Florida. Tessie rather welcomed it, yearning for some everyday communication. The way things were going at home and around the neighborhood, she felt resigned to conversations that pertained only to her so-called wrongdoing and her need to repent.

Mamma had taken the team up the road after dinner to visit with Rhoda Kurtz, where she was joining with Rebecca Lapp and Mattie Beiler to make pies to sell at market tomorrow. For once, Mamma had not invited Tessie along. Feeling as isolated as her sister Mandy said *she* felt at times, Tessie went to sit in the front room near the heater stove, where she had been finishing up some sewing.

She looked down at the letter in her hand, suddenly hesitant. Eventually, though, curiosity overcame her, and she opened Levi's letter.

Dear Tessie Ann,

I promised I'd write to you, but I'm not the best letter writer. So please bear with me.

How are you? And how's everything in Hickory Hollow? Are you getting more snow? It's hard to believe how warm it is down here in Florida, and I'm beginning to understand why my grandparents and so many others like to come to this tropical community for the winter. It's an escape, I'm thinking. A way to keep warm during Lancaster County's lengthy cold snaps.

Like I told you on our first date, I'm noodling the idea of going deep-sea fishing. My grandmother frowns at the notion, as you can imagine. To be honest, I'd rather not give her cause for worry, though I think it would be quite the adventure. I'll be sure to tell you all about it if I do go, but I keep myself so busy caring for my grandparents presently, Grandmammi especially, I don't have much time for fanciful ideas.

He shared with her the sights he'd enjoyed since arriving, as well as mentioning a rather competitive Scrabble game. Levi also described the large tricycles many of the Amishwomen rode up and down the narrow streets in the little village of Pinecraft. He seemed to enjoy being one of the few young people there this time of year as he tended to his beloved grandparents.

Tessie could picture quite clearly what he was writing about and was surprised there were three pages to his newsy letter. He even talked about a particular type of peanut butter spread the Amishwomen there made. He wondered why the womenfolk in Hickory Hollow didn't make it quite like this, *with oodles of extra syrup.* He put a smiley face next to that particular line.

Tessie finished reading, sad to see the letter end. It was obvious how fond he was of her; otherwise, why would someone who didn't enjoy writing letters want to pen such a long one? She sincerely hoped he had a pleasant time during his stay in Florida, soaking up the sunshine and exploring the sea in what free time he might find.

A single young man like Levi deserved a reply, yet Tessie knew that she must be forthright about what she wrote — he needed to know about her condition. It was apparent by his letter that none of their church members had broken the required silence and spilled the beans about Tessie's attempt to confess last Sunday. *At least not yet.*

Levi will be relieved I'm writing, once he learns the shape I'm in. . . .

Finding her stationery box, she pulled out a single sheet and began to write by lantern light.

Dear Levi,

Thank you for your thoughtful letter. I've enjoyed hearing about your experiences there in Florida . . . and I pray your grandmother is getting along much better very soon.

What I want to tell you here is ever so important, Levi. You see, I'm going to have a baby in July, and because of this I don't expect you to keep writing to me, kind though you've been. . . .

As had been the case month after month, Mandy was devastated once again to learn she wasn't pregnant. *I just want to cry,* she thought, and she went right to her room and did so.

Everywhere she went, she seemed to encounter expectant mothers — at Preaching service, at market, at quilting bees . . . and Tessie Ann.

Growing up in her family's home with four sisters, Mandy had never known such a silence there, and it made her jittery. The place had become the opposite of a refuge — the empty rooms a constant reminder of what she longed for and did not have.

Since her cooking and cleaning was caught up by midafternoon, she roamed upstairs, trying to decide where she'd put together a nursery when the time came. *If* it did. "Oh, dear Lord, what's wrong with me? Am I barren?" She assumed it was her problem and not Sylvan's. No, surely their lack of children could never point to him.

Trying not to give way to despair, Mandy

decided to do some piecework and begin to cut small squares for a baby quilt. Such a project made the silent confines of her home more bearable, at least for the moment. The dear Lord knew she needed something, because the walls were pressing closer with each passing month. She simply did not fit in with a community that put such a high value on children — many children per household, in fact. The failure to conceive isolated her, whether in reality or in her mind.

Mandy picked up her basket of fabric and scissors, weary of tears . . . yet she never permitted her husband to see inside her heavy heart to her ever-present sorrow. Her life with Sylvan had become little more than waiting for the day their love might spring at last to life.

Sitting down to work in the kitchen, Mandy decided that, if nothing else, she could give the quilt to Tessie for *her* baby. A lightweight coverlet would be ideal since Tessie's little one must surely be coming in the heat of summer. *Perhaps my own life will be different by then. . . .*

Mandy had not expected a visit from Mamma just now, but there she stood at the back door, nonetheless. Only an hour or so had passed since she'd gotten the idea to make a baby quilt, and the project was all laid out on the kitchen table.

When she heard the knock, for a moment she considered quickly gathering up the evidence. But there wasn't time, and here came her mother, walking right in the door, as family typically did.

"Hope ya don't mind me just appearin'," said Mamma, eyeing the squares and going directly to look at the pretty pattern Mandy had created. "That's right nice." She lifted her eyes to Mandy's, then came over to give her a quick hug. "For *your* baby?"

Mandy sucked in a breath and shook her head. "Not just yet, Mamma, but soon . . . I hope, very soon."

"Ah . . . for Tessie, then?"

"Maybe so."

Thankfully, her mother let that go and sat herself down at the opposite end of the table, folding her pink hands in front of her — like Dat often did when his mind was working on something heavy.

"I'm awful worried." Mamma frowned.

" 'Bout Tessie Ann?"

"Can't put my finger on what it is with her. I'm concerned that Marcus's death has affected her terribly."

"I've wondered that, too."

"Well, I wonder if something's snapped, maybe, in her mind."

"She seems normal enough to me."

"But to say what she did in front of the whole church?" Mamma shook her head. "I can't get over it. Neither can your father. He's on his knees prayin' every night now, pleading with the Lord Gott to help our poor Tessie think straight."

Mandy certainly hadn't noticed anything wrong with Tessie's mind, and she wished her mother wouldn't say such things.

"Since you and Tessie were always closer than the other girls, I've been wonderin' what you think 'bout this."

Mandy shook her head. She guessed her mother hadn't sensed the difficulties between her and Tessie these past couple of years. She went to the sink to lather up her hands, using some homemade soap she and Tessie had made a few months ago. She let the warm water run and run, then finally turned off the faucet and dried her hands. "Would ya like a piece of pie or something to eat?"

"Kumme sit by me," Mamma said, tapping the table. "Why do you think Tessie didn't confess her sin . . . havin' a baby out of wedlock?"

They were getting into dangerous territory, speculating like this. "Not to be disrespectful, Mamma, but we shouldn't be talking 'bout this, should we?"

"Well, it wasn't just at Preaching. She's been mum on that point with me when I've asked, as well — hasn't admitted to any wrongdoing. Other than saying she was disobedient to me and your father, that is."

"Ach, then, I just don't know."

Mamma fell silent, shaking her head slowly.

"We must pray for Tessie, Mamma. Something's troubling her . . . and not just her pregnancy."

Her mother looked at her, eyes shimmering. " 'Tis a mystery, and your father and I fear it will be her undoing."

Is Tessie too mindful of the past to be fully aware of the present? thought Mandy sadly.

She brought out some peanut butter and a stalk of celery, washing the latter and cutting it into smaller sticks. Then, carrying a tray over to the table, she managed to get her mother to agree to have a snack, and for the longest time they sat and nibbled, mercifully without saying more.

Chapter 26

The first thing that crossed her mind when Tessie spotted another letter from Levi two days later — another snowy Friday afternoon — was that he was wasting time writing to her. *Surely he hasn't received my own letter just yet.*

She experienced concern and a speck of sadness at seeing her name on this envelope. Had he gone deep-sea fishing, she wondered, giving his Grandmammi more gray hairs? She pondered his longing for adventure and managed a faint smile.

She appreciated his thoughtfulness, if that's what it was. Levi Smucker had always been the sort of fellow a girl might expect to be exceptionally kind, even sympathetic, back when she'd first known him at the one-room schoolhouse up the road. Levi often wore a caring expression, especially when one of the younger schoolchildren needed help. She recalled seeing him assist one of the little boys who'd fallen and hurt himself during a rather rough corner ball game at recess. And while Levi most likely didn't know of Tessie's present state, he had expressed concern early on for her loss of Marcus. *Yet Marcus was the very beau who kept Levi from having a chance with me. . . .*

Hurrying up the lane toward the house, Tessie was thankful she'd thought to bring her woolen scarf this short distance, wrapping it around her neck and part of her face, the way Dawdi Dave did this time of year. She made a mental note of promising Mamma to go over and clean his place tomorrow, before she went to the Bird-in-Hand shop to help out Mandy and Cousin Emmalyn.

Meanwhile, she had Levi's second letter to read, but it could wait till she helped make supper — no sense in raising eyebrows by rushing to her room. She folded the envelope in half and pushed it into her black woolen coat before finding her allotted peg in the outer room, near the kitchen. Quickly, she removed her snow boots and scarf and made her way into the house with the rest of the mail — two circle letters for Mamma and some odds and ends, mostly ads from Englisch-owned stores in Bird-in-Hand, as well as one for the Amish Village down in

Strasburg.

"Not much mail today, looks like," her mother remarked with a glance at the two letters that interested her most. "I'll read them later — something to look forward to." She placed them on one of the bookshelves on the far wall.

That was the last thing Mamma said the whole time they worked together to peel a batch of potatoes for mashing, then scraped carrots and chopped onions. When it came time to brown the round steak, Mamma said she needed to get off her feet for a spell and headed into the sitting room with her letters in hand.

Adding flour, a can of mushroom soup, and a bit of water for the steak to simmer in, Tessie considered why Levi would write her again so soon. Her curiosity grew as she contemplated it further while setting the table for Dat, Mamma, and herself.

While the steak and gravy cooked, Tessie was tempted to go and read her letter, as well, but there was a stir at the back door, and her sister Marta came in with twins Manny and Matthew. The little boys came running over and hugged Tessie's knees. "Well, hullo there," she said, leaning down to hug them collectively. "Nice to see you both!"

Marta's strawberry blond hair was perfectly parted down the middle and looked like she'd just washed it. Still wearing her heavy black coat, Marta set a large basket of canned goods down on the counter. Snowflakes graced her shoulders like sprinkles of flour. "Thought I'd stop in and share some of my extras," she said, explaining that she'd gone to BB's Grocery Outlet in Quarryville, where she'd bought up lots of dented, bent, and bargain canned goods. "Especially tomato sauce, since I can be lazy sometimes." She rolled her eyes at her own remark and laughed.

Mamma appeared around the corner, carrying her opened letters. "Well, aren't you nice!"

Marta glanced again at Tessie, and Tessie took the cue that perhaps her sister had come to talk with their mother. "Come, let's go an' see what we can find to play with in the front room," Tessie said to the boys, who still had on their coats and hats.

She could hear Marta take right up with Mamma, rattling away in Deitsch the minute she must've thought Tessie was out of earshot. Tessie caught just this much: "There must be far more to the story, ain't so?" Instantly self-conscious, she was glad she'd brought the twins in here to play awhile.

Let Mamma go ahead and talk to Marta, instead of me, she thought crossly.

After Marta and the twins left, Tessie put supper on the table, and Dat came into the kitchen to wash up. When they said amen after the silent table blessing, he stated, "It's time we're more careful with lamp oil and whatnot. Need to be more frugal all around, I daresay."

Tessie nodded her head, wondering.

"Are things goin' all right with the family business?" Mamma asked.

"Oh, ain't the steers a'tall, May." Her father cast a look at Tessie, as though waiting for her to speak up. "Want to be prepared if your baby's born with . . . well, serious problems," Dat said kindly.

"I don't expect ya to —"

"Don't be *lecherich* — ridiculous. Families do what they have to." He sounded more stern now, an irritated look on his lined face. He didn't have to say, *"If you'd just listened to me in the first place, we wouldn't have to scrimp on candles and gas for the lamps and who knows what all in the future."*

So now, on top of everything else, Tessie felt guilty she might potentially sap her parents' financial resources. She felt so miserable during Bible reading and rote prayers, she slipped in a prayer of her own from her heart, asking the almighty One to help mend her broken relationship with Dat. *Somehow or other, as You see fit.*

For the longest time that evening after family worship, her father sat and read *The Budget* beside the heater stove in the front room. Mamma simply sat rocking, her eyes drooping closed now and then.

Tessie wondered what things were going round in her mother's head, glad to see her relaxed for a change.

When they decided to call it a night, Tessie went around behind her parents and turned off all the gas lamps. Then she went to the outer room to locate her coat and pulled out the letter from Levi Smucker. Remembering what Dat had suggested earlier — about taking care to be thrifty — she went to sit in the dark on the floor near the stove, which was dying down and soon to be mere embers. She reached for the flashlight on the table near one of the more comfortable upholstered chairs and turned it on.

Once again, she was taken aback by the length of the letter, with accounts of some time spent at a nearby park, where Levi had played volleyball with a few visiting youth his age. For hours they'd played, he wrote, till he was tuckered out and decided to return to his grandparents' cottage-like residence to write to her. *Dawdi sure found a* gut *deal on this rental cottage.* He didn't admit to being homesick after only a few days away, but she could read between the lines and knew he was lingering only because of his concern for his grandmother's health. So very fond he was of her.

When she finished reading, she returned the letter to its envelope. It would be ever so difficult if she ended up alienating someone who had turned out to be such a caring friend. *If only Mamma and Dat weren't so aloof when I need them most.* Still, if she was honest with herself, she knew the distance between them was largely her doing. After all, she'd made her choice to marry Marcus, unknown to her family.

Tessie made her way back through the large front room, where in June they were scheduled to host Preaching service. *When I'm great with child.*

In the kitchen, she perused her mother's shelves of inspirational novels and pulled out one she hadn't read, *Love Comes Softly.* She returned to the front room with it and the flashlight and read nearly the whole first third of the book while lying on the floor near the heater stove. She connected at once to the young and desperate main character.

Hours later, when Tessie at last headed off to her room, her thoughts were still captured by the compelling prairie love story. And for the first time since Marcus's deadly fall, she found herself thinking about something other than her own sorrow.

Chapter 27

Tessie felt a faint moistness in the air the next morning, a promise of approaching spring — still a few weeks away but present all the same. When she and her sisters and Dat and Mamma were still living in the big farmhouse up the road, there had been Saturday mornings similar to this when she'd gotten up before dawn. She would often awaken to the sounds of the goats bleating and their raucous rooster, Wilder, crowing like his lungs might rupture.

This was truly the best time of day, so fresh and new and filled with hope. She typically liked going around next door to cook breakfast for her grandfather. This day, however, she prayed Dawdi Dave would not bring up the effect her child might have on the family, as her father had at the table yesterday.

"How would ya like your eggs cooked?" she asked Dawdi after she'd greeted him and hung up her coat and scarf.

"Over easy — all three of 'em." He was grinning, wide awake and sitting over on his rocking chair in the rather dark house. Was he also conserving gas? The thought crossed her mind, but she doubted her father had requested that of Dawdi.

"*Three* eggs, ya say?"

Dawdi nodded enthusiastically. "For some reason, I'm mighty hungry this mornin'."

"All right, then." She asked if he wanted toast or pancakes, and he smiled, choosing the latter. Moving over from the small sitting area with the help of his cane, he urged Tessie to cook enough for her, too, saying he preferred not to eat alone if he didn't have to. "I'll be happy to stay for breakfast," she told him, observing him as he slowly pulled out a chair and eased himself into it.

Once settled, his attention turned back to Tessie. His scrutiny didn't bother her, nor did it make her feel uncomfortable, though she guessed that something was heavy on his mind. And, while they sat together, sharing the meal, he asked her a shocking question that set her back.

"Did ya know your Mamma lost two little girls 'tween Mandy's birth and yours?"

She gasped as the truth clamped down on

her. She shook her head. "No, I never heard this."

"Your mother took it awful hard, I can tell ya that." He moved his graying head up and down, eyes blinking repeatedly. "Not sure she'd ever want me to say a peep, though." He drew a slow breath. "Even so . . ."

Tessie said she understood.

"Might just be the reason your Dat was so worried 'bout you and Marcus King getting hitched up. One of your stillborn sisters had a terrible disease. Your mother told Mammi Rosanna as much." Dawdi's shoulders rose and fell at the mention of Tessie's deceased grandmother. He looked away, toward the window and the rising sun. "The Good Lord knew 'twas best. We can trust in that."

Trust.

Tessie could only agree by nodding — she wasn't up to discussing any of this. Oh, the worry she already had for this tiny soul she was carrying . . . yet she must trust her babe was completely in God's hands, at His mercy.

"Don't mean to upset ya." Dawdi reached for his coffee cup. "Thought someone oughta tell ya, though."

"Jah," she whispered. Things began to make even more sense in that moment. No wonder Mamma had been vexed earlier, when Tessie first told of her own pregnancy.

She simply could not hold back the tears and excused herself to get some more maple syrup warming on the stove, where she managed to compose herself without being seen by Dawdi. Bless his heart; he'd only wanted to be helpful.

When Dawdi had eaten his fill, Tessie cleared the table, did the dishes, and swept the kitchen floor.

"Mamma will come over and strip your bed like always early Monday mornin'," she told him. "Now I must get ready to go to work at Mandy's little shop."

He frowned and suggested she'd done enough for one morning. "Aw, must ya?"

"You don't need to coddle me, Dawdi," she said, leaning down to pat his shoulder. "I'm a healthy young woman."

He smiled with his eyes. "You'll keep to yourself what I told ya, jah?"

"You can trust me," Tessie said, then headed to get her coat and scarf. It struck her just then; did he also trust that she'd told the whole truth last Sunday at church? Thankfully, none of that had come up.

Tessie made her way up the snow-swept walkway into the darling shop in Bird-in-

Hand, thinking how to make the new one Sylvan wanted to build just as pretty. She could help Mandy plant a small front garden on either side of the entrance with box shrubs and bright blue morning glories on a white trellis. Perhaps add some yellow tea roses to round things out. *If Mandy likes the idea . . .*

The tiny bell on the door rang as she entered the shop. Right away, Tessie noticed the fragrant potpourri. Cousin Emmalyn had been making a variety of packets with different scents and reported to Tessie when last she'd come to work that already sixty-some packets had sold. Evidently it was all Emmalyn could do to keep up with customer demand.

"Hullo, Emmalyn," she called, pushing her woolen mittens into her coat pockets before hanging her coat, along with her scarf, in the narrow closet behind the main door.

"*Gut* to see ya, cousin." Emmalyn's smile had an extra lift.

"Feels nice getting out of the house."

"That's what Mandy says, nearly every time she comes to work."

"Oh?"

Shrugging, Emmalyn went to open the curtains, letting the sunshine in to slant across the old floorboards. "I daresay havin' the shop is a godsend." She made her way to the next window.

"For me, too," Tessie said before thinking.

"I've wondered . . . well, *hoped* so." Emmalyn stepped back to see if the ties on the draped curtains were even, then went to Tessie, took her hand, and led her to sit on one of the two chairs near the counter. "No need standin' when no one's here just yet."

Tessie Ann was grateful to sit down, still absorbing her grandfather's surprising family news as she was. She looked at Cousin Emmalyn, realizing again how very caring she'd always been. "Seems like an especially long week since I saw ya last."

"No doubt." Emmalyn sat next to her, glancing up at the little black-and-white wall clock behind the counter. "Looks like we've got ourselves a few minutes before the customers arrive. They tend to swish right in on the weekend, ya know."

Tessie smiled, glad for the quiet. Such peace here!

Emmalyn leaned nearer. "I hope ya won't mind, but I had the opportunity to talk privately with some of my Mennonite cousins this week — an older couple over in New Holland. I didn't mention names or many details, mind you, only that someone I love dearly might need a place to stay . . . just maybe."

"How kind," Tessie said. " 'Tween you and me, I just don't know what's going to happen anymore." It was possible things might heat up between her and Dat again, especially after next Preaching Sunday. And Mamma certainly wasn't as cordial or agreeable as Tessie had always known her to be; clearly her mother believed she was making a serious spiritual error in not confessing completely. Things were just becoming plain awkward at home. Well, everywhere, really.

By the look of compassion in her cousin's eyes, she didn't need to tell Emmalyn more of this. "This means so much to me," Tessie said.

"I won't let you be an outcast with no place to go," her cousin said, touching her hand again, patting it like Ella Mae Zook sometimes did.

A few minutes later, the door opened and a half dozen or so Englisch ladies came inside chattering, carrying stylish purses over their shoulders, their coats and brightly colored scarves bringing in the cold dampness. *The promise of springtime,* Tessie preferred to think, wanting to grasp the positive side of things, although right now it was nearly impossible.

As Tessie rode home from the shop in their driver's van, a smattering of birds flew in a perfect line across Nate Kurtz's meadow, a little ways from her father's house. *Another sign of coming spring,* she thought, aware of her ever-expanding stomach. *And my little one has been growing inside me all this time.* She wondered what might be suggested at her consultation this Monday at the Clinic for Special Children in Strasburg. She'd already lined up this same driver to take her there but hadn't said a word to anyone, not even Mamma, who'd have to manage the laundry alone.

Turning away from the window, Tessie realized her lips were pressed together, as if deep in thought. Thanks to Dawdi's revelation this morning, she was seeing her mother in a completely different light, one that reflected great loss. *Mamma lost two babies . . . were there more?*

It was excruciating to dwell on such things. No wonder Mamma hadn't felt comfortable telling her. Tessie's older sisters, if they knew, had never breathed a word to her about it, either. Surely, the Wise Woman knew, but she was a keeper of secrets and could be trusted implicitly.

Tessie Ann shifted in her seat as the driver pulled into the lane. Looking over at the front porch, she gasped softly. Bishop John and her father were standing together, their collective breath turning wispy white as they talked. She shivered at the sight, but they were seemingly so caught up with whatever they were discussing that they didn't even look her way when she quickly paid the driver and hurried toward the house.

"Did ya have a nice day?" Mamma asked as Tessie came in the back door, even before she had a chance to hang up her outer garments. This seemed peculiar, and Tessie waited till she went into the kitchen to say that she'd had a fine day, indeed. "Did *you,* Mamma?"

"S'pose so." Mamma looked befuddled. "Till just now."

"I hope the bishop's visit hasn't upset you." Tessie reached for a warm chocolate chip cookie on the plate situated in the center of the counter.

Mamma craned her neck toward the front room, gawking for a moment. "Ach, looks like they're still at it out there."

Still at it . . .

Tessie wasn't sure she wanted to know what was going on.

"Seems the bishop has changed his mind."

"Oh?"

"He says since ya started to confess last time and didn't finish that you oughta do so before the brethren mete out discipline. He's not forcin' you, though. That wouldn't be right."

Bowing her head, Tessie remembered all too clearly, last Sunday rushing back to her on wings of sadness. She'd started to lie and say she was sorry for making love with Marcus, to give the bishop what he'd asked for. But the way things ended up was far better in the sight of God than confessing to the wrong thing.

"Mamma, I tried tellin' Dat the whole truth."

"Tessie Ann . . ."

"And I'm sorry for disobeying you and Dat in following my heart with Marcus," Tessie said, her voice rising. "But Dat has discouraged me from revealing all that I told him. He forbade it, actually."

"Ach, the things you say make me feel *verlegge* — troubled, daughter. I see with my eyes you're going to have a baby, yet you haven't confessed as much to the membership. How can you be with child without having sinned?"

"Mamma, *please.*"

"Makes my poor head spin. Gives me a

Koppweh." Her mother rubbed her poor aching head, looking at Tessie with growing alarm. "All of it points to sin, plain and simple." She put her head down for a moment and then whispered, "The bishop says it's a downright terrible example for the other courting-age young women here."

"I'm not lyin' to ya, Mamma."

Her mother's face was as pale as pasta. "Bishop wants you to seek God 'bout confessing *all* your deceitfulness and your rebellion . . . along with everything else that must've transpired. Ya need to do so next Preaching service."

"What I had to confess, I confessed to Dat already. And the Lord God before that. I've told the membership all I can." Tessie felt a prick of guilt at Mamma's obvious consternation. If only she dared to tell her mother what she'd told Dat!

Tessie noticed the book she had been reading last night still out on the table in the sitting room and went to pick it up. She could still feel Mamma's eyes on her as she rushed up the stairs with it, feeling like she was being chased.

Chapter 28

Tessie Ann made sure the bishop was gone before she crept out the back door, looking all about and spotting her father out hitching the horse to the family carriage.

She made her way toward the road, remembering the little stream that ran along their lane, hidden now beneath melting snow, and the lovely way it ran gently over the small rocks. It made her yearn for summer . . . and the coming birth of her babe. Sometimes she felt sure the child she was carrying was a boy — she hoped this for the sake of Marcus's memory. Other days, she didn't mind either way. What she desired most of all was a miracle for her child's health, if that was God's will. And if not, the willingness to embrace whatever the Lord allowed with a caring and patient heart.

Just then, she saw her sister Mandy along the roadside, coming this way, and if Tessie wasn't mistaken, it looked like she was crying. Tessie held her breath.

What's the matter?

She hurried toward her sister. "You all right?" she asked. "Ach . . . I can see you're not."

"Don't tell anyone you found me cryin'," Mandy pleaded.

"What's wrong, sister?"

"I just weep sometimes privately, that's all . . . so Sylvan won't see."

Tessie considered that. "Maybe he should know, so he can comfort ya." She was momentarily uncertain what to say, then, "Can I help with anything?"

"Just walk with me a ways, all right?"

Tessie was glad to and told her so. But Mandy was quiet as they slowed to a shuffle, the way Dawdi Dave did on days his rheumatism acted up. And Tessie didn't think she'd be wise to continue prying. Knowing Mandy, if she didn't want to talk about something, she simply wouldn't.

Some time later, their father came rattling up Hickory Lane with the horse and carriage, and Mandy looked away, even though Dat gave a quick wave. "He's in an awful hurry," Tessie remarked, hoping that might loosen Mandy's tongue.

"Jah . . . just seems to be the way he is."

Tessie felt the weight behind Mandy's comment and would not touch it. She could not bring herself to open up layers of past hurt. "Daylight's lasting longer, have ya noticed? Little by little."

"Sylvan pointed that out to me just yesterday."

"Feels *gut,* really." The receding sunlight caught the blue of Mandy's eyes, but Tessie didn't stare. She looked instead at their neighbors' pretty barn, newly painted white last fall and blending with the remaining snow. "I wonder how many more snowstorms we'll get before spring arrives."

Mandy laughed softly. "Honestly, I'm ready for the thaw."

"And all the upcoming auctions and farm sales, no doubt."

"Heard Paul Hostetler's two uncles are havin' a big one in a few weeks. Are ya goin'?"

"Don't know." Tessie shrugged. "Are you?"

"Sylvan thinks we should — says it'd be *gut* for me to get out more."

Smiling, Tessie agreed with that. Looking at Mandy, she thought of Dawdi Dave's revelation and wondered who their tiny unborn sisters might have resembled had they lived. She felt besieged with sudden sadness, not feeling close enough anymore to Mandy to divulge such a family secret. But she wouldn't have, anyway, having given her word to Dawdi.

"Some days I think I'd like to trade places with you, sister." Mandy glanced at her.

"Why on earth?"

"To be expecting a baby. Not, well, other things . . ."

The exchange was plain awkward. And for the life of her, Tessie had no idea how to smooth it over, if that was even possible. She simply said, "I hope and pray you'll be with child real soon, Mandy."

"If only wishing made it so" came the downhearted reply. Mandy sighed, then brushed a gloved hand across her eyes. "Will Mattie Beiler deliver your baby?"

"Haven't talked to her, not just yet." Tessie was shivering with cold but didn't want to complain, lest her sister think she was anxious to end their conversation. She hadn't bundled up very well, thinking she was just making a quick run out to the mailbox.

"Maybe you should speak with her, don't ya think? To make sure things go all right."

"Well, things just might *not* go well at all, according to Dat," Tessie blurted out, feeling the old surge of anger.

"Ach, what do ya mean?" Mandy looked aghast as she stopped on the road. "What's Dat sayin'?"

"Well, that my baby could be born with an awful bad disease — a rare genetic disorder, maybe." She paused, thinking now might be a good time to reveal what she knew about the charts, for Mandy's sake, too. "Not to worry ya, but that's the reason he didn't want me marryin' Marcus."

"Oh, Tessie Ann . . ."

"And," she continued, "the reason why Dat was so opposed to Norman Byler . . . for you."

Mandy's eyes widened. "How do ya know?"

Tessie quietly told her about the secret family listings. "Guess Dat didn't want to just tell us about them, since the bishop's against such things."

"Ach, I wish I'd known back then," Mandy said ever so softly. "Would've helped a lot."

"Sorry if this upsets ya."

Mandy shook her head. "Was awful hard then . . . not understanding what happened. My beau just up and left, ya know."

"I remember. It was a difficult time for ya."

"Norm never breathed a word 'bout why."

Tessie wasn't sure even Norm had known

then. She almost wished she hadn't brought it up, yet it wasn't fair for Mandy to be kept in the dark. Not then and not now.

At that moment, she made the mistake of looking back at Mandy's farmhouse, their childhood home. She stared up at the window that had been her and Mandy's bedroom all those happy years. The old, familiar disappointment hit her hard. She shook her head. "I really miss our close days together," she said softly. "Honest, I do."

Mandy nodded and smiled wistfully. "Jah . . ."

"Remember when we played dolls for hours and dressed them in matching clothes?"

"Even the little sleepers Mamma made for them with leftover fabric," Mandy said. "Aw . . . so soft."

"Always white or yellow, never pink or blue," Tessie recalled.

"Guess we didn't care if they were boys or girls, jah?"

Tessie pondered that, having forgotten. "I can't wait till you and Sylvan have a little one to cuddle together."

"Denki, sister."

"With all my heart, I mean that." Tessie held out her hand. "And I'll be very happy when ya tell me it's true."

They walked quietly, hand in hand, Tessie almost forgetting the chill weather. And she couldn't help wondering if her sister would willingly give up the old homestead if only she, too, were expecting her first child.

Mandy was relieved to have a little time left to scrub her face good before Sylvan came in for supper. When she was satisfied he couldn't possibly know she had been crying, she went to check on their oven meal of hearty chunks of tender beef, potatoes, sliced carrots, and onions. She was glad to have gone walking, even out in the cold, after staying indoors all day, except to feed the chickens, which Sylvan insisted on keeping, even though they seemed to be more bother than they were worth.

The way she and Tessie had talked so openly just now had soothed her. These past many months, she'd sometimes felt an undercurrent of tension between them. She felt awful about Tessie's worry over her coming child. What could their father know about the possibility of such dire diseases?

She set the table and recalled Tessie's dear hope that Mandy would become pregnant soon. And that, too, gave her comfort.

Surprised at her and Mandy's renewed

closeness, Tessie headed back toward the house, walking carefully along the road, still shivering. Would she always feel this cold? She remembered what Levi had written about enjoying the balmy weather down south, and for a moment wished she were there. *Anywhere but here,* she thought, yet the idea of going anyplace in her condition was unlikely.

She fondly replayed her walk with Mandy and soon realized she'd forgotten to get the mail. She hurried back to discover the mailbox was quite empty. "Mamma must've come out here," she mumbled, feeling terrible her mother had risked this weather.

Hurrying inside, she found Mamma sitting at the kitchen table with a letter. "When you didn't return right away, I thought you'd disappeared . . . like the other day."

When I went to see Ella Mae, Tessie thought.

Mamma pointed to the letter on the table. "By the way, this came for ya."

It was another letter from Levi Smucker, and when Tessie looked at her mother, she was surprised to see Mamma's eyes were moist.

"Could be right promising, really," Mamma said softly, though she did not smile.

"Mamma . . . Levi Smucker will never be anything more than a friend," Tessie let it be known. *He feels sorry for me, that's all.*

"Well, a *gut* friend's all it takes sometimes, dear," Mamma said before returning to reading her own mail.

Tessie considered the fact that he'd written three letters since leaving for Florida yet had received only one reply from her. What motivated him to keep writing now, knowing of her predicament?

The notion that he might feel sorry for her made her bristle. No, she did not want sympathy from Levi or anyone.

Chapter 29

Long after supper, Tessie slipped away to her room with the letter. She found herself deeply touched, even tearing up, as she read.

> I'm cutting my visit short, Tessie Ann . . . lining up some local help here for my grandmother's care. If I can get in touch with a driver, I plan to return to Hickory Hollow right away, instead of waiting for the next bus. In fact, by the time you receive this letter, I might even be home, Lord willing.
>
> And if it's all right, I'd like to see you as soon as possible. Maybe even Sunday afternoon, since it's an off-Sunday from Preaching there.
>
> Your friend always,
> Levi Smucker

Tessie let her tears come. For sure and for certain, she hadn't expected this. Not at all.

To think Levi still wanted to see her. This was the kindest gesture. *Ever so dear, really.*

Oh, but she felt terribly out of sorts. What was wrong with her emotions? Levi's latest letter was complicating everything, wasn't it? Tessie really did not deserve his attention, but her heart was soft to this young man in good standing in the Hickory Hollow church. Softer than she'd ever intended.

Sleep escaped Tessie — the worst night since Marcus's funeral — and she paced back and forth in her room. In her weariness, it struck her that just maybe Dat was somehow behind Levi's letters and his hasty return from Florida. But would her father be able to interfere like that, considering?

She stifled a laugh, not wanting to awaken her parents this late. Certainly, her father would go to great lengths to get his way. Hadn't he always wanted to get Levi Smucker in the family? The thought took all of the joy she'd felt while reading the recent letter.

Yet could even her father still hold such sway over Levi, when Levi knew she was carrying another man's baby? The idea bewildered her. No wonder she wasn't able to relax. Well, Tessie decided, if that were the case, then she'd rather not be anywhere near this house tomorrow afternoon, when the People went visiting — and when Levi wanted to come see her. If it meant wrapping up but good and shivering her way over to see Ella Mae, she'd do well to be gone. She couldn't expect him or any man to take on the responsibility for such a financial burden, if her baby was born with serious problems.

Levi has no idea what he's pursuing, really. Surely he's better off without me.

When Tessie fell asleep at last, it was fitful. Several times in the night, she awakened with a jolt and sat up in bed, disoriented, trying to familiarize herself with her whereabouts, even thinking once that she was back in Marcus's house, sharing his bed. But when she looked, the room was terribly, dreadfully vacant.

Shaking herself, Tessie rose and walked downstairs to pour some milk into a glass, then wandered to the back door and looked out. She began to pray, *Lord, Thy will be done in all of our lives. And, if it is possible, please let Marcus know I'm doing the best I can to take care of our baby . . . and to preserve his love for me.*

She paused, again recalling her mother's miscarriages. Somehow, Mamma had bravely gone on to birth another healthy child.

"That child was me," Tessie whispered, also remembering Ella Mae's courage to have more children, not knowing if they would be vigorous or struggle like her tiny baby Joseph, buried in the hard, frosty ground in the same cemetery as Marcus.

"I give my little one to Thee, O Lord," she said softly, eyes fixed on the sky. "I will trust and not be afraid."

Finishing the milk, Tessie set the rinsed glass in the sink and returned upstairs to bed without praying for Levi Smucker, come to think of it. *He says he's coming home early. For me?*

Ever so tired now, she pushed all of that aside for another day, unable to think clearly.

Why am I in such a bad mood? Mandy walked the hallway upstairs, struggling with insomnia that Saturday night. She was so sleep deprived, she'd even considered putting on her coat and boots to walk the short distance to her parents' house, hoping to slip indoors to locate the bottle of sleeping pills she'd given to Mamma.

She glanced at the door to her and Sylvan's bedroom and realized she'd left it ajar.

She'd never known her husband to not sleep peacefully all night. He fell asleep directly and did not awaken till around four-thirty, when he pulled on his clothes and hurried outdoors to meet Mandy's father and a few other men, all of them working hard till they could fall exhausted into bed at eight-thirty or so at night. Day after day, week after week, the People lived according to the seasons and their animals' care. *Our predictable life.*

Mandy pictured herself walking the floors with a restless infant and had the good idea to put a small daybed in the empty bedroom nearest her and Sylvan's room. *The perfect nursery.* At first, of course, she would have their newborn in their room with them, in a handmade cradle her mother-in-law had said they could have *"whenever you say the word,"* giving Mandy a gentle smile. Everyone was like that — encouraging and hopeful, though she was beginning to be weary of too much encouragement.

Poking her head into the unfurnished nursery, Mandy went to stand in the middle of the vacant room and bowed her head, folding her hands. In that moment, she felt God was calling her to pray about her poor attitude toward Sylvan. It seemed odd, really, to consider such a thing when she never had before. She had not heard a voice from heaven, but in her spirit, a still, small voice was urging her, and Mandy did not doubt whatsoever that she ought to answer. *O Lord, make my heart anew and soften it for my husband's sake, according to Thy will.*

She didn't expect to feel differently, but when she returned to bed, she yawned and was aware of the scratchiness behind her eyes. Mandy was more relaxed as she pulled up the covers and settled onto the pillow. Sighing deeply, she fell swiftly to sleep.

An hour or more before dawn on the Lord's Day, Tessie Ann lay quietly in bed, contemplating next week's Preaching service. She pressed her hand against the pillow and drank in the peace of the house — the familiar silence of it. Next Sunday at this hour, she would be getting up and preparing to go to the house church gathering, brushing her hair and putting it into a slick, neat bun.

She rolled over and sighed. Could she even attend that service without being considered as defiant by her parents and the People? *Yet not going might seem still worse. . . .*

Oh, to take a long walk today, despite the cold, she thought. Here lately, walking seemed to calm her. Reading did, too. She was nearing the completion of her book, captivated by the young woman's ability to throw herself on the mercy of God and marry a man she scarcely knew. Such a hopeful story. *One of bravery, too.*

Tessie Ann sat up in bed and realized she had not had a single grief-filled dream last night. For all these months, her nighttime dreams had often lingered into the morning, but not today. She breathed a sigh of thankfulness for that as she reached for her Bible and the small flashlight on the little table next to the bed. Until she heard her mother up and padding down the stairs, she had time to read from several psalms. In many ways, the lack of a scheduled church gathering on this particular Lord's Day was a relief and a blessing of sorts.

Later, once she was dressed, Tessie fidgeted in her seat at the breakfast table, next to Mamma, glancing at her father now and then. She'd helped make a hot breakfast rather than the typical cold cereal and fruit they were used to having on a Preaching Sunday. There sat the three of them, enjoying the delicious German sausage, pancakes, and baked oatmeal.

Tessie Ann wondered if it was a good idea to bring up her question while they were eating. She took a few more bites of pancake, then forged ahead. "Dat?" she said, trying to sound as polite as she ought to be. "Would ya happen to know anything 'bout Levi Smucker's return from Florida?"

He glanced up with a frown, then looked at Mamma and shook his head. "Why do you ask this, daughter?"

"Did ya contact him before he left, maybe?" She had to know.

"I did not." His flat words were no comfort.

"It just seems ever so peculiar, really, that —"

"Tessie Ann, you heard your father," Mamma intervened.

Feeling embarrassed, Tessie hushed up and nodded. When would she ever learn that to confront her father was a mistake? Even so, she'd gotten her answer. "Sorry, Dat," she murmured. "Never mind."

He didn't even bother to ask why she wanted to know. Dat just kept eating and smacking his lips, seemingly relishing the meal, which was really all she guessed they ought to care about right now, anyway.

Following breakfast, Dat left to go see Sylvan for a while, and Tessie took the opportunity to tell her mother of her doctor appointment tomorrow morning. "I thought you'd want to know, 'specially since I won't be around much to help with the washing."

"I see," Mamma said, studying her. "I'd actually thought of hanging it in the cellar. Last week the clothes froze like boards out on the line. Who'd have thought the beginning of March would be so cold?"

Tessie remembered how cold it had been, glad there was no conflict over the appointment.

"I s'pose you don't mind goin' by yourself, then?" Mamma asked, looking a bit disappointed, actually.

She shook her head. "This is the consultation appointment with a pediatrician at the Clinic for Special Children. Our doctor recommended it very strongly."

Mamma said she knew of the well-known clinic. "Samuel Lapp's nephew has a daughter who sees a doctor there for her autism. And the Mennonite farmers over near Harristown Road are getting help for their girl who suffers with Pretzel Syndrome."

Tessie wasn't surprised. More and more Amish and Mennonite families were being seen and helped by the renowned doctors, some for the rarest disorders.

"I've been prayin' for the health of your baby," Mamma said quietly. "Wanted you to know."

"That means everything to me." Tessie was pleased to hear it. "I'll admit I'm awful scared at times, but I believe with all of my heart that having a special child is a gift from God. Just as all the People do." She blinked back tears. "If that happens, I'll learn much patience, jah?"

Mamma nodded slowly. "And compassion."

"Ach, I already love my little son or daughter so very much."

Mamma fixed her eyes on Tessie. "Mothers write love on the hearts of their children before they're born, no matter how they come to us. I see how careful you are, dear. 'Tis so admirable."

"I'm doin' all I can, with our heavenly Father's help. And I'll know more after my appointment."

"We're called to bear each other's burdens," Mamma reminded her.

Tessie agreed, believing it might just be God's calling for her to care for a disabled child.

Mamma mentioned the convenience of having a summertime baby, and Tessie agreed. Her mother's expression was a blend of concern and confusion, but Tessie felt it best not to talk about the confession she was sure her parents, along with the bishop, wanted from her.

Much later, after the kitchen was clean and everything put away, Tessie mentioned the possibility that Levi might drop by that afternoon. "If I'm in the house, I'd prefer not to see him."

"Prefer not or absolutely not?"

"Both."

"You could come with us to visit Mandy and Sylvan, then," suggested Mamma. "How's that?"

Tessie wasn't sure it was such a good thing for her to see Mandy today, not when her sister was so longing for a child of her own. *Don't want to be a reminder . . .* "Well, but Dat's over there right now, ain't so?"

Mamma seemed to sense her hesitancy. "Well, ain't the same as all of us sitting down together and havin' a nice long visit, though."

Tessie nodded. "Still, I'd really like to go over and see Molly's little Michael Abram. Haven't even held my nephew yet."

Mamma smiled. "He's growin' like a bean sprout, I'll say."

Tessie would not ask again to visit Ben and Molly instead of Sylvan and Mandy — it wasn't her place to suggest where her parents headed on a Sunday afternoon.

Somehow or other, she would manage to steer clear of Levi Smucker today.

Chapter 30

Mandy served up some warm sticky buns and hot coffee to her husband and father as the two men sat at her table. It seemed curious there was this much talk going on, especially when they worked together most of the week.

She never interrupted them — did not even speak — when Sylvan and her father were in discussion. And they certainly were not discussing business on the Lord's Day. She happened to overhear snippets of their conversation as she moved back and forth between the table and the counter, topping off their coffee and offering fruit and sweets.

It was a dance of sorts, and the longer they sat and talked without including her, the more she felt she ought to just keep taking food over there. After all, Dat and Sylvan were eating everything she set before them. *Didn't Mamma feed Dat before he came?*

Her ears perked up at the mention of Levi

Smucker.

"Levi Smucker's back in town," Sylvan was telling Dat. He blew on his coffee before taking a sip. "He's interested in Tessie, is what I hear."

"Well, someone's gotta be, else her child will have no father," Dat stated with an edge to his voice. "And Tessie Ann *needs* a husband in order to form a fitting family, under God."

"Still, it's hard to figure why Levi'd want to take that on."

Mandy felt awkward — it wasn't easy being right there and hearing things pertaining to Tessie Ann. Even so, she stayed put.

"Is anyone urgin' Levi to reach out to Tessie?" asked Dat.

"It's all his doing, according to his father." Sylvan scratched his chin through his beard. "Reuben is mighty perplexed, as are Levi's brothers."

"Not any more than we are over Tessie." Dat glanced now at Mandy, who was leaning against the sink, wringing her hands.

At this point, Mandy stepped out of the kitchen, but she could still hear much of what they were saying.

"Heard Levi came back quick-like from Florida because he heard Tessie is with child," Sylvan said. "Interesting, ain't?"

"Sure is. Levi's always been a mighty *gut* fella. 'Tween you and me, I never thought Tessie Ann would give him a chance, so caught up with Marcus King, she was."

"How do ya know she will . . . even now?"

"That's just it; who's to know?"

"And Tessie's goin' to have her first beau's baby. That's surely a stumbling block to any man."

"Levi's not just any man," Dat replied. "Let me tell ya."

Mandy had to smile at that and wondered if, just maybe, her father was up to his old matchmaking tricks.

Tessie and her parents were eating leftover pumpkin pie for dessert when her father brought up the family charts that Tessie had inadvertently discovered. "I struggled some years ago with being faithful to God's sovereign will . . . wanted to confess this to you both," he said, looking mighty serious. "Thought you should know, daughter, that it went against the grain to just stand by and watch you — and Mandy, before Sylvan — get involved with young men from families where genetic disorders are all too common."

Tessie sat quietly, surprised he was being so blunt.

"The will of almighty God comes first round here," he said. "Sadly, I failed to trust in that, secretly keepin' my family charts for all my daughters, not wanting uninformed choice to dictate who ya ended up with for a mate."

Tessie listened, wondering why he was sharing this now. *Too late.* Yet, knowing her own strong will — and her love for Marcus — would she have heeded Dat's warning in the long run?

Mamma spoke up softly. "What's done is done, Ammon."

"Still, there's the matter of a particular confession next Sunday." He directed his gaze to Tessie once again. "I've already made mine to the bishop, and to God, for disobeying 'bout the lists."

That was all well and good for her father, Tessie thought. And while she'd felt tender-hearted toward him for opening up like this, she didn't want to speak again about what was expected of *her* after that same service. She questioned now whether it was wise to go visiting with them today. Why set herself up for more confrontation, a sitting duck in her parents' buggy?

Anymore, Mamma's life seemed to be ruled by the many work frolics planned by the womenfolk. And when they stopped over to see Molly and family — supposedly for Tessie and her father to hold the new baby — the upcoming gatherings were nearly all Molly and Mamma wanted to talk about as everyone sat in a circle in the kitchen. Tessie tuned Molly and Mamma out as they jabbered contentedly.

The ring of chairs included Molly's husband, Ben, and their two little girls, Mae and Marian, who perched on their own chairs without fidgeting while the adults conversed leisurely, all of them wearing their clean church clothes. Tessie wasn't aware of the topic of conversation between Ben and her father, who this minute appeared to be making over tiny blanketed Michael Abram, sound asleep in his strong arms.

Tessie found momentary joy in the precious sight of her father with his new grandson. It was hard to imagine Dat holding her own tiny infant son or daughter. *Will he even want to, the way he is pushing for my confession?*

Dat had never looked as comfortable as now, she thought, finding it a lovely yet strange thing to behold. Had he ever held his baby granddaughters so lovingly like this?

"Go on over and have your turn," Molly

said, leaning around Mamma to encourage Tessie Ann. "That one's the most relaxed of my three," she said with a bob of her head toward Dat and the baby. "He's already tryin' to sleep through the night, if ya can believe that."

"My, my, aren't you fortunate," said Mamma, all smiles.

Uncertain if she wanted to scoop the infant away from Dat's embrace, Tessie sat there a few minutes longer, and Molly began to talk now about Mary Beiler's cousins from Apple Creek, Ohio, who were coming in for a visit soon. Nate and Rhoda Kurtz had relatives on their way, as well, from near Harmony, Minnesota. Tessie kept her ears peeled for talk of Levi Smucker, but no one said a word — no doubt Mamma was careful not to mention him in this setting, lest it embarrass Tessie. She wondered if she'd made a mistake by escaping from the house with her parents to avoid Levi. *If I'd stayed home today, I could've nipped the whole thing in the bud.*

About the time she rose to get the baby from her father, four-year-old Mae slid down from her chair and walked over to take her by the hand, leading her over to the kitchen table. "Can ya sit with me and color awhile, Aendi?" she asked, eyes bright.

"All right," Tessie said. Just then, Dat handed the baby to Molly, who carried him straight to Tessie and placed him, still sleeping, in her arms. *Does she think I need practice?* Tessie mused, looking into the tiny face, long eyelashes lining his eyelids like minuscule feathers against his fair face. "Do you like to help Mamma with your baby *Bruder*?" she asked Mae.

"*Alsemol* — sometimes." Petite Mae explained that she really liked when Mammi May came over to help. "Then I can color more . . . like now." She disappeared to go over to one of the drawers close to the floor, pulled it out, and rummaged through several coloring books before finding one she preferred, along with a plastic container of crayons, all the while babbling to herself in Deitsch.

Looking down at the sweet baby in her arms, Tessie Ann thanked the Good Lord for giving her sisters healthy children, thus far. *Will mine be the first special child in the family, besides Mamma's lost babes?* She glanced over at her mother and caught her eye, feeling shy. Had she and Molly been talking about her? By now, Tessie should be used to Mamma's furtive glances. It was unquestionably difficult for Mamma to see her youngest daughter in such a state, unaware that Tessie's baby was not a product of sin but of legitimate, sanctioned love. *Just not by the church.*

There was a slight commotion at the back door, and when Tessie turned to look, she saw Sylvan and Mandy removing their coats. Mandy spotted Tessie holding the baby and looked away right then.

Oh, this isn't such a gut *idea.* Tessie wished now she'd stayed home for sure!

Chapter 31

Tessie missed Marcus. For one thing, Marcus would've known what to do when Mandy sat in the circle of chairs, her eyes sad and hardly talking except in one-word responses. Meanwhile, Sylvan had planted himself on the other side of Dat, and he, Ben, and her father were already having themselves a fine time conversing and chuckling.

Concerned for her sister, Tessie continued coloring with little Mae, and now Marian, too, one page after another. Baby Michael scarcely moved in her lap. Such a darling little one he was — she could hardly keep her eyes off him.

At young Marian's request, Tessie helped finish one of her scribbled pages, and goodness, but Tessie felt Mandy's solemn eyes on her all the while.

No wonder she's hurting, surrounded by all

the children as I am.

Later, when Molly, wearing her prettiest blue Sunday dress and matching apron, brought out the plump angel food cake she'd baked yesterday, along with coffee for everyone, Tessie offered to put the baby down in a cradle around the corner from the kitchen. There was also a comfortable rocker and an upholstered chair nestled in the cozy smaller room. A nearby magazine rack was filled with periodicals, including *Die Botschaft* and *The Diary,* and the lovely four-color *Ladies Journal.* The little girls followed Tessie Ann into the separate room and helped by holding the crib quilt and hovering near while Tessie placed the baby in the cradle.

Going to sit in the large, upholstered chair, a matching pillow in the crook of its wide arm, Tessie decided to relax a bit. Her little eyes twinkling, Marian climbed onto her lap and leaned her head against Tessie's shoulder, resting her small hand on the bump on Tessie's middle.

"Our baby grew inside Mamma's tummy, too," said Mae, sitting wide-eyed on the rocking chair, pretty in her rose-colored dress and white organdy apron. She leaned forward to make the chair rock ever so gently.

Tessie was at a loss for words — *what to say?*

She pointed toward the cradle, smiling. "Just lookee there at your baby brother. See how tired he is?"

"Mamma says new babies need to sleep a lot," Mae announced, sounding very much the big sister. Mae got down from the rocker and knelt beside the cradle, her dimpled hands resting on its wooden railing.

As she sat there observing, Tessie soon realized that cuddly Marian had fallen asleep right there in her lap — she'd just have to stay put awhile, dessert or no. And when Mae sang a quiet hymn in Deitsch to the sleeping infant, it was all Tessie Ann could do to stay awake herself.

Mandy had half hoped they would go and visit Miriam or Marta this afternoon. She'd had an inkling her parents and Tessie Ann might be over here at Molly's, taking turns holding the baby, since she was fairly sure her father hadn't yet seen his new grandson. And even though the tension with Tessie had greatly diminished, Mandy had wanted to shy away from expectant sisters and new babies.

But Sylvan had settled on Ben and Molly's place, and now there sat Mandy, trying not to stew at his evident lack of consideration, not hungry while the rest of the adults enjoyed dessert and coffee. She wondered if Tessie Ann realized she'd gathered the children to herself, of all things.

Does she think that will make things easier on me, maybe? More than anything, Mandy yearned right now to hold Molly's new baby, but Tessie Ann and the children were still around the corner. So Mandy waited awhile longer, giving her youngest sister plenty of time with their baby nephew and sweet little nieces. When Mandy could stand it no longer, she excused herself from the table and made her way to the smaller space behind the kitchen.

When she peered around the corner, what she saw took her breath away. It was the sweetest scene — her pregnant sister sound asleep while holding Marian, who was all curled up in her arms. Mae was leaning her little head on the cradle, droopy eyed, and one of the baby's tiny pink fists had managed to find its way out of the blanket and was moving, his pale blue eyes blinking open just now.

She dared not speak lest she awaken them, and she tiptoed over to look down into the gleaming wooden cradle, touching the baby's soft cheek with the back of her fingers. *"Biebche,"* she whispered. Just that quick, Mae's head popped up, making the cradle rock. Mandy stilled it and reached down to pick up the darling bundle, then sat down in the empty rocking chair, sighing with deepest pleasure.

On the ride back to the house, Dat and Mamma talked about their grandchildren, primarily the new baby, whom they seemed to agree equally resembled both Ben and Molly. "Tiny Michael has Ben's eyes and the shape of Molly's mouth," Mamma said, and Dat chuckled with a fond glance at Mamma.

Tessie Ann sat behind them, observing her parents, anxious to get warm again at home. The late-afternoon sun made brilliant dots on the terrain as they passed first the deacon's house and then David and Mattie's enormous expanse of land . . . then finally Ella Mae's Dawdi Haus attached on the far end of David and Mattie's old farmhouse.

Dat and Mamma continued their steady banter about the upcoming hog butchering this Wednesday and the colder weather, and Mamma mentioned a number of work frolics she was planning to attend, including a quilting bee at Mary Beiler's.

Tessie Ann paid little mind, still cherishing her time with Molly's little ones. She could hardly wait to hold her own wee one and was thinking ahead now to tomorrow's doctor appointment. *How will things go?* she mused.

"Well, lookee there," her father said, slowing the horse. "Just see who's comin' this way."

"You missed havin' a visitor, Tessie, dear." Mamma smiled over her shoulder.

Not having to wait even a minute to guess, Tessie heard Levi's voice. "Hullo, Ammon. Wie bischt?" he said, like they were old friends. Tessie was glad she was well hidden toward the back of the buggy.

One of the horses neighed; Tessie couldn't tell which.

"I was just over at your place," Levi told Dat.

"Well, why don't ya turn around . . . follow us home," Dat suggested.

"Is Tessie with ya, then?"

"Jah, in the back here," her father was quick to say.

Tessie groaned quietly, and Mamma turned again to look at her, though not any too kindly this time.

"Well, only if it's all right with Tessie Ann" came Levi's gracious reply.

Mamma craned her neck at Tessie again, eyebrows raised high.

It wasn't like her to be impolite. Besides, hearing Levi's voice and realizing he'd gone out of his way to see her today, perhaps even shortened his time with his grandparents in Florida for her, Tessie suddenly believed she owed him this visit.

"All right, then," she said quietly, glad her father hadn't been the one to turn around and inquire of her. "Tell Levi it's okay."

Mandy's husband walked alongside her to their enclosed carriage after they bid farewell to Molly and family. Sylvan waited silently till she was settled, then helped pull the heavy lap robe over her before walking around to the driver's side and hopping in. This was one of the rare times he'd done this since they'd married, and the thoughtful gesture was not lost on Mandy.

After the mare pulled out of the long driveway and they were heading down Hickory Lane, Sylvan asked, "Ya didn't have such a *gut* time at first, did you?"

She was surprised he'd noticed. " 'Twas a challenge, I guess."

"Thought so." Sylvan glanced at her and

offered a quick smile.

"Tessie Ann just attracts children, is all. Like bees to honey."

He was silent.

"I was glad I eventually got to hold the new baby," she said. But he'd known that, having found her all tucked away in the small room near the kitchen, baby Michael's head resting innocently on her shoulder and little Mae at her feet. So very caring of him to come searching, she'd decided at the time.

They talked of other things for a while, making more conversation than usual. *Another nice change,* she thought. Then, after waving at some folks in a carriage as they passed, Sylvan mentioned he'd heard from Norm Byler, who was thinking of returning to Indiana. "He wants to try and win Glenice's heart again."

She listened, not sure it was right to reveal the poor woman's impromptu visit to see her.

"Just thought you should know." Sylvan kept his hands on the reins, his eyes on the road ahead.

"How soon will he be goin'?"

"He's sorting through his things presently, is what he told me. Said this Sunday would be his last at church."

"Tessie's confession day . . . if she decides to tell all."

"Hard to know 'bout that sister, jah?" Sylvan said.

Mandy nodded, curious about her husband's willingness to share his thoughts today, and his little asides. "I just keep remembering her in my prayers," she said.

"*Gscheit* — wise."

And she agreed.

Chapter 32

Mamma's intentions were comically evident when she suggested Tessie get comfortable in the rocking chair on the far end of the kitchen, near the coal heater stove, almost the minute they arrived home. Dat announced they'd make themselves scarce, and Mamma skedaddled off to the front room while Dat hurried back outdoors — it sounded like he was out there helping Levi tie his horse to the hitching post. Tessie, feeling a little nervous, could hear them talking and taking their time coming in.

A bit later, Dat reappeared in the kitchen, having removed his shoes and coat. Then, without looking at her, he darted out of the way, joining Mamma out of earshot of the kitchen. Tessie shook her head, amused by this rushing about.

Presently, she heard the thuds of Levi's boots coming off in the outer room, and then the pause for him to remove his coat and hang it, she supposed. Soon he emerged, his light brown hair ruffled up some — she guessed he'd taken a moment to run his long fingers through it.

"Hullo, Tessie Ann." He moved quickly to her side and repositioned the vacant chair to face her before he sat down. "It's *gut* to see you again." He leaned forward, smiling at her, his hands folded between his knees.

"Hullo, Levi."

"You're a sight for sore eyes."

How can he think that?

She felt her cheeks redden and quickly said, "From what you wrote, it sounds like ya had a nice time in Pinecraft."

"I did, but you've been on my mind ever since I left. I couldn't wait to get back here." His eyes searched hers. "How're ya doin' . . . now?"

"I'm all right, I guess. How 'bout you?"

"Well, now that I'm here, wonderful-*gut.*" He leaned back in the chair and folded his arms, his smile ever so warm.

She was speechless. Hadn't he heard about her upcoming confession and discipline? Or that the bishop was urging her to come clean?

"Listen, Tessie, I'd like to take you out for supper again. What do ya say?"

She reminded herself that he didn't know

yet that her pregnancy was high-risk. "My baby . . . may not be healthy, Levi. In fact, it's likely that he or she will be born with a serious illness . . . or worse. And I —"

"A special child, then?"

"Jah, possibly."

He looked away, staring at the window. He was quiet awhile before he returned his serious gaze to her. "I'd still like to treat you to supper, if that's all right," he said.

The small sphere of a world she'd purposely created these past months, with dearest Marcus at the center, shifted with Levi's persistence. This fine young man just kept surprising her.

"It's nice of you to ask me, but I'm not sure." She wished their visit wasn't so very private. "I hope you understand."

Not to be deterred, he mentioned that his father's warm family carriage was available Friday night. "My parents have plans on Saturday . . . the traditional night for courting, ya know." His face brightened hopefully. "I'd really like to get to know you better."

"Honestly, it'll serve you no purpose," she replied, though she felt herself hesitate.

He frowned and studied her hands. "All right, then. Maybe all you need is a listening ear, Tessie . . . what 'bout that?"

This startled her and pointed away from the notion that her father had anything to do with Levi's rush back home. Knowing that this visit was likely all Levi's doing gave her some reassurance, despite her inner resistance. "Could I give you my answer later this week?" she said finally. "Would ya mind?"

He smiled and reached for her hand, giving it a brief squeeze. "I'll look forward to that."

"Denki."

"Good-bye, Tessie Ann — take *gut* care," Levi said, then left the kitchen to retrieve his coat and boots.

All this before she'd ever thought to offer him coffee and something sweet to eat.

Upon awakening early Monday morning, Tessie stretched her arms until they touched the headboard. She got out of bed to kneel and ask God in prayer to help her through the consultation in Strasburg that morning, wanting to trust fully and not give any place to anxiety.

Her local doctor had informed her that the cost for the first meeting at the nonprofit clinic would be low compared to hospitals involved with insurance networks. Since she and her family did not have medical insurance — something prohibited by their church ordinance — she was grateful to have saved enough money for the first visit, and possibly another later on. *Thanks to my work at Mandy and Emmalyn's little shop.*

Presently, Tessie made her way into the post-and-beam building that housed the clinic. Situated on a two-and-a-half-acre slope overlooking a snowy field, the property had been owned years ago by an Amish farmer whose granddaughters suffered from debilitating genetic disorders. Tessie's primary doctor had shared with her that the clinic was raised in a single day by sixty Amish and Mennonite men working together, much like a barn raising. As she entered, Tessie noticed the quaint feel to the porch and the pretty springtime wreath decorating the door.

The receptionist was soft-spoken and cordial as she led Tessie Ann down the hallway to a consultation room. A large framed painting of a seated Amish family, their heads bowed before a meal, touched her. The familiar scene was depicted from a different perspective — from high above, as God must see them. "This was painted by one of the founders' daughters," the woman told her.

The considerate doctor breezed into the small room and sat behind a desk near her chair. "Why are we seeing you today, Tessie Ann?" he asked. His hair was peppered gray on the sides and he sported a short mustache and a close-cropped beard. The kindness in his eyes helped her to relax.

She told of her doctor's referral, which he seemed aware of, and then referred to her father's list of families of concern in her church district. "Turns out I married into one of those families without knowing," she explained, saying she wanted to do everything she could to give her baby the benefit of the well-known clinic. "You've helped so many little ones in the Plain community." Tessie's breath caught in her throat, and she tried not to tear up.

"Is this your first pregnancy?" the doctor asked, and she replied that it was.

The astute doctor also inquired about the surnames in her family tree, as well as her husband's, then asked the location of her church district. "Has your family lived in the same area of Hickory Hollow for two or three generations?"

"Oh, jah, and even farther back than that. My husband's family, too — Marcus died in October of last year, unfortunately."

The doctor offered his sympathy and

asked how long they'd been married. "You're so young to be a widow, Tessie."

She nodded, saying they'd only had a few weeks together as a married couple. "Marcus fell from the rafters at a barn raising," she said, her throat tight.

Again, the doctor's expression was one of genuine kindness, and he shook his head with obvious regret. "Have you had any complications during your pregnancy, thus far?" he asked.

"None that I know of. Just some anemia, but I took some supplements for that."

The meticulous doctor named a list of other, more worrisome symptoms, but she had not suffered with any of them.

Intrigued, Tessie Ann watched as, with her permission, he took a moment to rapidly type her answers into a nearby computer. Later, the good doctor clarified that over twelve percent of all Amish living in Lancaster County shared the surname King, which was certainly cause for concern for Tessie's baby.

"We offer easy access and affordable therapeutic care that can effectively limit the possibility of suffering for your child," the doctor said. He also urged her to have her newborn tested as soon as possible. "Ninety-five percent of the diseases we see present symptoms during infancy," he explained. "But merely screening your baby won't guarantee a successful outcome," he added with a professional smile. "If we diagnose early, a follow-up plan will be absolutely essential in addressing any issues for your baby."

She listened, trying to grasp everything.

"We can also mix special formula for babies who test positive for certain disorders, so do come with your newborn to the clinic for early screening." He confirmed the name of her doctor and contact information.

"Do you know my chances of having a sick baby?" she said, asking the question that had plagued her for so long now.

"Given the circumstances, I would say you're at medium to high risk." He reiterated that bringing her baby in for screening and diagnosis was vital.

Feeling a bit overwhelmed but also thankful to know there was help if she should need it, Tessie thanked the doctor, then returned to the waiting room to await her driver.

Mamma sat Tessie down in the kitchen and offered some freshly made peanut blossoms and hot cocoa, full of questions about the visit with the expert geneticist. Tessie was glad for the chance to rehearse what she'd learned, although it wasn't exactly easy to put into simple terms the things the helpful doctor had explained.

Later, Mamma did a bit of fishing, no doubt trying to find out if Tessie had given any thought to Levi Smucker's visit. "I dare-say he likes ya, honey-girl — and quite a lot."

"Seems so." But that was all she had to say about it, given that she wanted to pray more before deciding to accept his supper invitation. And, too, she wished to walk over to the tranquil little Amish cemetery. It helped her to speak her thoughts into the air and pretend Marcus was still alive, especially now that she felt so close to him, with his baby growing and moving about more each and every day.

Mamma rose and got some mending, divided it up between them, and mentioned there was a small amount of ironing. It seemed Tessie wasn't free to take her long walk until after supper that night, once the sun had already gone to bed. So she would wait till tomorrow, needing the sunshine.

Besides, there's no need to hurry my decision for Levi, she told herself. *And if I'm facing the shun . . . or a shaming, that'll put the kibosh on a relationship.*

For sure and for certain!

Chapter 33

Tuesday morning, while dusting and redding up, Mandy noticed a new devotional book lying on the small table next to Sylvan's side of the bed. It obviously belonged to him, because he'd written his name on the inside.

Thumbing through, she opened to a random page and was surprised to see yellow highlights on various lines, and in some cases, complete paragraphs. She read some of those same passages and quickly realized they portrayed an understanding and thoughtful husband, one pleasing to God.

She was astonished to think Sylvan was studying such guiding principles. *He must be taking the words to heart, too.* Several times here recently, he'd spent more time in the evenings with her, coming in from the barn earlier than ever before. And he was smiling at her more, too. This realization warmed her heart.

In the same moment, she felt sad, even remorseful. *Have I made things hard for my husband, considering I cared deeply for someone else before him?*

She carried the book across the hallway, cherishing her discovery, and leaned against the doorjamb of the vacant room where she prayed their baby might sleep and play one day.

Standing there, dreaming her longed-for hopes, she lost track of the hour. *A baby will draw Sylvan closer to me,* she thought. *A baby will be God's blessing on us . . . make us a family.* Oh, she was ready and waiting with all of her heart.

Her older sisters came to mind. Mandy was glad she'd gone to see baby Michael Abram, so dear and trusting, though holding him had made her ache all the more for a baby of her own. *A little gift from heaven.*

Then, hearing her husband coming into the kitchen downstairs, Mandy quickly made her way back to their room to place his book on the small square table right where she'd found it.

Before dinner that noon, when Mandy went over to invite her to join them, Great-Aunt Elaine claimed she was completely satisfied to have her own meal in her own kitchen.

"I'm making toasted cheese sandwiches and homemade tomato soup."

Sylvan seemed pleased to have Mandy to himself today, surprising her by stating how happy he was, having his wife at home more often. " 'Specially when you're the best cook I know," he said, blue eyes twinkling. His compliment took her off guard, but she rather liked it. He also seemed eager to talk with her . . . and not just today, now that she considered it.

How on earth could a mere book work such wonders?

After the noon meal, Tessie Ann pulled on her boots, even though the snow had largely turned to slush. After the months of seemingly endless cold, she breathed deep of the fresh, almost-springtime air and raised her face to receive the sunshine as she walked up Hickory Lane toward the fenced-in cemetery, past where Mandy and Sylvan resided. She did not stare at her childhood home as fondly, not coveting it as much today. Rather, she kept her attention on beseeching God about her future and whether to accept Levi's recent invitation. Why was this so hard?

Dat had mentioned at breakfast that today's warm spell was to be only a short reprieve from late winter's chill, because a cold snap was blowing in this very evening. It was a mighty good thing, too, considering the hog butchering would go better in colder temperatures. Most butcherings were done in mid-December or early January for that very reason.

"The Lord knows just what we need," Tessie whispered, deciding she would not go with her parents to the Smuckers' work frolic tomorrow. Reuben and his sweet wife, Sarah, would welcome her help, of course, as they would many others', but Tessie wanted to catch up on some maternity dressmaking, and then possibly go over to see Dawdi Dave. She was fairly sure her grandfather would not venture out to the butchering at his age, but then, who could say?

The cemetery looked nothing like it had in the height of spring when they'd buried her dear grandmother. She recalled the leafy trees shimmering in a wide veil of new green — their deacon and his younger brothers had planted the trees years ago. Sadly, the People had buried two of their small children, as well, on that day last May, one of them Marcus's aunt's little straw-haired boy, seriously ill for all the days of his young life. Tessie had never witnessed so many silent tears. The scene came back to her as she opened the wide wooden gate and turned to latch it behind her.

She knew right where to find Marcus's small white gravestone, but she avoided making a beeline there, though she was ever so drawn to it. This was the first visit she hadn't cried so hard it was difficult to see where she was walking.

Locating her grandmother's grave marker, Tessie peered down at it; the stone was darker than many that had been there for decades and longer. "I miss your comforting arms, Mammi Rosanna," she whispered, smiling now at the lovely memory. "Do ya ever run into my Marcus over there in Gloryland?" She let the question hang in the air, knowing it was pointless to ask questions of the deceased. "If so, will ya tell him I love him dearly . . . and always will?" She let it go with that, lest she make a fool of herself to the cluster of robins preening and twittering on the nearby fence.

She moved along, past Great-Aunt Elaine's husband's clean white stone, recalling how comical a man Pappy Amos had always been. Green-eyed Pappy had been like a grandpa to everyone, including those he wasn't related to even a speck. "My sister and Sylvan are lookin' after your widow,"

Tessie Ann said softly. "Doin' a *gut* and loving thing by her, too." She let her gaze roam over to Marcus's plot but still hung back. "So no worries . . . that is, if you even have any over in Glory. The bishop says all is joy, peace, and blessedness where the Lord Jesus is."

Tessie took her time as she finally walked to Marcus's grave, imagining a few more weeks from now, when this serene spot would burst into leaf, bidding winter goodbye. She could nearly taste the smell of fresh black earth and newly plowed soil.

"I've been talkin' to the Lord a lot," she said right out at her husband's graveside. "Mamma says she thinks Levi Smucker really likes me, and quite a lot, too. Maybe even enough to marry me and help raise the baby." Tessie had started more quietly, but her voice was more confident now as she went on. "I've told ya a-plenty 'bout this tiny sweet one growing inside me, Marcus. If it's a boy, I'll name him after you, my love. I hope you're pleased and think this is as fine an idea as I do."

She didn't say more, her words drying up as she enjoyed the light breeze, the sounds of birds, and the awareness that the earth was holding its breath for the next season — the glorious season of rebirth.

Life, she thought, struggling very hard not to let emotion overtake her, not sure she could manage to keep the secluded world of her and the baby and Marcus's memory intact. Would Levi's interest in her weaken it? she wondered. Tessie decided to try her best not to let it do that as she headed for the cemetery gate and home.

Chapter 34

The cold blast, a distinct return to winter, swept in right about the time Mamma was putting the steaming hot food on the supper table — a big platter of roasted turkey and all the side dishes. She was quite chatty as she told Dat and Tessie Ann how she'd "had this hankering for some delicious turkey meat and thick gravy." Naturally, Dat wouldn't think of arguing with that.

Tessie could hear the wind roaring against the eaves and rattling the windowpanes at the north end of the kitchen as they all sat down together and bowed their heads for the table blessing — that reverent and elongated silence before they passed the food.

Waiting till her father had taken a few bites of mashed potatoes with plentiful gravy, seasoned as only Mamma could, Tessie said she had a favor to ask Dat. He looked up at her, his fork filled with moist turkey.

"I've been thinking . . . and I wondered if you'd relay a message for me," she said. "To Levi Smucker."

Dat's eyebrows rose slightly, but he seemed to maintain control of his expression. "Be glad to."

Her parents exchanged a glance, and now it was Tessie who tried not to smile. "Tell him I accept — he'll know what that means."

"All right, then," Dat said.

The rest of the meal was taken up with talk of her father's plans to help Nate Kurtz oil and repair some farming equipment before the Lord's Day. " 'Course there's the hog-butchering workday tomorrow, too," Dat said. "Should be quite a doin's."

"Maybe ya oughta reconsider going — help with cooking head scraps for liverwurst or some such," Mamma suggested. "That way, ya can give Levi your message in person."

"Honestly, 'tis better like this," Tessie insisted as she enjoyed the scrumptious meal. She had no wish to belabor the point.

Thankfully, her parents let the matter be.

That evening after supper dishes were

washed and put away, Mandy sat down with her embroidery projects. She was lost in thought when she heard Sylvan wander into the utility room, then the kitchen. He came over to the table and pulled up a chair next to her beside the heater stove, folded his arms, and leaned back, watching her. "My work's all done for the day," he said, sounding relaxed.

"So early?"

"Had some extra help." He didn't twiddle his thumbs like usual, or seem in any hurry to go and do anything else in the house, either. "Would ya mind if I dropped by to see your shop sometime?" he asked.

She stopped her work and looked over at him. "You want to?"

He smiled. "I'd like to see how it's laid out — got an addition to plan, after all."

"I'd like that just fine."

"Well then, so would I."

This pleased her down to her toes.

And for the longest time, they sat and just talked. Sylvan mentioned Preacher Yoder's planned expansion of his general store. "He's doing it real soon, even before summer. Wants to bring in more odds and ends of things."

"It'd be nice if he'd stock bolts of dress fabric," she said, surprised Sylvan was still listening and not yawning or distracted.

"I'll put a bug in his ear, how's that?"

"Denki." She mentioned that she wanted to go over to Maryanna's greenhouse sometime this week and pick up her garden seeds. "It's already getting to be that time, ya know."

He nodded and brought up the farmers who were itching to start plowing and cultivating the ground for summer's crops. "There's always a bit of competition to see who'll get the mule teams out first." He chuckled.

"Like we womenfolk, when we see who gets their washing out earliest in the morning," she said, knotting off the last strand. "Why, I've heard of an Amishwoman in upstate New York who gets up before dawn to hang out a bunch of dry, clean clothes, trying to pass them off as already dry before the other womenfolk even have time to get their washing out on the line. Wants to make it look like she's won that week's competition, I guess."

Sylvan laughed heartily at that. "Not fair!"

She decided to put away her needle and embroidery floss for the evening. Mandy could not have predicted that she'd feel so comfortable with him. She was truly enjoying herself.

Sylvan leaned forward in his chair, startling her a bit, and reached for her hand. He cradled it in both of his and searched her face with his eyes. "I hope you know how much I love ya, Mandy." His expression was earnest. "I truly do."

She smiled back, speechless. Never before had he spoken to her like this, not even during their short courtship.

"And I'm sorry for treating you poorly, takin' ya for granted." He paused and looked down at their interlaced hands, then back up at her. "I could kick myself for not being mindful of your pain over . . . well, the past — you know what I'm talking 'bout." He sighed, shaking his head. "That day you burned your old letters behind the woodshed . . . I should've . . ."

"*Ach*, Sylvan."

"*Nee* — no, I wasn't thinkin' of you," he admitted. "I was wrong, Mandy."

Her breath caught in her throat, and she rose to go and wrap her arms around his neck. "Oh, Sylvan . . . *I* was the one who was wrong," she cried, cupping his face in her hands. "I was."

He sat her on his lap, and they wept shamelessly in each other's arms. "I want to be a better husband to ya. More than anything, I want to make you happy," he said and kissed her when she raised her face to his.

She felt an unexplained joy in their embrace, a longing she had not known. And their tears soothed their fragile hearts.

Not a lot more talking went on that evening, and later, after she'd turned off the small gas lamp on the dresser, Mandy recalled what Ella Mae Zook had once said to her. *"We oughta be thankful the Lord doesn't answer some of our prayers, jah?"*

Mandy couldn't help but smile at that, and as she looked over at her sleeping husband, she knew it was ever so true. With all of her heart, she did.

Very early the next morning, Mandy made Sylvan's favorite breakfast of homemade waffles and fried eggs with Swiss cheese melted on top. Sylvan's perpetual smile made her feel ever so lighthearted.

Mandy didn't inquire about his work for the rest of the week but was anxious to share her own plans with him. "Tomorrow I'm going to clean this big ol' house but *gut,*" she said, excited at the prospect. "Spring cleaning, you know."

Sylvan looked up from his meal. "Ya mean you haven't been cleaning *gut* before now?" He grinned at her.

"Well, not the way I will *this* week."

"It ain't our turn for Preachin' service, is it?" He was becoming a tease — even winked at her.

She shook her head. "Our turn's comin' early next summer. Sometime around the end of June, I think."

A faint smile touched his lips as he tilted his head, obviously enjoying the sight of her. "You look mighty nice today, dear."

It was almost like Sylvan was seeing her for the first time, but how could that be? Blushing, Mandy felt like a teenager. Was she falling in love with her own husband?

She decided she would not only scrub and scour the main level of the house tomorrow, she would cook and bake, too, making Sylvan's favorite foods.

When Sylvan hurried out to the barn to tend to a few things before they were to head over to the hog butchering, she went to sit in the front room. The sun shone in through the easterly windows as Mandy read from the Psalms, thankful for the transformation between them — and clear out of the blue, too. Truly, she could hardly wait to see her husband walk in the back door once again.

Later, once they arrived at the Smuckers' big farmhouse, Mandy waved to Sylvan before she headed off to work with the womenfolk. With a wink, Sylvan waved right back.

He seems so different. Then she wondered if it was really all him. *Or have I changed, too?*

"No matter," she whispered to herself. "Mamma was right . . . love has come a-callin' at last."

Tessie hadn't meant to be late for breakfast, but she'd overslept for the first time in years. When she walked into the kitchen, Dat and Mamma were already sitting at the table eating, their heads nearly touching. She paused in the doorway, her presence still unknown. She watched as they talked privately, the way two people do when they've known each other for nearly a lifetime.

Then Dat looked over at Tessie and motioned her in. "Kumme have some breakfast, won't ya?"

"Plenty's left over." Mamma pointed to the skillet still on the stove.

"Your Dawdi's been askin' for ya," her father said.

"Funny, I'd thought of goin' over to see him while you're at the butchering," Tessie replied. "Is he under the weather, then?"

Mamma shook her head. "Just lonesome's all."

That makes two of us, Tessie thought. "Jah, I'll head over once I finish hemming a dress."

She reached for a clean plate in the cupboard and dished up some scrambled eggs. Hesitating, she went to sit opposite Mamma, where big sister Miriam had always sat growing up, being the oldest of the girls. Tessie could see the hazy sunlight against the cold, stark trees from this particular spot, though she was surprised neither Dat nor Mamma seemed to mind that she'd rejected her usual place at the table.

Mamma looked over at her. "We're prayin' for ya, daughter."

"Denki." Tessie suspected who and what her parents were praying for. *No need to guess about that.* And, too, her upcoming confession must be looming in their minds. She was ever so sure.

"*Gut* of you to drop by," Dawdi Dave said while Tessie Ann slipped out of her warmest coat. "Won't be needin' that much longer, jah?"

"Spring's just down the block, though ya wouldn't know it today." She sat across from him in his small, rather empty front room. "Would ya like some hot coffee, maybe, or cocoa? I'd be happy to make some."

His gaze moved slowly around the place, like he was expecting her parents to come in and join her. Then he shook his head. "I've eaten my fill already, thanks to your Mamma."

"She came over to cook for ya earlier?" This surprised Tessie. "Guess I really slept in today."

"Well, you need plenty of rest. Ain't?"

"That's what Mamma says."

"And you're heeding that, I hope."

Tessie assured him she was doing everything in her power to be strong and fit for her baby.

"Have ya got any names picked out? Or shouldn't I ask?" he said, showing his teeth when he smiled. "Guess there are still a few left startin' with *M,* ya know." He grinned.

"Plenty of time yet," she said. "It'll be Marcus, of course, if the baby's a boy."

"And if a girl — what then?"

"Not sure, really." She didn't say what she was thinking at that moment.

Dawdi looked at her for the longest time, breathed in slowly, and said, "Ever wonder who named ya, Tessie?"

"Jah, sometimes." She laughed softly. "You

must know me well."

"That don't surprise me none. We've got the same blood flowin' in our veins, ain't?" He frowned a little then. "You and your father were always something real special together when you were just a little bitty thing. Do ya recall that, Tessie Ann?"

She shook her head — she scarcely remembered a time when she had felt so close to Dat. "I was somethin' of a tomboy, maybe?"

"Not only that — as spoiled as a rotten apple, too." He described her father's joy that Tessie was born healthy in every way after the loss of two babies. "Your Dat was determined to name you himself, let me tell ya. Wanted something to set you apart, 'cause that's what he felt sure you were — mighty special. What a blessing it was, the dear Lord seein' fit for you to be born full-term. Ever so healthy, too."

Dawdi's words were lovely to her ears. If she'd been told these things before, it must have happened in the wee hours, while Mamma's whisperings crept into her newborn ears as she was nursed and rocked to sleep. "You're full of secrets, Dawdi Dave," she said, smiling at him.

"Your father named you after your great-aunt Tessie Ann. He loved her dearly. She gave him his first Deitsch Bible before she died."

"Was she your older sister, Dawdi?"

"Jah, and goodness but she was a lot like you. Outgoing and fun loving — and fiercely determined. She was even caught sitting in a tree a time or two, till her babies started a-comin' . . . then, well, I s'pose she had to grow up. Not that she wanted to, mind you. But I think her husband was relieved." Dawdi let out a chuckle.

"Goodness, do I ever understand that!" Tessie felt pleased, knowing her father had named her. *Tessie Ann . . . a name to cherish.* "Denki for tellin' me, Dawdi." She rose to stand at the narrow window looking out to Hickory Lane. "You know so many things 'bout our family."

"Well, and someday you'll be the one tellin' the stories to your grand-youngsters," he said softly behind her. "And, Tessie girl, will ya also have to tell them how you refused to confess to the church?"

She spun around. "Dawdi, I —"

He waved his hand in front of his wrinkled face. "No need to fret, dear one. Just think 'bout what kind of legacy you want to pass on to the next generation . . . and the next." He smiled here. "Ponder this before Sunday, won't ya?"

Tears filled her eyes until the sight of him began to dim. "I love ya, Dawdi Dave." She hurried to him and knelt next to his rocking chair. "Ach, I love ya so."

Chapter 35

Before Mamma left for the quilting bee at Mary Beiler's on Friday morning, she tried at the last minute to get Tessie to change her mind and come along, but Tessie opted to stay home. Afterward, she got busy scrubbing the kitchen sink and the counters, then wiped down all the appliances before going to dust the bookshelves. She removed the books on the shelves one by one, taking care to dust the tops of each before returning them to the gleaming shelf.

While doing so, she recalled again the sweet love story she'd read and wondered if she might end up just as happy if she let Levi court her, for surely that's where this was headed. She'd witnessed the affectionate look in his eyes when they'd last talked, here in her mother's kitchen. She didn't honestly know what would come of their second date, though, especially with next Preaching Sunday still ahead of them. Any minute now, good sense might hit Levi smack-dab between the eyes. And he had older brothers who could influence him. Siblings had a way of doing that — parents, too.

Ach, I know that as well as anyone, if not better.

At five o'clock sharp, Levi Smucker arrived in his father's enclosed gray buggy. He bounded up to the back door and met Tessie there. She greeted him with a smile, saying she was just fine when he asked, "How are you, Tessie Ann?"

They walked to the waiting horse and carriage, where he helped her inside. "Can't tell ya how much I've looked forward to this night," he said. "Seemed today would never get here!"

She hardly knew how to respond, not used to such attention anymore. Once she was seated, he walked quickly around to the right side, got in, and picked up the driving lines.

Levi was dressed in nicely creased black trousers, and she could see his white Sunday shirt peeking out of his black winter coat, open at his throat on this mid-March night. Had he also worn his black vest and frock coat beneath?

She'd bathed and shampooed her waist-length hair, which was still rather damp, although tucked into its tidy bun beneath her prayer veiling. She was thankful for the portable heater, not so commonly used amongst the People. *So thoughtful of him to bring it.*

"When was the last time you ate at Dienner's Country Restaurant?" Levi asked, leaning toward her.

She couldn't remember and shook her head. "I don't recall."

"Well, I thought we'd go there tonight."

She smiled. The buffet was splendid, but she knew better than to think they were going merely for the good eats — especially when Levi reached for her hand.

"I'm awful glad you agreed to go out with me again, Tessie Ann."

His soft tone and pleasant remark left her without words, and she remained quiet for most of the ride.

It's like he trusts me . . . as if he somehow believes I did not sin with Marcus. Why?

Tessie smiled when Levi chose a private table in the side room, out of the way. He pulled out the chair for her and raved about the tender and tasty roast beef he'd had here on another occasion. She agreed and mentioned how wonderful-*gut* the buttered cut corn and lima beans had been last time, though she couldn't put her finger on just when that was. Even so, she was certain it hadn't been with Marcus.

After going through the buffet line, they brought their full plates back to their little corner, and she and Levi bowed their heads for the silent prayer.

As they ate and talked, she wondered if he might speak as much about Pinecraft as he had during their first date, but she quickly discovered he had other things on his mind. In fact, during the first half hour, he didn't mention Florida a single time, nor did he give an update on his grandmother there. He seemed more interested in discussing the possibility of dating her. "How do *you* feel 'bout serious courting?" he asked, his eyes on hers.

His letters had been one thing, but having him right before her, asking this question — however anticipated — she found it hard to breathe. It was important to slow down, wasn't it?

"It's something to think and pray about first," she said, hedging a bit.

"Well, I've thought and prayed about nothin' else for months." His expression was tender. "You see, I've cared for you, Tessie

Ann, for a very long time. A baby doesn't change that."

Unexpectedly, tears sprang to her eyes, and she looked down quickly. "Ach, I hardly know what to say."

"Only what's in your heart." He smiled and moved his hand slightly forward, then back, as if he were about to reach for her hand on the table.

And Levi did not have to declare his love; she saw it inscribed on his handsome face. Yet he didn't pressure her for a response, and she was thankful.

Later, after he'd indulged in two offerings of delectable desserts, including warm apple crisp à la mode and chocolate-covered strawberries, and then paid the bill, they returned to the horse and carriage, parked behind the restaurant at the first hitching post.

On the ride back toward Hickory Hollow, Levi headed west on the Lincoln Highway, then north on Ronks Road. Instead of turning east on the Philadelphia Pike, he took narrow and winding Irishtown Road. He was clearly choosing the long way back to Hickory Hollow, Tessie realized, but it didn't bother her in the least.

In the near distance, she could see a solitary light shining in one of the farmhouses. She stared at it, thinking the flame on the wick must've been turned down very low, because the light was rather faint. Something about the sight reminded her of the way she'd felt ever since Marcus's fatal fall . . . as if her spirit had sunk within her.

The moon was gliding behind the trees as she and Levi slipped into a comfortable cadence of conversation. Tessie began to relax again, though she was not ready to address his earlier question. Knowing how persistent Levi was, she assumed he would press for an answer eventually. Even so, she wondered if he'd still want to court her once the People had their say, once she was put under the Bann for refusing to confess.

Levi made her feel special, very special. And the longer they rode, the more things Tessie began to share about herself at his urging — how she looked forward to planting the family vegetable garden, entertaining moments while helping at Mandy's shop, and the kinds of pies she liked best to bake. "And I enjoy climbing one particular tree — well, I haven't lately, of course, but it's something I've done since childhood," she confided.

"My younger sisters do that, too."

"I'm honestly goin' to miss it," she said. "A lot."

"Well, maybe your baby will also grow up with a hankerin' to climb trees. You just never know."

"Maybe so." She paused, wanting so badly to forge ahead, yet flustered as to why she felt so at ease with him. She went on to hint that the circumstances surrounding her pregnancy weren't what people thought, an echo of her failed attempt to confess in church almost two weeks ago.

"You know what?" Levi glanced at her in the dim buggy. "I believe you, Tessie."

"Is that why you're askin' to court a young woman who is expecting another man's baby?"

"Well, I know you. And there just has to be more to all of this than meets the eye."

She felt then that it was all right to tell him how very much she and Marcus had cared for each other — that her father had forbidden them to marry for what were unknown reasons at the time. "But I now know why Dat felt it was so important to keep us apart. And I've forgiven him for what I thought was an unjustly harsh stand against Marcus."

"You two dated for a long time." Levi said it matter-of-factly.

"I loved Marcus dearly."

Levi paused, not speaking for a moment. "Even now . . . do ya still?"

"I'll always love him."

Levi nodded thoughtfully. "And what if you were to release his memory? Is it time to let it go, just maybe?"

"What do you mean?"

He smiled faintly. "I s'pose if you have to ask, then maybe not quite yet." Levi reached for her hand and held it for a long time before saying more. "I'm here to love you, Tessie Ann. Please remember that."

She couldn't stop the tears that rolled down her cheeks.

He promptly directed the horse to a wide shoulder in the road and pulled over. "I'd give most anything to win your heart," Levi said softly, firmly, as he turned to face her. "And I'm willin' to help you raise Marcus's child as my own." He raised her hand to his lips.

She sighed, watching him. Part of her wanted to shrink back, to pull away.

"But I can never take Marcus's place in your heart," Levi went on. "I wouldn't even want to try."

Instead of her heart singing, she felt a sting, the pain as her carefully crafted sphere of security and Marcus's memory started to crack apart.

"I'm here to love you. . . ." Levi's dear words rippled through her.

The silence in his father's buggy was so dense, it filled her ears.

"Would you consider havin' me as your husband, Tessie Ann?"

She breathed deeply. "Ach, Levi . . . I'm married already," she blurted. "At least I was." Then, struggling not to cry through the words she so wanted to say, she began to share with him what she'd held so long inside. "Marcus King and I secretly eloped back last September."

Levi did not respond one way or the other, still holding her small hand in his. His eyes were gentle and kind, and before she could consider what was happening, he opened his arms, and she leaned into them as he drew her quietly near.

Softly, sadly she wept away her secret while he stroked her wet cheek with his free hand.

"You are so precious," he whispered, leaning his head against hers. "Honestly, I don't think there's anything dishonorable about Marcus takin' the loveliest girl in Hickory Hollow as his bride . . . but he would've wanted the People to know about it by now. Surely, he would." He squeezed her hand ever so gently. "Now, Tessie, have ya thought of telling the church membership on Sunday everything you've just told me?"

She sat up straighter, drying her eyes.

"Can ya do that?" he asked tenderly. "For the sake of making peace with God and the congregation . . . and continuing in the Amish way?"

Doubtless, it made sense, at least from his perspective, but from her own, she wondered, because she still didn't have any proof of their marriage. Telling all might only make things more strained for her and her relationship with the bishop and the membership — especially with Marcus's family. And she couldn't help recalling how her father had acted when she'd attempted to tell him this very thing. Why on earth would the bishop and others respond any differently when she had no more evidence of her and Marcus's legal union than she did then?

Levi released her and picked up the reins once again. "I trust you'll confess fully this time. The People are quick to forgive when repentance is offered. Please do it . . . for the sake of harmony in the church," he urged, his voice ever so earnest. "I'll keep you in my prayers till the Lord's Day."

She didn't know what to do with all this

tenderness, having missed out on Marcus's love these months. "Denki, Levi. That means a lot," she whispered. "But I can't promise anything."

CHAPTER 36

Mandy baked enough chocolate chip cookies that Saturday for the entire church gathering the next day. She lost count after two hundred and fifty cookies and guessed she had enough for the youngsters to have two or more each, though since quite a few older folk had a sweet tooth, as well, she'd just kept baking cookies all afternoon.

Mamma had been over earlier, a sparkle in her eyes as she said, *"Somethin' wonderful*-gut *might just be happening to Tessie Ann."* But she didn't reveal what, and when Mandy asked, Mamma simply said they'd all have to wait and see. But it was a consolation to Mandy that her mother's face was beaming with happiness — and this in spite of tomorrow's hoped-for confession.

Mandy glanced at the wall clock and guessed Sylvan might be home in another hour or so. Meanwhile, she washed up the cookie sheets and wiped down the counters, then dried them nicely.

While she was washing her hands, she heard a knock at the back door and went to see who was there. She opened the door to see Norm Byler standing there.

"Is Sylvan around?" he asked, looking a bit sheepish.

"He's over at Nate Kurtz's place."

Norm nodded and handed her a black book. "I found this in the very back of Marcus King's former bureau drawer when I was packing up my things. Thought you could give it to your sister, maybe." He hesitated a moment, then went on. "It belonged to Marcus, but out of respect, I didn't feel I should read it."

She glanced at the book. "Is it a journal?"

"I think so." Norm's face was expressionless. "Well, would ya mind tellin' Sylvan I dropped by?"

She said she would, and a silence fell between them. She made no gesture to invite him inside, given Sylvan was gone, and she was keenly aware of the faintly mulch-like smell of plowed soil hanging in the air behind Norm.

"I'll be goin' now," he said, turning, then stopped. "I'm awful sorry for any pain I caused ya in the past, Mandy," he said with a quick look back. "I truly am."

She raised her hand to her cheek — she understood now that life's losses ultimately brought an unsought yet profound sense of release. She experienced this again even now as he expressed his embarrassment at leaving her without explanation those years ago, asking her to forgive him.

"No worries, really," she replied. "I've already forgiven you."

He glanced at the sky, then continued. "Did ya know it was your father's worry that pulled us apart — his grave concern at the possibility of genetic diseases in our offspring if we married?"

Tessie Ann had shared that very thing. But Norm had never spoken to her about it, and Mandy felt the need to lighten things up. "I daresay Dat's more of a worrywart than any of us knew."

"It's why I left so hastily back then."

"Understandable," she said.

Norm nodded, then waved to her.

"Have yourself a *gut* and happy life out west," she said.

"Same to you, here in Hickory Hollow, Mandy. *Da Herr sei mit du* — the Lord be with you."

"You too. *Hatyee!*"

He bobbed his head and said so long to her, as well.

Not lingering, she closed the door and went to the kitchen table and sat down with Marcus's ledger. Carefully, considerately, she handled it — *words from the recent past* — then she opened it, not expecting to see what looked like a legal document of some kind tucked inside.

When she looked more closely, she let out a gasp. "A marriage license? What on earth did Marcus and Tessie do?"

Seeing the date — September twenty-seventh last year — and realizing that her sister had gone and married Marcus King, Mandy couldn't help herself. She began to read his first entry: *Went to Chester County with Tessie Miller to apply for our marriage license.*

Mandy did not stop until she'd read every page, including Marcus's last entry, written on the morning of his fatal fall.

"Ach, Dat needs to see this!" She closed the journal and took it upstairs to put in her own dresser drawer. "So Tessie Ann was right all along — she did not commit a terrible sin."

Why didn't she just say so?

Immediately following breakfast the next morning, Tessie slipped on her coat and went to the bishop's place without telling her parents. She must hurry, as there was little time before Dat wanted to hitch up to leave for church this Lord's Day.

Mamma had said yesterday that it behooved Tessie to let the bishop know one way or the other what she planned to do about his request. In any case, Tessie would be considered rebellious if she didn't "come under" and make her contrition known to the Gmay.

With everything flitting around in her head, she hadn't slept well. Levi's words were like a pealing bell, beautiful and strange. *"I'm here to love you. . . ."*

The fact that he'd believed in her before he even knew the full truth stirred something up in her, moving her repeatedly to tears. Now, as Tessie hurried across the road to the minister's lane, she searched for the right words to say to the man chosen by God to shepherd them. Oh, she could not bear the thought of his piercing eyes studying her yet again.

Today was close to the coming season of preparation for their twice-yearly church council meeting, which would be followed on Good Friday by a day of fasting and prayer. *"It's imperative the membership be in one accord,"* Mamma had said, not mincing words.

There was ever so much to ponder this Sunday morning.

After her visit to the bishop, Tessie Ann took a reverent posture outside the house where worship was to be held, stepping into line with the other womenfolk, right behind her sister Molly, who was holding her little girls' hands. Oh, to have a small child's hand in hers, Tessie thought. *And to lead my own little one into the Preaching service . . .* She daydreamed of the name she'd picked out for her son. *Marcus.* Her sweet baby stirred within her, and just then, Tessie dreaded hearing the outcome of the People's vote, wondering just how long her excommunication might be.

Inching forward as the women's line expanded behind her, Tessie was relieved her moments with the bishop and Mary were behind her. She glanced around discreetly, wondering where Mandy was, because she always sat to the right of Tessie, since they filed in by gender, according to age.

Tessie happened to notice Mandy uncharacteristically standing over near the men's line, trying to catch their father's attention. It looked like she was giving something to him — a black book, maybe — prior to the menfolk going into the house by way of their separate entrance. Bobbing his head right quick, Dat looked embarrassed that Mandy had ventured over there, seeking him out that way.

What's she doing?

Then, just as quickly, Mandy rushed back to take her place beside Tessie, not saying a word.

The women and children began to move forward, heading inside to find their seats on the long benches facing the men on the opposite side of the room. Tessie watched her father and saw his head go down in prayer the minute he was seated. Then, oddly, he looked up and caught her eye for the longest time before bowing his head once again. Was he perhaps reading whatever Mandy had given him? All of this was so very strange.

The ministers headed upstairs for their usual *Abrot* meeting prior to the sermons while the congregation began its familiar ritual of singing for the next thirty or so minutes. Tessie tried to focus, to get herself into an attitude of humility and prayer. Now wasn't the time to speculate on whatever Mandy had given Dat, nor to whisper a question to Mandy, seated beside her. Tessie had never whispered during church that she could remember. *I wanted to do everything right, under God,* she thought, knowing she'd fallen short. She was beginning to think she and Marcus had been proud before the heavenly Father, taking the timing of their marriage into their own hands. *Weren't we?*

She felt weighty conviction during the singing and as each reverent moment passed.

Levi had encouraged her to tell today what she'd revealed to him two nights ago — *"for the sake of harmony,"* he'd said. No matter what, she would have to endure a temporary ex-communication, which would prohibit her from attending church — the place where she drew the divine strength she so desperately needed.

Trying not to concentrate her thoughts on what was to come, Tessie lifted her voice with all the others, singing "The Praise Song" — *"Das Loblied"* — their sacred hymn. The ancient song had twenty-eight lines, long enough for her to move into a better stance for adoration of the almighty One. " 'Your goodness exalt,' " she sang, hearing Mandy's clear soprano voice next to her.

Tessie yielded her thoughts to God, keeping her head bowed. *His goodness,* she thought as *der Vorsinger* — the song leader — rose and blew the pitch pipe for the next hymn. She realized the ministerial brethren had not returned from their meeting just yet, taking longer than any time she could recall.

They're deciding about my discipline. With that sobering thought, she bowed her head even lower.

CHAPTER 37

Mandy could feel the tension coming from Tessie next to her. All during the singing, their older sister Molly had shared the *Ausbund* hymnal with little Manny while his twin brother, Matthew, helped hold another hymnal with his mother. Mandy wondered why Tessie hadn't helped him with it. *Is she all ferhoodled?* Mandy hoped not, because Tessie needed to finish what she'd started last time — Sylvan had said as much earlier as they'd ridden to Preaching service. *"You must not know my sister very well,"* she'd replied, and her husband had given her a noticeably serious look.

There had been no further talk of it between them, and Mandy had spent the rest of the trip to church praying for a swift end, worried her sister was seemingly determined to stack sin upon sin — at least in the eyes of the People.

They were already singing another lengthy

hymn, which meant the ministerial brethren must be having a difference of opinion during their upstairs meeting. Preacher Yoder and Bishop John were the more strict of the four men, so no doubt there were at least two stern opinions vying for precedence. It had been a very long time since any young woman had caused such a stir as Tessie. Everyone just assumed she was with child out of wedlock, Mandy was sure, so it wouldn't surprise her if they decided to make an example of her sister. *If only she'd speak up and tell what really happened!* Mandy thought, recalling the lines from Marcus's journal.

Mandy searched for Sylvan across the room and saw him singing animatedly, sitting with his next older brothers, all of them in a row. Her heart swelled with love for him; she was still getting used to these new yet very welcome emotions. It was a puzzle how all of this had come about between them — there had to be more behind it than Sylvan's reading a book. *Surely Gott had a hand. . . .* Nevertheless, Mandy could hardly wait to have supper alone tonight with her husband, since Aunt Elaine had already said she was expecting company later. The thought made Mandy smile so big, she was afraid someone might think she was not being worshipful in church.

At that moment, the four ministers at last came filing down the row to take their seats in front. They sat quietly for a few moments till one of them stood and made introductory remarks about the order of service.

Mandy wanted so badly to reach over and clasp Tessie's hand, but poor Tessie had her hands folded on her lap . . . clenched and bright red.

O God our Father, we praise You and Your goodness exalt, Tessie thought, rehearsing the first line of "Das Loblied," the hymn they'd sung earlier. The words ran through her mind as the first minister gave the opening sermon, introducing the biblical topic for today's meeting — "the declaration of guilt," he called it.

She trembled.

Then the deacon rose and read the eighteenth chapter of Matthew, beginning with the third verse, " 'Verily, I say unto you, Except ye be converted, and become as little children, ye shall not enter into the kingdom of heaven. Whosoever therefore shall humble himself as this little child, the same is greatest in the kingdom of heaven. And whoso shall receive one such little child in my name receiveth me.' "

Tessie folded her hands all the more tightly as she listened. The People were so still, she could hear Mandy's breathing beside her.

Once the deacon had closed his Bible and quietly sat down, Preacher Ephraim Yoder got up from his seat and stood before the congregation. As he began to preach in a singsong voice, he also paced, flawlessly weaving Bible stories together to demonstrate the eternal consequences of one's life journey — the sins that so easily besieged folk and the victories they had over them in Christ Jesus. His caution to flee from temptation at all costs and to practice obedience daily, along with acts of humility, penetrated Tessie's heart. The long sermon eventually pointed out the importance of being willing to yield to God's supreme will, and to the church.

Dawdi Dave's words rushed back to her as Tessie and all the others turned and knelt, leaning their prayerful hands on the wooden bench where they'd just sat. *"Think 'bout what kind of legacy you want to pass on to the next generation . . . and the next,"* her grandfather had admonished.

After the closing hymn, when the unbaptized youth and children had left the room, the members' meeting began. Tessie answered the bishop's call to go forward, and she dropped to her knees near the ministerial brethren. Quickly, she lowered her head and folded her hands.

Behind her, she heard the scrape of a chair, and when the bishop touched her shoulder and pointed to it, she knew she was expected to offer a sitting confession instead, reserved for a lesser offense. *Of all things!* She was so surprised, she could hardly speak.

Bishop John commenced to ask the same questions of her as two weeks ago, and Tessie acknowledged she was ready to give a complete confession. "I wish to be in fellowship and faith with the church, under the Lord God."

The bishop went to sit with the other ministers, and Tessie felt the unspoken approval of the congregation as she began. "Marcus King and I were secretly married last fall on September twenty-seventh," she stated. "We disobeyed my father and ran off together — eloped."

There was sheer silence in the room.

She heard whispering then from the men's section, and an unexpected commotion followed. Looking up, she saw Marcus's father stand, a deep crease of a frown on his face. "That is *ummieglich* — impossible," Lloyd

King said sharply. "I knew my son, and he would *never* do such a thing! *Nie net* — never!"

Bishop John rose to his feet.

Tessie Ann cringed. *What will he say to that?*

"Let our sister proceed," the man of God said firmly.

But now Tessie's father was getting up out of his seat, also, two rows in front of Lloyd. He held a piece of paper in the air, waving it high. "I would like to say, if the bishop and the membership permit, that I humbly admit to having failed to believe my daughter." He paused and glanced down at something in his other hand. "But now I stand corrected, as I hold the proof of it all right here."

"Please bring this proof to me, Ammon," the bishop requested.

Her father moved into the aisle and came forward. "This is Tessie Ann's marriage license, signed by two witnesses." Dat handed the paper to the bishop.

An audible murmur, like a rushing wave, ran through the length of the room. Stunned, Tessie was relieved, yet unsure what to do.

Marcus's father raised his voice. "I'd like

to see that so-called document," he declared.

Just that quick, Tessie was ushered out of the room by the deacon, who followed behind her down the narrow aisle, through the kitchen, and into the utility room. There, she was left alone, though she could still hear Lloyd King's voice inside. Shaking her head, she tried to grasp what had just happened.

In a minute's time, Mandy had joined her, asking if she was all right.

"I'm fine. What a blessing, truly," Tessie whispered. Then, looking at her sister, she searched her face . . . her eyes. "It was you who saved the day, wasn't it? *You.*" She remembered seeing the peculiar exchange between Mandy and their father earlier.

"Norm Byler dropped by our house with Marcus's journal," Mandy explained. "The marriage license was inside. I spared no time in reading it and knew right away I must get it to Dat . . . for your sake, and your baby's."

"Denki . . . ever so much," Tessie said, holding back tears. "I don't know what I would've done without such evidence."

"Jah, such wonderful-*gut* timing."

They embraced and Mandy remained there with her, waiting for the members to decide what to do. The longer it went, the more anxious Tessie became. After all, she had not waited to marry Marcus in the Amish church, under God and the bishop, as was expected of engaged couples. There was just no other option . . . ever.

Finally she got cold and leaned down to sort through the pile of coats for her own. When she found it, she slipped it on, still shivering with nerves and the chilly air. "Spring can't come any too soon," she murmured.

Mandy touched her arm. "It'll be that much closer to knowing 'bout the health of your baby, too. Jah?"

Tessie shared about her meeting with the doctor at the Clinic for Special Children. "It gave me hope, really."

"We'll all breathe a sigh of relief when we know if your baby is all right."

"Either way, he'll be welcomed into the family," Tessie said.

"So, you're havin' a boy, then?"

"Jah, I think so . . . for Marcus."

They watched a train of birds gracefully dip and sway over the tops of the nearby trees, and then the deacon returned, saying quietly that the membership's discussion and voting were finished.

Mandy stepped aside, and Tessie, still

wearing her coat, followed dutifully behind the deacon, back to the bishop, and once again sat down on the chair at the front.

"Our sister in the Lord, due to Marcus's untimely death and our grave concern for your unborn baby's health, the People feel you have suffered enough," the bishop began, much to Tessie's amazement. Moreover, Bishop John explained that her father had testified on her behalf about her faithfulness to God and to prayer. "And you were truthful in the end."

She caught Cousin Emmalyn's warm look of encouragement from where she sat in the congregation.

"We do not endorse such hasty behavior, however, for any other couple," Bishop John stated clearly. "Lest anyone else get the idea to do so."

There was no audible amen, but many nodded in the affirmative.

The bishop asked if Tessie was sorry she had not allowed patience to do its work, according to the Scripture. "Do you regret not waiting to marry in the church, Tessie Ann?"

"I am very sorry, jah."

"Do you confess this sin before God and the People?"

She said she did, tears falling.

"In the name of the Lord and this church, peace and fellowship are extended to you. You may continue in full membership," the bishop announced before he reached for his Bible to read once again from Matthew. " 'Verily I say unto you, Whatsoever ye shall bind on earth shall be bound in heaven: and whatsoever ye shall loose on earth shall be loosed in heaven. Again I say unto you, That if two of you shall agree on earth as touching any thing that they shall ask, it shall be done for them of my Father which is in heaven. For where two or three are gathered together in my name, there am I in the midst of them.'

"Our sister, Tessie Ann, go forth and accept the forgiveness and compassion of the Hickory Hollow flock."

She rose before them, still glad for her coat. The bishop's wife, Mary, came up to her and offered a handshake and a holy kiss.

When Tessie turned to join her sisters in their row, she caught her mother's sweet gaze and cherished it most of all.

Hours later, after the shared meal, Levi managed to pass a note to her without being seen, or so Tessie hoped. *I'm mighty happy for you,* it read. *My prayers were answered.*

She, too, was happy . . . and sincerely thankful. The People truly cared for her, just as Mary Beiler had said.

Later, after the shared meal, when Mamma was standing with Tessie waiting for their horse and buggy, she reached for Tessie's hand and squeezed it gently. "Your father and I love you very much, Tessie, dear. And your baby, too — our grandchild."

"I know, Mamma. And it means so much hearin' ya say so."

She saw a tear on her mother's cheek and looked over to see Dawdi Dave hobbling this way with his sturdy cane. She released Mamma's hand and moved to make a spot for the dear man between them.

"Tessie Ann," he said softly, eyes shining. "Blessings on ya, my dear girl."

Now *she* was the one struggling with tears, knowing exactly what he meant.

On the buggy ride home, there was not a speck of talk about what had transpired at church, a sign that all had been forgiven — the Amish way. Neither, though, was any comment made about Levi Smucker.

As the buggy wheels rumbled over an uneven patch, Tessie unfolded his note once more where she sat behind Dawdi Dave.

She found it curious that Levi had not asked to see her again.

Chapter 38

It wasn't until midweek that Tessie received another note from Levi — a supper invitation to his parents' home this upcoming weekend. Such a surprise!

> I realize this isn't the way most couples court round here, but we aren't most couples, jah? My parents are eager and willing to host us for the meal, where you'll get better acquainted with the rest of my family, too. It'll be one big feast, for certain. Let me know if this is agreeable to you, my dear Tessie.

"His parents want me to come to their home even before I agree to marry him?" she whispered, astonished as she put on her coat and outer black bonnet. She wanted to walk over to the cemetery and say one last good-bye to Marcus; it seemed like an appropriate time to do so.

Truth be told, she was feeling more interested in everything now, including attending the farm sales that week. Best of all, she'd enjoyed some good fellowship with Mandy both at the house and once at the little shop. Mamma must've noticed they were on better footing, because when Tessie caught her eye at the store, where Mandy stood right next to her, Mamma looked to be brushing back tears of joy.

Tessie's time in the cemetery was short-lived; she just didn't feel as comfortable there anymore, and it wondered her. She did catch herself looking back, glancing once more over her shoulder before heading for the white gate.

"Good-bye, dear Marcus . . . I'll see you in heaven, when it's my turn."

The weekend supper at Smuckers' farm arrived quickly. Tessie amazed herself by eagerly anticipating the chance to spend some time with Levi's parents. His devoted mother, Sarah, was every bit as encouraging as he was, and a wonderful hostess.

When she and Levi arrived together that evening, Sarah greeted her at the back door and offered to help by hanging up Tessie's black shawl. "Come in and make yourself at home, dear." Then she whispered, "You'll be sitting next to me at the table."

"Denki, sounds nice." To be recognized in such a warm way by Levi's family after all the secrecy she'd experienced with Marcus, well, it nearly seemed like a lovely dream.

Even Levi's black-and-tan coonhound, Trickie, thumped his long tail each time Tessie Ann passed him on the porch that most pleasant springtime evening. "Guess our hunting dog likes ya, too," Levi's father said brightly.

Sarah Smucker remarked how the littlest children were drawn to Tessie. "You're a magnet for Kinner," she said before they all sat down to eat.

" 'Tis a *gut* thing," Levi put in quickly, and his father glanced his way, his raised eyebrows giving way to a warm smile.

"We'll have as many children as the Lord God permits," Levi told Tessie later, on the ride home. "That is, if you ever get around to answering my question." He winked and slipped his arm around her, holding both reins with his right hand. "What do I have to do, my darling?"

"Guess I'm just bein' cautious," she said softly. "Are we rushin' things?"

"Well, we've known each other our entire lives. And it's obvious both our families approve."

" 'Tis true. It's *gut* to have the support of our families, that's for sure."

"And no one loves you better than I do. So what do ya think — will you have me as your husband?"

"I do miss ya when we part ways," she admitted.

"That's one *gut* reason." He held up his pointer finger.

"And I've seen you enjoyin' my cookin', too, after Preaching and whatnot all."

He put up a second finger. "And?"

She enjoyed his company very much, but surely he knew that already. "I've prayed about it, not wanting to get ahead of the Lord God . . . this time."

Levi held up three fingers.

She smiled; he was such a joy to her. And looking at him and watching his face burst into a grin, she laughed out loud. The devotion she'd cherished for Marcus's memory — and now their baby — seemed to somehow merge with the love she felt for Levi, creating a very different, very special kind of affection.

"When would ya like to go an' ask for my father's blessing?" Tessie ventured.

"Why don't we go together . . . when the time's right?" he suggested. "We'll wait a little while, if you prefer that."

She agreed, remembering how the rush to marry Marcus had led to heartache.

A little patience can only bring blessing.

And Tessie was thankful again for this wonderful young man beside her.

It was an especially warm afternoon six weeks later when Tessie spotted Levi at market. The afternoon customers were slowing to a trickle as he nearly ran across the aisle to where she was seated. Having spent every Saturday evening with him since the meal at his parents' house, not to mention other times in between, she was beginning to realize that each time she saw him, her heart fluttered. And, too, thoughts of Marcus were fading, although she'd promised herself she would never forget him.

"Would ya like to ride back to Hickory Hollow with me?" Levi asked. "We can stop and get some ice cream on the way, if you'd like."

She laughed softly. "How can I refuse?"

"That's just what I was hopin' to hear." He leaned near and whispered, "I love you, Tessie Ann," making her blush but good.

"I'm not goin' to say it back, not in front of everyone." She smiled at him, too aware of the other Amish vendors, who were trying not to stare and not succeeding.

"But you'll say it in front of God and the People . . . at least in the way they'll expect, ain't so?"

"And soon, too, I 'spect."

He grinned at her as she eased out of her chair. "Of course . . . just as soon as we talk to your father." They'd agreed recently that it was time.

Levi kept his hand on her elbow as they walked to his buggy, and he gently helped her in. "You know what I think?" Tessie asked.

"Hmm." His eyes twinkled. "You're ready for ice cream?"

"That's not what I was goin' to say, but sure." She couldn't help but smile again. "I honestly think Marcus would be very happy for me . . . and for you."

He nodded wholeheartedly. "I think you're absolutely right."

They pulled into the ice-cream shop, and Levi tied the horse to the back hitching post, then stood near the carriage to help Tessie down. "Sweets for the sweetest girl ever."

"You're just full of sugary words today, ain't?"

"And every word's true." Levi slipped his arm around her as they walked around the side of the little building.

"We should have plenty of homemade ice cream on hand for the wedding feast, jah?" she suggested.

"Whatever you'd like."

She smiled. "Well, in that case . . ."

"Within reason, of course." He chuckled as he opened the door to the cozy shop and they stepped inside.

I'll be the plumpest bride in Hickory Hollow! thought Tessie.

CHAPTER 39

When Levi took her home later that evening, he accompanied Tessie into her father's house. Mamma was nowhere to be seen, but Dat was sitting at the kitchen table working a crossword puzzle.

Levi went right over and sat down at the table beside him. "If you don't mind, I'd like to ask ya something," Levi began.

Dat looked over his glasses at him, then reached up and deliberately removed them. "What's on your mind, Levi?"

Levi glanced at Tessie, who stood near, then back at her father. "I'm here to ask for Tessie's hand in marriage . . . and for your blessing, Ammon."

Dat's lower lip quivered slightly, and he cleared his throat, gathering himself somewhat. Then, with what appeared to be tears welling up, he quoted from the book of Tobit: " 'And he takes the hand of the daughter and puts it in the hand of Tobias.' " With that, he reached for Tessie's hand and placed it in Levi's right hand, cupping their hands in both of his before praying silently.

May Thy will be done, O Father God, Tessie prayed, as well.

When Dat raised his head, he was unable to squelch his grin. He called for Mamma to come downstairs. "Such *gut* news," he said. "When's the wedding?"

"We'll set a date as soon as we talk with the bishop," Levi said, a broad smile on his handsome face as Mamma joined them. "We want his consent, too."

Tessie agreed, scarcely able to contain her own happiness.

"Surely bishop'll dispense with havin' ya wait till the fall wedding season," Mamma said, coming over to give Tessie a hug and Levi a handshake. "And if so, we can have the wedding feast here for just the two immediate families. If that's what yous want," she added.

There was a twinkle in Levi's eye. "Well, we won't be runnin' off to elope, that's certain."

Tessie poked his arm. "Oh now, aren't you a *gut* one!"

No one mentioned it was right smart to get plans under way, considering the baby was coming in a couple of months. Even so, that was definitely on Tessie's mind as she cradled her stomach and walked with Levi to the outer room. She closed the kitchen door behind them. "I love you, I hope you know," she whispered as he took her into his arms.

"So you'll marry me, then?"

Tessie laughed softly. "What do *you* think?"

He kissed her cheek. "My father told me just today he's ready to hand over the farm to me — lookin' to retire. So we'll live in the big house there, not far from your beloved childhood home."

"Not as beloved as the one I'll move to . . . with you."

He smiled into her eyes. "I hope you'll be happy there, Tessie Ann."

Nodding and trying not to cry, she said, "Wherever you are, that'll be home to me."

He drew her near again and said how pretty she was. And always had been.

"Well, you must be blind just now." She glanced down at her middle.

"Not blind at all, my love." And with one more kiss on the cheek, Levi turned and waved good-bye. "We've got us a weddin' to plan."

"Not before we talk to the bishop, remember." She watched him go, glad for the solar yard light her father had installed with Sylvan's help last fall. "Till I see you again," she whispered, her heart full.

Oh, goodness, she hadn't expected to like Levi this much. Like him, *and* fall in love with him, too. Why, she hadn't expected to care deeply for anyone ever again, after Marcus. But the Lord certainly had worked in wondrous ways — if not miraculous ones — and Tessie was thankful for the surprising gift she'd found in her wonderful-*gut* husband-to-be. *A precious gift, indeed.*

A few days later, as they rode around in his black open buggy, Levi asked if Tessie was ready to go and apply for their marriage license now that they had the bishop's permission. He, too, had agreed the wedding should take place sooner rather than later.

"I want to be sensitive to your feelings about that, ya know."

She glanced at him, glad for his understanding spirit. "Ach, I appreciate you for it, Levi. I've come a long way, believe me."

He held the reins as he turned to look thoughtfully at her. "I believe you, love." He reached for her hand. "I do."

Tessie felt self-conscious as they entered the

Chester County courthouse later that week. She looked about, then ducked her head, hoping no one would recognize her and feeling squeamish at being there as a pregnant bride-to-be. *And for a similar purpose to last September.* This time, though, she would gladly follow the church ordinance and marry in front of the bishop and the People.

Thanks to the Amish grapevine, more of the Hickory Hollow Plain community had begun to express interest in attending their wedding. Eager whispers and hopeful smiles were offered at the marketplace and farm auctions, as well as at various gatherings for the womenfolk. It wasn't long till Mamma told Tessie Ann that their original plan for a small guest list simply would not do.

So, two weeks before the Thursday wedding, Tessie's father cheerfully stood up in church and invited all of the membership to his house for the wedding.

Four hundred and fifty guests came to honor Levi and Tessie that lovely, sunshiny May morning, including Tessie's four sisters and their spouses, and Mamma's and Dat's many siblings and their families, too.

After the three-and-a-half-hour Preaching service, as was their custom, Tessie and Levi went to stand before the bishop with their four wedding attendants, including dear Cousin Emmalyn.

The bishop read a Bible quotation from Ephesians chapter five: " 'Husbands, love your wives, even as Christ also loved the church, and gave himself for it.' " Then he read further. " 'For this cause shall a man leave his father and mother, and shall be joined unto his wife, and they two shall be one flesh.' "

Next, Tessie answered the important questions asked of a bride, including the very last one: "Do you confess, our sister, Tessie Ann Miller King, that you accept this, our brother, Levi Emmanuel Smucker, as your lifelong husband, and that you will never leave him until death divides you?"

Tessie was momentarily distracted by Marcus's last name — her former married name — and paused, though she kept a solemn expression. "Jah, I do," she said, looking into the bishop's face. "With all of my heart."

Levi was then asked the same questions, his words serious as he immediately answered.

Tessie thrilled to hear Bishop John declare them husband and wife at the end of his prayer. "Go forth in the name of the Lord

Jesus Christ. Amen."

The couple returned to their appointed chairs, and Tessie looked forward to what was to come as they sat patiently through the testimony of one of the church members. Next, several ministers were invited to comment on the sermons, as well as to offer good wishes to the couple. Hearing her new last name made Tessie Ann smile a little, although she was careful to maintain an attitude of respect in the house of worship — today, her father's home.

When everything was accomplished in an orderly manner, her Dat got up and thanked everyone for coming and also those who'd helped cook the upcoming feast or assisted with the horses and carriages outdoors. Once Dat was seated, Reuben Smucker walked to the front, hands folded and eyes glistening. Reading his comments from a small piece of paper, he, too, made a short statement of gratitude, thanking everyone in attendance.

After the final prayer, given by the bishop from the old *Christenpflicht* prayer book, the People waited for the benediction to come, and the last song, which told of the marriage supper of Jesus Christ, the Lamb.

Levi waited till they were alone upstairs in her old room to take Tessie in his arms and kiss her tenderly. Smiling, he admitted, "I've waited since seventh grade to kiss you like that, *mei lieb.*" He did not stop with one, and Tessie embraced the fervency of his affection, thinking she might just melt right there in his arms. "Ach, I love you so," he said between each kiss.

"I'm ever so happy," she finally breathed.

"Well then, I am, too." Levi pulled her gently near again.

It was impossible for Tessie to count her blessings. *Blessings and mercies. Ach, so very many.*

Later, when she spotted Mandy in the kitchen helping to set the long tables, she noticed a sweet smile on her face. Was her sister just delighted for Tessie and Levi — was that it?

Yet the more Tessie looked her way, the more she wondered if Mandy had something special to tell her, just maybe. Oh, she could scarcely wait to find out!

At the wedding feast, Dawdi Dave was grinning to beat the band, happier than Tessie had seen him since before Mammi Rosanna's passing. After a couple bites of the delicious wedding cake, she even briefly left Levi's side to tell him so.

Levi's family members were ever so cordial, though the grandparents he'd traveled to Florida to see in early March had stayed put, due to his grandmother's ongoing health struggles. Levi had told Tessie that he'd confided in them about her while there and was nearly pushed out the door as they'd encouraged him to hurry home to Hickory Hollow . . . and to Tessie. "Yet another confirmation we were meant to be together, don't ya think?" he added, and she wholeheartedly agreed.

Lloyd and Hannah King, Marcus's parents, were also at the feast and the afternoon Singing offered by the youth for the older folk. The youth sang two of Tessie's favorite faster songs, "What a Friend We Have in Jesus" and "He Leadeth Me."

While they sang, Tessie considered the wisdom of her mother, who'd encouraged her to seek out Lloyd and Hannah to invite them to be involved in Marcus's and her child's life . . . when the time came. Lloyd had humbly apologized to Tessie Ann that day for saying she'd lied about eloping with his son. And Tessie had shaken his hand, encouraged by this change in their relationship. *Marcus would have been glad to see it,* Tessie thought, remembering.

Ella Mae Zook sat there in the front room with her daughter Mattie and son-in-law

David, singing along and obviously enjoying the lovely old hymns, moving her little head slowly from side to side, eyes closed.

From her place next to Levi, Tessie noticed Dawdi Dave glance over at the Wise Woman every so often. She couldn't help but smile at the sweetness all round.

She turned her attention back to Levi, and her new husband looked fondly at her. Oh, she could scarcely grasp the many blessings of this never-to-be-forgotten day.

Tessie remembered the psalm her father had read at family worship just last evening and embraced it as her own: *He healeth the broken in heart, and bindeth up their wounds.*

Epilogue

A couple days after the wedding, I was just itching to go and visit Mandy. Passing by the old tree, I made my way into the familiar house. It wasn't until then I realized I'd failed to look up longingly at my old oak.

I found my sister sewing the prettiest baby quilt in the kitchen, near a big black pot of stew simmering on the stove. "That's real perty," I said, eyeing it.

"Well, it's for *you.*" Mandy held up the cradle-size quilt, displaying both sides. "For your baby, I mean."

My heart dropped. "Oh."

"Wrong color, maybe?"

"Ach, not at all."

"*Gut,* then, 'cause that'll leave me plenty-a time to make one for *my* little one, too." Mandy smiled mischievously.

"Puh, aren't you a tease!" I pulled out a chair and sat down beside her, reaching for her hand.

"If the midwife's correct, our baby'll come in December."

"A wee Christmas gift?"

"Close to the day, maybe." Mandy nodded. "And just think, my little one will only be a few months younger than yours, Tessie Ann. Our two should be dear, close cousins, jah?"

I leaned to embrace my sister. "I'm ever so happy for you."

"Sylvan's been walkin' around like we're havin' twin boys or some such thing."

"Twins, really?"

"Might be. Mattie Beiler says she doubts it's only one baby I'm carryin'."

It wondered me how the midwife could know this so soon, but I didn't question. Mattie had delivered oodles of babies, so she would know, if anyone did. Besides, twins would surely be a double joy for my sister after her long wait for a babe of her own.

When my labor pains grew on that early July afternoon, Levi fairly flew out to the phone shanty. Soon enough, our good driver, Thomas Flory, arrived in his van and rushed us to the hospital, where in just a few more hours we welcomed tiny pink May Sarah Smucker into the world, named for both

Levi's Mamma and mine.

I remembered the *gut* doctor's advice, and a week later Levi and I took our baby to the Strasburg clinic to be screened for genetic diseases. Wonder of wonders, little May was as healthy as could be, free of the dreaded genes that might've caused her brain damage, terrible pain, or even eventually taken her life.

Dat and Mamma reckoned it a divine miracle, and Levi pronounced it an added *Sege* — blessing. I held baby May close to my heart as we rode back home, then placed her in the rocking cradle Levi had made. It was soothing to me, watching her sleep and breathe, and I offered up a prayer of thanksgiving in gratefulness for this answer to the many prayers I'd offered these past months. How this day might've turned out, bringing with it a far different outcome! But really, what mattered most was trusting our heavenly Father. *"The trials only come to make us stronger,"* Cousin Emmalyn had encouraged me recently.

There was more to living a devout life than striving to follow rules — trying to do everything right. Jah, ever so much more.

I knelt at the cradle, rocking it slowly and gently. And I peered down with wonder at this precious new life. "I'm here to love ya, baby May," I whispered, eager to teach her to trust wholly in the Lord and to appreciate the power of patience.

And to embrace and know the beauty of grace — God's glorious grace.

AUTHOR'S NOTE

Pieces of my heart must surely reside in Hickory Hollow, at least part of the time — the story people who "live" there are that precious to me. Perhaps, if you haven't had the opportunity to view the footage of this lovely and very real setting (with a fictitious name), you'll want to watch "Glimpses of Lancaster County with Beverly Lewis" on YouTube. The area is splendid, if not heavenly.

I am grateful for the continued encouragement and insight of my editors, David Horton and Rochelle Glöege. Thanks, as well, to my most supportive first reader, David Lewis, my novel-writing husband, partner, and collaborator for our upcoming book, *Child of Mine,* which releases June 2014.

My heartfelt appreciation also goes out to the Amish and Mennonite parents and children who suffer with severe genetic diseases. From them, I was blessed to glean not only vital information but plentiful doses of sweet-spirited consideration. I am forever grateful, as well, for the reams of enlightening information I consumed over many months prior to the writing of this story, numerous articles (found in the *American Journal of Medical Genetics*) by renowned Dr. D. Holms Morton and his wife, Dr. Caroline S. Morton, as well as Dr. Kevin A. Strauss and others, each associated with the remarkable Clinic for Special Children in Strasburg, Pennsylvania.

The character of Ella Mae Zook, Hickory Hollow's Wise Woman, has been inspired by two devout and endearing women, members of my father's Lancaster congregation when I was growing up: Edna Keller and Helen Kline. Not only were they particularly wise, but they were warm and wonderful in all respects. Even now, I am taken by the extraordinary way Jesus' love was extended through each of them to others. Their legacies continue to live on in the hearts of all who knew them — and in the imaginary narrative and wit of Ella Mae Zook.

May we daily demonstrate the tender compassion the dear Wise Woman offers so readily to Tessie and Mandy in this book, and to others in the novels I've set in Hickory Hollow. There, perhaps, in that very special place, we can meet ourselves anew.

Soli Deo Gloria!

ABOUT THE AUTHOR

Beverly Lewis, born in the heart of Pennsylvania Dutch country, is the *New York Times* bestselling author of more than ninety books. Her stories have been published in eleven languages worldwide. A keen interest in her mother's Plain heritage has inspired Beverly to write many Amish-related novels, beginning with *The Shunning,* which has sold more than one million copies and was recently made into an Original Hallmark Channel movie. In 2007 *The Brethren* was honored with a Christy Award.

Beverly has been interviewed by both national and international media, including *Time* magazine, the Associated Press, and the BBC. She lives with her husband, David, in Colorado.

Visit her website at www.beverlylewis.com for more information.

The employees of Thorndike Press hope you have enjoyed this Large Print book. All our Thorndike, Wheeler, and Kennebec Large Print titles are designed for easy reading, and all our books are made to last. Other Thorndike Press Large Print books are available at your library, through selected bookstores, or directly from us.

For information about titles, please call:
(800) 223-1244

or visit our Web site at:
http://gale.cengage.com/thorndike

To share your comments, please write:

Publisher
Thorndike Press
10 Water St., Suite 310
Waterville, ME 04901